Sept 14th, 1990

A QUESTION
FOR
HEAVEN

Kathleen O'Connor

Glencree Publications Ltd.

First published in Ireland 1989 by Glencree
Publications Ltd, 10, The Mall, Waterford

© Kathleen O'Connor
I.S.B.N. number: 0 9515271 0 X

Print origination by Irish Typesetting &
Publishing Co. Ltd, Galway

Printed and bound in Great Britain by Richard Clays
& Co. Ltd, Bungay, Suffolk.

To all nuns in convents all over God's earth—
for they are heroines all.

To my husband and four sons with all my love

and

To Niamh and Ursala without whom the manuscript
would never have been typed.

Prologue

Mac's bar was the focal point for the poor inhabitants of the little village of Glenbeg. It was inside its whitewashed walls they drowned their sorrows, celebrated their victories and joys, and it was there also that the affairs of the big wide world outside were debated at length, and ultimately solved. Hurling and football matches were replayed there, with every goal and point replayed in every detail. Songs were sung, verses of poetry composed and rendered, and religious dogma and political affiliations and views fearlessly aired and threshed out, very often resulting in blows and punches being thrown here and there from time to time.

It was Friday evening, and the week's toil was over. Neil O'Grady sat there on his high stool in his own special spot in the corner at the end of the counter, under the large picture of his hero, de Valera.

'Fill them up again, Patsy lad,' he said, handing two empty pint glasses to Patsy McCarthy, the owner's son.

'That'll be my call,' protested Ted O'Gorman, as he rooted deep in his pockets for the money.

'Forget it,' said Neil. 'I'm standing. My old nag came romping home today in the three-thirty, at five to one.'

'Begor!' Ted said. 'That was some luck. Had you much on him?'

'Two shillings a win,' Neil was proud to say.

'You're in the money so, in earnest,' replied Ted, and

they lifted two frothy pints to their lips, celebrating Neil's great luck.

They were well and truly inebriated, when Hugh O'Grady walked into the bar, a startled expression on his face. He came over to his father and tapped him gently on the shoulder.

'Can I have a word with you outside please, Da?' Neil looked quizzically at his son.

'Have a word with me here, boy. I am among friends and I have no secrets from them.' Hugh hesitated. It was plain to see that he was highly embarrassed. He was, after all, a teacher in the local school, and a very shy, retiring lad.

'What have you to say, boy? Speak up will you. I'm listening.'

'Well, Da,' he muttered as quietly as possible, 'Dickie Doyle is above at the cottage and he wants to see you urgently. Ma is very upset, so you had better be coming home with me now.'

Neil put down his glass with a thump on the counter and looked around at his drinking companions, now agog with curiosity.

'Do you hear that, my friends? Dicky the Dasher Doyle, that vile miserly moneylender is at my home looking for his pound of flesh, and terrorising my wife and son.'

'The blackguard!' 'Be damned to him!' were comments loudly shouted.

Neil stood up, now feeling really hard done by.

'He has the nerve and gall to summon me from my place of recreation after a hard week's work, but Neil O'Grady will not bow and scrape to this extortionist. Am I right gentlemen?'

There was a loud cheer of assent. 'That's the spirit Neil, old boy,' said Ted O'Gorman, clapping his friend on the back. 'I'm proud of you, and proud also that your fine handsome son here is courting me daughter Nessa.'

There was another louder cheer, followed by words of praise and encouragement from all. Neil could feel his courage mounting to a crescendo, and turning to Hugh, he said.

'Tell Mr Dicky Doyle to come down here to my office, and talk to me in front of my friends.' Another loud cheer arose amid thunderous applause, and Hugh walked out, promising to say as he was ordered.

'There's breeding in that lad,' remarked little Mick Dunne.

'Where would he be got, boy,' answered Tom Driscoll, 'and his father the finest, bravest man in these parts, and he to stand up to Mr Dick Doyle.'

'Hear! Hear!' every voice in the bar shouted in unison, and drinks were called by all for the fearless Neil O'Grady.

Spirits were high and tempers soaring, when the bar door opened to the sound of the little bell, and there, standing in their midst, was the formidable Dicky Doyle himself, the little man, who up to now had them frightened out of their wits.

'Where's Mr Neil O'Grady?' he asked.

'Right here,' answered Neil, standing up.

'Come outside please, Mr O'Grady,' he demanded.

'I'll do nothing of the sort,' replied Neil, going towards him brandishing his walking stick and shouting 'Get to hell out of here and don't ever again show your face in these parts.'

Neil was joined by all his friends and neighbours, and they chased the little man down the road until he was at the other side of the bridge. He never returned to Glenbeg after that day, and Neil O'Grady was there and then proclaimed their hero.

PART I
1905 – 1934

Chapter 1

Nessa O'Gorman thought Glenbeg was the most beautiful place in the world. Never in her wildest dreams could she even contemplate living in any other part of God's universe. Situated in the south west of Ireland, and surrounded by green hills, it was a quiet, picturesque little paradise, and very sparsely populated. As small as it was, the little river 'Cush' divided it in two. North of the river, Rosebud Cottages nestled at the foot of the hill, almost on the banks of the Cush. Here also lived all the working class community in the shadow of St Fintan's catholic church, while south of the river, the big wealthy farmers and business people resided. The physical divide of the river could be crossed by a little timber bridge; but the social division of the inhabitants, north and south, was a deep-rooted, insurmountable barrier, which put them poles apart.

Nessa very rarely crossed that bridge and never went abroad. She preferred to mix with her own class and kind; but today was Nessa's big day. She was crossing the bridge to go into service in the large home of Jack Dan O'Mahony, one of the biggest farmers in the area. She had been packing her bags for hours now, mooning and day dreaming as was her wont, for at fifteen, she was a deep thinker, and a creature of routine, who didn't like change of any kind. Who would take care of her father now that she was going away? True, Ellen O'Grady would feed him; but he was in the habit of drinking a bit at night, and smoking in bed. 'My God! What would happen if he fell asleep with a cigarette lighting? Why, he could be burnt alive in his bed! Her heart was beating rapidly and her face was flushed with anxiety. Holy Mother of God! Please mind him for me and don't let anything happen to him, for he is all I've got. She heard the key in the door.

'Is that you Da?'

'Who else, me pet? Are you ready yet? They'll be here for you any minute now.' He came into the bedroom to her and noticing her tear-filled eyes, he took her in his arms.

'What ails you, a chroí? 'Tisn't lonesome you are, a big lass like you, and sure you are not going miles away?' She looked up at him with her big, blue eyes.

'I'll be worried about you, Da, and you all on your own here.'

'Don't fret your little self one bit my pet. Sure, I'll miss my only girl, but I'll be fine, and I would be long sorry to deprive you of your independence, and the chance to earn a few bob. And anyway, every girl should be trained in household affairs and management.'

'If you say so, Da.'

'Finish packing your things now, and be ready when himself comes, for he doesn't like to be kept waiting.'

Her father was right. No sooner had he pulled up outside in his pony and trap, than she heard the loud knock. Her father answered the door to him.

'Come in Mr O'Mahony, sir?'

'Is the girl ready? I'm in a hurry man, no time for dawdling about. There's lots of work to be done. Where is she? I must be on my way.' Nessa came out with her two bags in her hand, and a furtive smile on her face.

'There she is Mr O'Mahony sir. This is Nessa, and I can tell you, you are getting a gem if ever there was one.'

'We'll soon see. Come on girl; look smart.' Nessa looked at her father, as she mounted the trap, and she could detect

4

the hurt and the sadness in his eyes. Ellen O'Grady and a few other neighbours came up and shook hands with her.

'You'll be fine, love,' Ellen said, 'Don't worry about a thing. You'll be a credit to your father.'

'Thanks Mrs O'Grady and goodbye.' As they went down the road, she could see her father standing there waving, until they went out of sight.

As the trap rolled down the Ashe Road, Nessa saw several of her school friends, laughing gaily by the side of the ditch, and basking in the warm August sunshine. She envied them from the bottom of her heart, and wished she had decided to spend another year at school, for she didn't feel ready for this break. But she was sixteen years of age, and girls like her were supposed to go into service. As they passed the Church she saw Hugh. He was posting a letter in the little green box beside the post-office. He looked up and saw her, and her heart missed a beat. He dashed out in front of the pony and put up his two hands.

'Stop a minute, sir. I want to say goodbye to Nessa.'

'Out of the way boy,' shouted Jack Dan O'Mahony, as he gave the horse a lash of the whip, and nearly killed her Hugh. She didn't like him from that moment, and she was toying with the idea of jumping out herself, and running back home with Hugh.

As they drove into the yard of the big farmhouse, Nessa felt numb with fear and apprehension. He stopped the cart outside the back door. She sat there motionless.

'Get off girl, and look lively. Go inside to the kitchen, and Nanny Black will tell you what to do.' Nessa walked through the back door, into a large scullery full of churns, and then she lifted the latch of the door that led into the kitchen. She was taken aback by the largeness of it, and by the long black range full of pots and pans and kettles of all sizes. A small frail looking slip of a girl was taking cakes of brown bread out of one of the ovens, and Nanny Black was busy slicing ham on the large table in the centre of the stone floor. Nessa hesitated at the door for a moment.

'Come on in girl. We won't bite you. You must be young O'Gorman, Ted's girl?'

'That's right Mrs. Black. I'm Nessa.'

'Put your bags down there on the floor for a minute, and sit yourself down until Lizzie is ready to take you to your room.' Nessa liked Nanny Black. She was abrupt but there was a kindness in her wrinkled face. She was tall and stately in appearance, and her grey hair was swept back from her forehead and formed a bun at the back of her head. She poured Nessa a mug of strong tea, all the while instructing her on her duties and behaviour in the honoured position of parlour maid in the home of Jack Dan O'Mahony and his lady wife, Clare. As Nanny rambled on about the various duties contained in this important post, Nessa couldn't help noticing the servile attitude of this lovely capable old lady. The absolute importance, almost sacredness that Nanny attached to the most menial jobs and her very apparent obsession about pleasing the master and the mistress, filled Nessa with resentment towards these upstarts, but the crunch came when Nanny informed her that she must bend the knee to the master and mistress, and call the four year old son, Master Colin, and the two year old daughter, Miss Christeen. Nessa's face blushed with anger, for although she was quiet, humble and retiring, she was always taught to believe that she was every bit as important as anyone else. Nanny was quick to see her change of expression.

'Don't worry too much girl. You'll get used to all the formalities and they will become second nature to you.' She turned to Lizzie, 'Take Nessa upstairs now, and show her around, but don't be too long, because dinner must be served upstairs on the stroke of six.'

6

The room was small, but clean and airy, and Nessa's uniform was laid out on the bed.

'Try them on,' Lizzie entreated eagerly, 'I'm dying to see what you look like in them. You're a handsome girl you know, and much too nice for this lot here'

'Are they that bad?' enquired Nessa.

'Well, the master is OK, but the mistress is septic, and as for the two brats, they'd drive you demented.'

'I'll take no nonsense from them,' Nessa said indignantly.

'The best of luck to you.'

Nessa looked smart in her black dress, black stockings and little frilly cap and apron, but deep down in her heart she felt silly and stupid, and dreaded the thought of parading around the house in this formal garb. Such a lot of foolish grandeur, she thought to herself, but sure didn't Hugh always tell her that the gentry lived in a world of silly make believe. How right he was. The thought of Hugh made her lonesome and wistful. How she really was going to miss the nightly kisses and cuddles in the little boreen behind the cottage!

'You've gone all quiet and thoughtful all of a sudden,' Lizzie remarked, 'missing home already?'

'Ah no! just a bit anxious about everything. If I had the first week or two over me, I wouldn't be too bad.'

'You'll be fine. Sure you have a fine easy number compared to mine. That reminds me I had better scatter, or Nanny will do her nut. Don't forget to come down for your dinner.'

'Thanks Lizzie, I'll see you later.'

Nessa unpacked her bags, and carefully placed her clothes in the drawers of her dressing table. She then sat down and wrote a long letter to Hugh, and when that was done, she felt a lot better. He would write back to her immediately, and they would arrange to be together on her day off. After dinner, she helped Nanny and Lizzie with the wash-up and then retired to her room to be ready for an early start in the morning. She met the master on the stairs, and he summoned her to the drawing room to meet the family.

'This is my wife.'

'How do you do, Mam,' but she didn't bend the knee, nor would she ever. Young Colin was making a jig-saw puzzle at a large mahogany table, and Christeen his young sister was playing with bricks.

'These are my children, Colin and Christeen.' Nessa nodded to them and smiled faintly. Then she left the room.

'That's a pompous lass,' Mrs O'Mahony said to her husband, 'she needs her wings clipped. Anyone would think by her attitude that she was one of us.'

'Twill be easy to talk to her in a week or two,' Jack Dan replied.

'I sincerely hope so,' his wife answered, 'or else she won't last long here.'

Nessa did however last quite a long time, four years in fact. She carried out her duties meticulously, but always maintained her own dignity. Though perfectly respectful and obedient to all her superiors, she adamantly refused to bow or scrape for any of them, and although this irritated them at first, she eventually earned their respect, and the two children actually looked up to her. During the first week Colin tried hard to demean and belittle her, but on each occasion Nessa quietly and firmly got the upper hand. The night he put the bunch of nettles in her bed, and waited outside the door for her reaction, he suffered most himself. She lay down on the bed, and after a few seconds, felt the burning sensation. She jumped up, saw the nettles, and heard him giggle. Coolly and calmly she gathered them in her hands, and followed him to his room, where she took down the legs of his pyjamas and rubbed them onto his legs until little white blisters appeared. After that they became the best of friends and Nessa helped him with his homework every night. Lizzie couldn't understand for the life of her, how Nessa managed to win him over, without apparently even trying.

'By Gor! You are some operator. There was never a parlour maid lasted longer than six months here'

'If you put a value on yourself Lizzie, that's the value that will be put on you. My father always taught me that.'

'He was a wise man, for that was real good advice.'

'Always remember it,' said Nessa.

'That, I surely will,' Lizzie vowed, but unfortunately she didn't put it into practice, for she was brainwashed by poor Nanny Black.

Colin always waited at the gate for Hugh when he called for Nessa on Wednesday evenings and Hugh would kick a football with him while Nessa was titivating herself. The door of the house was always locked at ten o'clock at night, and everyone was expected to be in by then, but on Nessa's night off, Colin always left a back door key for her under the big black flower-pot. The only reward he asked for this, was that he be invited to her wedding to Hugh. 'He hasn't asked me to marry him yet, but when he does, you'll be the first to know, and the first guest on my list.' Nessa was telling Hugh all about him, as they lay together on the soft hay in the loft over the hay barn at the back of the house. He laughed, that short cynical laugh that he often did, and said.

'Ness, me love! He's young yet and innocent enough, but by the time our wedding day dawns, he'll be on his high horse and just as uppity as the others. You wait and see. They're all alike, girl.'

'I suppose you're right, Hugh! But anyway, so far, so good.'

'Oh! True, true, enjoy him while he's young.'

'Did you hear we're having Stations here on September 7th?'

'Oh yes, I heard something about that. Ma and all the other neighbours are saving their pennies in a jam-jar to have enough to pay the "dues" to the parish priest.'

'We're run off our feet inside. You never saw anything like the preparations, painting, wall-papering, white-washing and cleaning and polishing every inch of the house. I have a pain in my wrist from doing all the silver and the brass.'

'A lot of rubbish I call it. I hope they have plenty of porter and whiskey.'

'Oh! Nanny Black is taking care of all the provisions, and she's up to ninety at the moment.'

'September the seventh, that's the eve of the Immaculate Conception. That's an ideal day to have it, for I'll have a holiday from school next day.'

'I won't have much time to look at you, with the big crowd I'll have to dance attendance on.'

'Sure won't you be giving me plenty to eat and drink, and when they're all well drunk, we can slip away.'

Nessa smiled contentedly, and from that moment onwards she began to look forward to the day. It would be great to have her father, Hugh and his family and all the other neighbours here, and to be able to spoil them with plenty of good food and drink.

The altar was set up in the morning room, and was adorned with a spotlessly white starched laced cloth, vases of red chrysanthemums and silver candle sticks. The parish priest arrived at six-thirty, and was greeted by the master and mistress and taken to the drawing room. Nessa was ordered to bring in a silver tray with three glasses of hot punch with cloves. Her next assignment was to answer the front door and escort the parishioners to the morning room for mass. She was up in the clouds, with excitement and the

10

joy of greeting her own friends and neighbours, but time after time when she answered the door, she was disappointed at not finding any of them there. Where on earth have they gone, she thought to herself, as it was approaching seven o'clock, and the mass was about to begin. Nanny Black called her to the kitchen to help with the preparation of dinner, and to give her a list of duties for the night.

'I haven't seen one of my own neighbours. I don't know what has happened to them,' she said. Nanny looked at her aghast.

'Sure what ails you at all girl! Didn't Lizzie let all your folk in by the back-door.' She felt the blood rising in her veins, but she decided to keep calm, and not upset poor Nanny. Anyway what about it. Wouldn't she be serving them after mass, and that wasn't long now.

Lizzie came running into the kitchen with a basket full of brown envelopes containing the priests 'Dues', which she had collected during mass.

'I'm worth knocking down now,' she giggled.

'Less of that nonsense, girl,' Nanny Black said, 'and take that basket of money straight up to the drawing room.'

'Did you notice any of the folk there?' Nessa asked.

'Oh! they're all there. Sure, didn't I let them in myself, and they're all dressed to kill.' Nessa couldn't wait to see them and to show them how well she could serve at table.

'You may send in the soup now please, Mrs Black,' the mistress said as she entered the kitchen.

'Yes mam, right away.' Nanny filled the large tureen full of steaming, hot giblet soup with sherry. 'Take that in now, girl, and when you come out you can give me a hand to carve the turkey and ham.' Nessa took the soup into the drawing room, and to her absolute horror, only the big farmers and business people were seated at the long table with the parish priest, the master and mistress and the two children. There wasn't one of her own people there. This

11

was too much for her, and livid with anger she ran into the kitchen.

'What's happening around here? Don't my neighbours get any hospitality?'

'Of course they do. Isn't Lizzie looking after them in the servants' quarters, and didn't I send in trays of sandwiches and pots of strong tea?'

'That's not good enough! Why this big difference in treatment for my neighbours, and why aren't they seated in the drawing room enjoying the same fare as the others?'

'Have sense girl, and get a grip on yourself. Don't you realise that the people in the drawing room are wealthy and contribute large sums of money?'

'Did you ever hear of the widow's mite in the bible, Nanny? Well what we contribute is just as much, in proportion to our means. I think this is a thorough disgrace and injustice, and I refuse to be a party to it. My God! Will there be class distinction in heaven?' Nanny was shocked to the core at Nessa's reaction.

'Forget this stupid talk now, girl, and carry on with your work. The mistress will be wondering what's keeping the main course.'

'I don't give two hoots about the mistress or any of that crowd in there. I will not serve them, and I am going upstairs to pack my bags, and go home with my own folk.' She ran out of the kitchen, leaving Nanny high and dry and in a shocked and dazed condition. She had to call Lizzie up from the servants' kitchen and get her to do Nessa's job.

'That girl is gone out of her mind. My God! Is she in touch with reality at all?'

'Oh! she's in touch all right. Maybe 'tis the crowd in there that are not.'

'Don't you start now. Behave yourself, and go upstairs as fast as you can, and get into her uniform, for you can't serve in the drawing room with those old overalls.'

When Nessa was finished packing and dressed in her own clothes, she went downstairs and headed straight for the servants' kitchen. Her face was flushed with anger as she entered, and her father knew there was something amiss the minute he laid eyes on her. She came and sat beside him.

'I'm getting out of here right away,' she said.

'What on earth has happened that has upset you so much?'

'Oh! Da, are you blind or what? Can't you see the distinction that has been made here to-night, between us northside folk and those other big shots? Do you know that they are all sitting in state in the drawing room with the priest, wining and dining in great style? I can't stand it, and I never again want to see it.'

'Sure that's the way of life, girl, and you'll never change it.'

'Be that as it may, but I'll never be a party to it.'

Hugh came over, and putting his arms around Nessa, he asked, 'What's the problem love? Were you sacked?'

'No, I wasn't sacked, I just left.'

'She got upset, Hugh, when she saw us relegated to the kitchen area with tea and sandwiches, and the other crowd being treated royally upstairs.' Hugh's eyes lit up. 'I'm proud of you, Nessa, and I think you displayed great courage and loyalty to your own.'

They went home with Hugh and her father, and the others followed shortly afterwards. That was Nessa's first and last encounter with the gentry, and it made her a kind of heroine in Glenbeg. The story was talked about in the homes, pubs and shops for weeks afterwards.

Nessa looked around her little kitchen at No. 7, Rosebud Cottages, her haven of peace and solitude, where she was mistress of her own little manor, and where nobody could dictate to her, or order her about. She had just recently covered her settee and two little armchairs with lovely

13

colourful floral cretonne, and had made curtains to match for the small windows, one overlooking the back garden, and the other, the front. The willow pattern delft on the old pine dresser seemed to glow in the warm flames of the crackling log fire. On the table were the wire trays, laden with freshly baked buns and scones which she had just taken from the oven, and the sweet aroma of the baking still lingered.

She was feeling very pleased with herself as she looked through the front window. It was great to be home again amongst her own kith and kin, and she was happy and contented as the days were long. It was a dull October evening, and the little narrow road was almost carpeted with the damp leaves which had just fallen from the old elm and ash trees. How she loved this old place, where her neighbours in the other nine little cottages overlooking the river, were all like one big happy family. Her mother, poor Maggie O'Gorman, a delicate fragile piece of a woman had died at her birth, and Ted O'Gorman, though broken-hearted, had lavished all his love and affection on his 'golden girl'. She too loved him dearly, and had tenderly cared for him from the time she was knee high.

She looked at the old clock with the swinging pendulum over the bookcase. It was three-thirty in the afternoon. 'I had better go and tidy myself up,' she said, 'Hugh O'Grady will be passing by on his way from school, any minute now.' Nessa was a charming, Irish cailín, tall and willowy, with two big blue eyes. She had a head of glorious blonde curly hair, which reminded one of a veil draped over her shoulders. From the time she was a toddler she had loved Hugh, and now at twenty years of age, this love had blossomed and matured, and she had great hopes of becoming his wife. Oh God! How she adored him and always longed for the tender touch of his strong virile body. He had made love to her on several occasions, and she had

14

been wafted to heights of bliss each time. She needed him like the air she breathed, and was quite sure he felt the same way about her.

As she stood by the front door, waiting for him to pass by, the evening had brightened a little, and faint streaks of sunshine had begun to peep through the now almost naked trees which flanked the little road. When the clouds began to lift, the green hills, which completely surrounded the little town again became visible. They always gave Nessa a wonderfully comfortable feeling of security and safety.

Ellen and Neil O'Grady, Hugh's parents, lived two doors from O'Gorman's, in No. 9. Ellen was a small, plump, cheerful little woman, who was like a mother to Nessa, and Hugh was the apple of her eye. Neil, a dapper, slim, trim little man, worked in the post office, and strode proudly, almost army-like along the Ashe Road, morning and evening, winter and summmer, always managing to sport a flower on the lapel of his coat. He groomed immaculately, and though stern and stately in his appearance, he had a wonderfully unique sense of humour. He was a boy at heart and the most important function of his day was his flutter on the horses. Unfortunately, he more often lost than won, and because of the financial difficulties that followed from time to time, he caused himself and his family a good deal of trouble and embarrassment. The two daughters, Kate and Mary worked in the civil service in Dublin, and had bought themselves a beautiful house in the north side of the City. They came home often to Glenbeg, and 'twas they were the fashionable pair, with their swanky clothes at first mass on Sunday morning. They were prim and proper, and didn't appear to have the slightest interest in the opposite sex.

Hugh left the small, white-washed school-house, and began to walk the two miles home to Rosebud Cottages. He was tall and slim, with a mop of dark wavy hair, which he wore high, showing his large, brainy forehead. His eyes

15

were greenish-grey, deep-set and displayed great tenderness and compassion. He was sallow skinned, very much like his great grandmother O'Grady, who was a French woman, and known in the family as 'the Black Mammy'. He was later than usual so he decided to take the short cut across Buckley's field, then on to the Primrose boreen, and out to Ashe Road. As he crossed the little stream with the stepping stones, he heard the heavy thud of horses' hoofs. He looked up, and he saw the horse and rider skilfully and gracefully jump the high ditch about fifty yards away from him. As they came closer he noticed that the rider was a very striking looking girl, clad in brown and beige check jacket, beige jodpurs, black riding hat, and high black boots. The horse was a dark chestnut, and about eighteen hands high. She brought the horse to a sudden halt, dismounted, and leading her by the bridle, approached Hugh.

'I wonder did you see a black and white sheep-dog on your travels? He followed myself and the horse, and a little while ago I noticed he had disappeared. I have searched everywhere for him, but there's not a sign of him anywhere.'

'I'm sorry,' said Hugh, hypnotised by her strange beauty, 'but I haven't laid eyes on him.'

'He answers to the name of Tipp, and he is very dear to me, so if you see him, would you drop him into Flaherty's pub on Clover Road?'

'I'll certainly do that, and I hope you find him,' said Hugh, a strong wave of strange emotion coming over him.

'Thank you very much' she said, remounting her horse, and galloping off.

Hugh watched her, until she went out of sight, and his heart was thumping madly with excitement. He could not get her out of his mind, her slim frame astride the horse, those dancing eyes, and the frankness and candour in her manner of speech. The more he thought of her, and re-lived the whole incident in his mind, the more he realised that he

16

had fallen head over heels in love with her. He had often heard of love at first sight, but never dreamt he would experience it himself. How and when was he going to see her again, this strange but alluring girl that he had met only ten minutes ago, and who had already stirred up in him an urgent need to be with her again. She must be Peggy O'Flaherty, one of old Toby O'Flaherty's daughters. He had seen her name often on *The Trumpet*, for winning prizes in show-jumping and other equestrian events. She truly belonged to the upper class, big farmers and publicans, living south of the Cush. However, could he, a humble, small-town school teacher, match up to the high social standards and, indeed, the price that Toby demanded when suitors came to ask for his daughters?

In this thoughtful, dreamy mood, he arrived at Rosebud Cottages. There, standing at her own gate, looking more beautiful and simple than ever, was his own Nessa, her big blue eyes alight with the joy of seeing him.

'How's my girl to-day?' said Hugh, giving her a little peck on the cheek.

'You're unusually late,' said Nessa, 'I was beginning to think you had gone astray on me.'

'I could never do that. Sure, you'd find me anywhere.'

'That I surely would, but you look cold and drawn. Come on in and have a cup of hot tea.'

'That's just what the doctor ordered,' he said, holding her round her slender waist, and leading her in front of him, through the little porch, full of sweet smelling geraniums, and into the cosy warmth of the kitchen. Hugh stood with his back to the fire, soaking up the heat into his cold bones. 'Poor Nessa,' he thought, 'How could I ever hurt her, and she so very fond of me and I of her, and sure really isn't she more my class and type.'

Nessa was humming a little tune to herself as she fixed the tray, taking down the pink, flowery china from the dresser, and filling a plate full of her freshly-baked currant scones. She put the tray down on the small pine table in front of the fire.

'Sit down there on the armchair, Hugh', and enjoy this afternoon tea.' He rubbed his hands together in an effort to muster up the enthusiasm which he sadly lacked.

'Oh! this looks scrumptious,' he said, giving her a little hug of gratitude. 'You must be the best cook in Ireland.' Nessa smiled, that sweet, coy smile, as Hugh sat down, and began to relish the sweet, strong tea and fresh scones. She sat on the sheepskin rug in front of the fire, looking up at him with hero worship. She never doubted his whole-hearted love for her. Hugh, on the other hand was silent and pensive. Why did Peggy O'Flaherty look at him like that? Why did she have to spoil everything? and why, suddenly did he feel this strong magnetic draw to her?

'You're very quiet and strange this evening, Hugh, not at all your lively cheerful self? Is something the matter?'

'No pet, there's nothing wrong. It's just that little Johnny Casey had a nasty toss in the playground to-day, and I'm a bit concerned about him.'

'Ah! he'll be all right. He's a tough little fellow if he's anything like Bob, his father.'

'I suppose you're right,' said Hugh, sheepishly, feeling miserable and awkward for having deceived her. He got up to go. 'That was excellent Ness,' he said holding his tummy, 'I'm full to the brim.'

'Why don't you come over to-night after eight? Dad will be out, and we can be alone.'

'That will be nice,' he said, and kissing her again, he said 'I'll see you later,' then he left for home.

Chapter 2

Peggy O'Flaherty rode into the large yard beside her father's pub in Clover Road, and walked her chestnut mare to the stable. Dave, the groom, had just finished cleaning out the ten stables, which formed a semi-circle on a large concrete pad at the end of the yard. The other nine horses had been fed, and given clean beds of straw, and were looking contentedly over the half doors, neighing in welcome at the return of their stable companion.

'Walk her around for a bit, Dave, until she cools down. She's had a very long and hard gallop and she's sweating quite a bit as you can see. Oh! and don't forget to give her some water.'

'I'll do all that, Miss Peggy' said the thin, scrawny youth who worked for Toby since he was a very small boy, and who was by now, well trained to submission and obedience by his very hard task-master.

Peggy's heart was light, as she skipped cheerfully through the paddock, and into the large dreary house. In the back kitchen, she pulled off her long black boots, hung her jacket and riding hat on the hook at the back of the door, and then washed her hands and face in the large enamel sink. When she entered the kitchen, her mother, poor Brigid O'Flaherty was busy as usual, preparing the supper.

'Had you a nice ride, Peg?' she said in her kindly, gentle voice.

'Yes, Mum. Gypsy was in great form and went a treat;

she's getting better every day, and I don't think there's a horse that will beat her in next Sunday's trials.'

'I'm glad to hear that, and I bet your father will be too, for she cost him a pretty penny, and he will be expecting to make the price of her, and more, back in prize money.'

'Precious little of it we'll see,' said Peggy, 'Sure, he's the biggest hoarder in this land.'

'Hush now, chroí, and sit down to your supper. Maeve and Sheila are serving in the bar, and you are to take over as soon as you've finished.' Peggy sat to the big round table.

'I'm absolutely ravenous. There's nothing like a long gallop in the fresh air to give you a good appetite.'

'That's true, a chroí! Eat your fill, but be quick about it, for your father is due in any minute, and he'll expect you to be at work.'

'That's all he thinks about, for all the good it is to him. Sure, he hasn't the heart to spend a penny, and he can't bear to see anyone having fun or relaxing.'

'Don't speak of your father like that. Haven't they taught you anything about the fourth commandment in that posh finishing school in France?. And anyway, he's not a bad man. He provides well for all of us.'

Peggy studied the thin, tired face of her mother. What a quiet, docile, patient and tolerant woman she was, to endure the harshness and meanness of Toby, all those years. He never gave anyone a civil word or a kind look, with the exception of Jamie, her eldest brother, and of course, his pride and joy, her youngest sister, Maeve. He was by far the wealthiest man in Glenbeg, but he was a pathological miser. He kept the house fuel under lock and key, and allocated only a certain amount for each day. This would be left in a timber box in the back kitchen each morning, and you could not have more even in the severest day of winter. He would not allow the gas lamps to burn, except for a few hours each night, and you had to take a candle to bed with you. His God was money, and he could never amass enough of it. When small farmers got into trouble with the banks, he would buy their farms for half nothing, and later, sell for a handsome profit. He was not liked by anyone, and hadn't a friend in the world. He was a small, fat man, bald headed, beady-eyed, with a big handlebar moustache. What did her mother ever see in him? It was probably a match, but it was surely made in heaven, because marriage to him would definitely make her a saint. She slaved from dawn to dusk, and seemed to always wear the same black frock and coat.

'Mum,' said Peggy, 'while I was riding out today, I met a handsome fellow. I think he is a teacher in the national school, and lives at the north side of the Glen.' Brigid sat for a minute and thought.

'That would be young Hugh O'Grady, Neil O'Grady's only son. By all and every account he's a fine-looking young man, and a brilliant scholar; but you had better be forgetting about him, a stór!'

'Why is that Mum?'

'Well, because your father would have a seizure if he thought you were even talking to him. Neil, his father, is a terrible gambler, and they don't have any money. In fact, I hear the sheriff paid them a visit recently, and seized the furniture on account of Neil's gambling debts. They hadn't two pennies to rub together, but the neighbours in the other cottages rallied around, and made a collection for them.' Peggy liked Neil immediately. What a contrast to her own dull, boring, greedy father. She was adamant to see Hugh O'Grady soon again, and she was a very strong willed girl, who usually got what she wanted.

Toby and Jamie arrived in, as Peggy was still day-dreaming. Her eldest brother was good-looking, blonde and fair, and although he had his father's gruff, abrupt manner, deep down he had a heart of gold. He was thirty-five years of age, and had to do exactly what he was told by his father. He took off Toby's coat and boots, and brought him his slippers. Then he went about drawing water for his bath.

'What are you doing, mooning around there?' said Toby, 'Don't you know the Devil always finds work for idle hands to do! You should be in the bar for the past hour.' Knowing not to thwart or aggravate him, Peggy left the kitchen.

Maeve and Sheila were twins, and had just celebrated their nineteenth birthday. They were only waiting to reach the age of twenty-one to get out of Toby's clutches. They had plenty of boyfriends, and escaped out at week-ends to attend the local dances. The eldest daughter, Celia, was a nun, Sr Dominica in the local convent. She had been engaged to a fine doctor, Ned Casey, son of another big farmer. He still loved her, and paid regular visits to the convent, bringing her bunches of flowers, and always enticing her to come out and marry him. Toby was very proud of Celia, and of the status symbol attached to a nun in the family. He gave the convent a large dowry when she entered, and constantly supplied them with meat, poultry and vegetables. Celia was a very domineering person, and would come home at regular intervals to see that every member of the family was towing the line.

In the bar Peggy found Maeve and Sheila, flirting as usual with a few eligible bachelors.

'It's about time for you to come and relieve us' said Sheila, looking at her watch. 'We have a date at Doran's Inn, and we're half and hour late.'

'Whoever they are, they'll wait, if they think ye're worth waiting for,' said Peggy. Sheila opened the till, and took out two half-crowns. She gave one to Maeve and then the two of them went into the snug, where they changed into high heel shoes, and more glamourous clothes. 'If Pop is looking for us,' said Maeve, 'tell him we have gone to the Devotions in the church, and that we will be praying for him.' Then giggling to themselves, they sped out the door.

What an airy pair they are, thought Peggy, as she washed the glasses, and filled up the pints of porter as only she could do. She didn't like the idea of her two younger sisters drinking so much, and especially at Doran's, which was noted for its clientele of young fellows trying to pick up girls. They were naive and innocent enough in their own way, and she feared for them. She had never been to Doran's herself, because she wasn't interested in drinking and meeting fellows. She was more an outdoor type of girl, and she spent every spare minute riding the horses and preparing them for the various events. She had to admit to herself though, that Hugh O'Grady did interest her, and more than that, he had captivated her. Try as she might, she found it difficult to keep her mind off him, the way he looked at her, that fine face, full of character, and Oh! those lovely kindly eyes! Would she ever meet him again?

The bar was exceptionally busy, as it was Hallowe'en, and the farmers had a holiday next day. Peggy was run off her feet, and her eyes were smarting from the dense cloud of tobacco smoke. Her father rambled in to see that she was at her post, and she could detect the glint of delight in his small, mean eyes as Peggy was ringing up the cash into the till. She felt like screaming, and telling him there was enough work here for three others at least, but she knew it would be to no avail. The answer she would get was: You're a fine, strong, strapping girl, and what do you think I'm feeding you for? When I was your age... etc. etc. She couldn't bear to listen to that rigmarole.

Just then the bar door was thrown open, and in rushed young Danny Mulcahy, with Tipp, the black and white sheep-dog in his arms. 'I found your dog, Miss O'Flaherty. He was caught in a snare, and his paws are still very sore.'

Peggy dashed outside the counter and began to rub the animal affectionately.

'You're a great boy, Danny,' she said. 'Wait now 'til I get you a penny reward for yourself.' She went to the till, and as she was about to take out the coin, Toby caught her hand and stopped her.

'What do you think you're doing, Miss,' he said, 'you have no authority to give away my money like that.'

'But father, the young fellow surely deserves a reward for returning Tipp. Don't you think his honesty should be rewarded?'

'He'll get his reward in the next life. Meanwhile there are pints to be filled here and glasses to be washed; so get on with your work, and let the Lord do the rewarding.' Peggy was livid with this tyrant's attitude, and extremely embarrassed and upset at having to let the lad go away, very disappointed, but it was futile to argue with Toby O'Flaherty, as you couldn't win, and you would end up wildly frustrated and infuriated. She worked on until closing time, then cleaned up the bar, and, feeling tired and worn, retired to bed.

She was relieved to be in the quietness and privacy of her own bedroom, and as she lay there in the dark, her thoughts were on Hugh, her new-found love. She relived in her mind over and over again, her meeting with him, and as she did so, she began to feel pleasant but strange feelings stir up in her body — feelings she had never before experienced. 'I love you, Hugh,' she whispered to herself. 'Oh God! please send him to me soon again, for I have never felt this way before, and you must have sent him to me.' When at last she lapsed into slumber, she dreamt she was with him, and woke in the night tossing and turning in her bed, in a fit of intense passion, culminating in orgasm.

November was the month of the Holy Souls, and Hugh

24

always found it very lonesome and depressing. The days were short and often wet and foggy, and there was a lot of sickness around the school. It was three weeks since he had first met Peggy, even though he had come home through Buckley's field every evening since that first meeting with her. This evening he had returned as far as Clover Road, and had even peered into the yard, but no sign of her. As he turned the key in his own door, he heard his mother's voice. 'Oh! Thank God, you're home son, I am at my wits end here.' He thought she was tipsy, as she was very partial to a drop or two of whiskey; but when he entered the kitchen, he found her very agitated and distraught. 'What's the matter, mother,' he said, cradling her in his arms, for she was a very kindly loving woman, and he really adored her.

'Look at this,' she said, handing him a telegram. 'Your father went to the races in Mallow, yesterday, and this was delivered to me just a while ago.' Hugh took the telegram from her and read it: Please send two pounds immediately, to pay my debts, and to get me home. Urgent. Neil. There wasn't a penny in the house, and all Hugh had in his pocket was half a crown.

'Don't worry, mother,' he said, 'we'll think of something, although he deserves to be taught a lesson, and let walk home. Will he ever learn?'

Ellen knew that would do no good, and with all his faults, she dearly loved him, and couldn't bear to think of him stranded among strangers in those foreign parts. The money was to be sent to a public house in Mallow town, and if it was not there before closing time, he would be on the road.

Hugh lit a cigarette and began to think. Maybe Nessa would loan him the money. But, no; he could not use her like that, especially now that his heart was elsewhere. What was he to do? He had to do something soon, or his mother would lose her reason, and it was for her only that he was concerned. Then he thought of it. Yes! that was it!

'Don't worry, mother! Rest easy, there now, and I will bring father safely back to you.'

'How can you do that, son?'

'I can mother! trust me, and don't worry.' He kissed her on the cheek, and left the room.

'Take care of yourself, son, and may God speed you!'

Hugh donned his best suit of clothes, his new navy overcoat, and left the cottage. He walked quickly, with a spring to his step, down the Ashe Road, over the timber bridge, and out on to Clover Road. He stopped at Flaherty's pub, took a deep breath, whispered a little aspiration to God, and then he opened the bar door and walked in. There were about five or six men sitting at the bar, enjoying their drinks, all of wealthy farming stock, and when they saw Hugh, they stared at him in amazement. 'Good-day to ye, and God save you kindly,' said Hugh, as he riveted his eyes on Peggy who was serving behind the counter. His heart was beating wildly, and his voice quivered as he ordered a pint of porter. Peggy returned his gaze, and she too was excited and nervous, as she filled his pint, and then put it in front of him on the counter. He took a large slug of the soothing, black beverage, wiped his lips with the back of his hand to remove the white froth, and then, almost instantly, he felt reassured. There was a moment or two of tense, awkward silence, and then Peggy said.

'I haven't seen you around here before. This is a very pleasant surprise indeed.'

'No! I've never been here, but I came this evening on a dual mission.' At this stage he had almost finished his drink, and his courage was increasing by the minute.

'I came here, first and foremost to see for myself, that the beautiful winsome lass I saw riding in Buckley's field a few weeks ago, was real, and secondly, to ask a favour of this darlin' girl.'

'The lass you saw was myself, and I'm real all right,' said Peggy, the colour rising in her cheeks, and her eyes aglow with anticipation. 'But what is this favour that you need, for I would be most happy to help a charming lad like yourself.' He looked anxiously around the bar, for he could not discuss his personal business in front of these other men. Peggy, sharp as usual, saw his dilemma, and beckoned him discreetly into the snug. She opened the hatch on the counter, and held it up for him until he went through. 'I'll be missing for a while,' she said to the customers, 'so if anyone wants another drink, now is the time to call, and I'll serve you before I go.' She filled two or three pints for those who needed them, and then went inside to hear what Hugh had to say. They both sat down on the timber bench, and Peggy put a drink on the table for Hugh.

'Drink that up, and it will help,' she said, in what Hugh felt was a very considerate gesture.

'Thanks a lot. You are very kind indeed.' He then told her the story of his father's latest escapade, showed her the telegram, and told her how upset and anxious his mother was. No sooner had he finished the last word when Peggy was on her feet.

'We'll solve that problem,' she said, and, quick as lightning, ran out to the yard and returned with young Dave, the groom. He was to take care of the bar until she returned, and make whatever excuse he could think of to her father for her absence. Dave, puzzled and confused, didn't question her decision, and obediently nodded his assent. She then took two pounds from the till, led Hugh by the hand out to the yard, and headed straight for the stables. She led out a small dappled grey gelding.

'This is a job for Sammy, she said, harnessing him to her

27

father's trap. Hugh was flabbergasted at the speed and efficiency with which she performed this very complicated operation. There seemed to be leather straps and collars everywhere, and they all looked the same to him. She even thought of putting new candles into the lamps at either side.

'It will be dark in less than an hour,' she said, fixing them in position, 'and these candles don't last kissing time.' She opened the trap door, jumped up on the little iron step, and with one hand already on the reins, she pulled Hugh up with the other. Hugh was absolutely fascinated at her prowess in handling the horse, and watched her closely, whip in hand, as she manoeuvered the trap out through the gate, on into the Clover Road. In no time, she had the pony clippety clapping like lightning on the way to Mallow.

She wasn't good-looking, but Oh! God! she had a vivacious attractiveness which drew Hugh to her like a magnet. Her features were sharp, and she had a rather long, noble nose. Her hair was ebony black and shiny, straight and silky, and she had a fringe across her forehead. Her eyes danced brightly in her head, and displayed her every emotion. His eyes were riveted on her, as she, apparently quite oblivious of his presence, kept Sammy on his toes all the time. Her breasts were firm, and well formed, and she had long, graceful legs. He could feel his body rising to her, and a desperate urge arose in him to hold her tightly and closely to him, and to kiss her again and again. Would he ask her to stop, and drive into the woods, where they could be alone? No! he mustn't; but how was he to contain this torturous longing and desire for her. He couldn't! Yet, he must! But it was impossible. He was losing control. 'God! but she is beautiful and Oh! so very desirable!

'Peggy,' he heard himself call faintly, after a long, arduous struggle with himself. She looked around, her eyes aglow.

'Did you call me?' she asked, staring curiously at him.

She thought he looked pale and tense, but then she began to detect that urgent, loving look in his eyes. As if there was some hypnotic force at work, she instantly felt the same way. There was an intense love and passion between them, and they were both simultaneously, acutely aware of it.

'Drive down that lane there, and into the wood,' he said, at last. She turned Sammy off the road, and trembling all over with passion and desire, they fell into each other's arms. What a moment that was!! She returned Hugh's kisses with almost gluttonous passion, and then she felt the hardness of his strong body against her. He gently lifted her out of the trap, and laid her down on the rug on the soft grass beneath the sheltering trees. He took off her coat, then her frock and petticoat, and she clung to him like ivy to a wall. He was gentle and beautiful, and after a long ecstatic sojourn together, they became as one. They lay there for a while, wrapt lovingly in each other's arms.

'I love you with all my heart, Peggy!'

'Me too,' she whispered, in a soft, dreamy voice. 'I have never experienced anything as magnificent as this in my life.'

'I hope you will never change, my darling' said Hugh, 'for I am yours forever.' They then continued the journey, cuddled up close together.

Neil was well and truly inebriated in Sheehan's pub, in the main street, lapping up the free drinks of sympathisers who had heard the sad story of his bad luck at the races. Hugh walked into the bar, with Peggy held tightly by the hand. His father looked up from his pint glass, relief, combined with amazement written all over his jovial face.

'Hugh, me lad! 'Tis I'm the happy man to see you standing there before me, and who is this handsome cailín beside you?'

'This is Peggy O'Flaherty, Dad. Were it not for her kindness and generosity, you would have sore feet by now.'

29

Neil looked at the girl, and taking her by the two hands, he thanked her warmly and profusely, words of gratitude pouring out of him, even if the speech was slurred.

''Twas no trouble at all, Mr O'Grady. Sure there's nothing I wouldn't do for your fine, handsome son.'

Neil O'Grady was happy for Hugh, but couldn't help the feeling of anxiety that kept floating through the haze of drink, to the top of his mind. Hugh had a hard, tough battle on his hands, if he was harbouring any ideas about Peggy O'Flaherty. Old Toby was no easy man to talk to about love, if there was no money to back it. Ah! but all is well for today, and tomorrow will take care of itself. That was always Neil's motto, and he truly lived his life by it. He bade farewell to his drinking companions, and promising to see them all soon again, he left for home with Hugh and Peggy. 'God save us,' he said, as Hugh settled him in the trap, 'but if old Toby saw us now, he would surely have a canary.' Peggy and Hugh laughed heartily, and they had a very pleasant journey home, with Neil singing all his patriotic songs, and telling stories of his many adventures. He was, indeed, a very comical character, Peggy left them off at the timber bridge, south of the Cush, and discreetly enough, Neil walked on, while the young people bade each other a very intimate farewell.

'When will I see you again,' said Peggy, anxiously.

'Come to St Fintan's Church on Friday night at eight, and we will have a long talk about everything.' He kissed her once more, and watched until she was gone out of sight.

Chapter 3

Ted O'Gorman was the local Postman, and was aware of everything that stirred in Glenbeg. He had heard stories about meetings between Hugh and Peggy O'Flaherty, at the back of the church of God of all places. He thought this was grossly sacrilegious, but his greatest concern was for his own darling girl, Nessa. She had lost her mother the day she came into this world, and her heart and soul were stuck in Hugh. He was the only man she had ever loved, or indeed ever even wanted to love, and was she now about to lose him too. The idea of it didn't bear thinking about. Sure, his poor little girl would be devastated, and it would break his own heart to see her pine away for him. He must put a stop to this foolishness. After all, wasn't it pure senseless—Hugh O'Grady with his big ideas, reaching upwards for the hand of Toby O'Flaherty's daughter, and they the wealthiest and grandest family in Glenbeg. Who did he think he was anyway; and why couldn't he stick with his own kind, especially when he had the whole-hearted love of the prettiest flower in the Glen, even if she was his own daughter? What a great cook and housekeeper she is! Sure that Peggy O'Flaherty couldn't boil an egg, for she had plenty of servants to do it for her. All she is good for is prancing around the countryside on the back of a horse. A lot of good that would be to Hugh, and he not knowing one side of a horse from the other. She would definitely break him, and break poor Ellen's heart, and she having more than her share of problems with Neil. Yes! this was a very serious state of affairs, and it was his duty, before God, to put an end to the whole thing. He would tell Jamie O'Flaherty all that was going on between his sister and Mr Hugh O'Grady, the would-be big shot! That would put an immediate stop to his gallop, and maybe Jamie would stand him a few pints for putting him wise. With these thoughts rushing through his brain, he turned the key of his own cottage door and went into the kitchen. There, was his own little Nessa, sitting, as always, in her special rocking-chair, patiently awaiting his return. She served him up a fine, hearty dinner of spare ribs, flowery potatoes and fresh, green cabbage. She knew that was his favourite, and went down very well after five or six pints of porter.

'That's a fine dinner, me flower. I don't know what I would do without you. He'll be the lucky man that makes you his wife.'

'Thanks, Da, but sure you know who that man will be, and doesn't he really deserve me?' Ted did not reply, but he could feel the tears well up in his large, brown eyes. He was a rough, tough, brawny man, but when it came to his daughter, he was as soft as putty. Didn't he rear her himself, with the help of Ellen O'Grady, and he now saw her as the very image of his dear, departed Maggie. He was more adamant than ever to carry out his plan, and prayed to God in Heaven that it would work.

He finished his dinner, Nessa fussing around him all the while.

'I suppose you are going to Mac's bar to-night. I hear there's a whist drive on there, and maybe you would win the Christmas turkey.'

'Maybe I will. I could be lucky. Who knows?'

'If you see Hugh there, will you ask him to call? I havn't seen him for a while, and I cannot understand it. I hope he's not sick.'

'Don't worry, pet. I'll hunt him down all right,' he said,

as he shaved himself in front of the mirror over the kitchen sink. Nessa then handed him a clean, white, freshly ironed shirt, and he was ready to go.

'How do I look now?' he said, liking what he saw in the looking glass.

'As handsome a man as ever walked the roads in Glenbeg, and I am proud you are my Pa.' She kissed him affectionately, walked with him to the front door, and watched him as he walked down the road in the direction of Mac's bar, at the cross of four roads, about two miles from the cottage. It was a cold, frosty night, but there was a full moon in a bright, starry sky. She remained in the porch for a while, watering the multicoloured geraniums, and pulling a bad, withered leaf off, here and there. As she was about to return to the kitchen, she heard the musical whistle, and she knew it was her Hugh coming up the road. He always whistled as he walked along, and he was affectionately known among the villagers as 'Whistler O'Grady'. About time for him to call, she thought to herself. Pa didn't waste any time putting the skids under him. She was very excited though, and more than happy that he was coming at last.

She went to the front door just as he was approaching. 'Hello stranger! Where have you been hiding yourself?' His expression changed, and she thought he looked at her strangely. This made her feel unusually shy and awkward, and she had never felt that way before in Hugh's presence.

'I've been busy, Nessa, correcting papers for the Christmas tests, and helping mum with odd jobs around the house. You know how fussy she gets coming up to Christmas.'

'But where are you off to now, dressed up in that lovely, navy overcoat? You look more like Dan Moynihan, the bank manager, than the local teacher. He laughed at that, but it was a strained, false and forced laugh, and somehow, she felt as though he had become a stranger to her. This was

33

a very queer, frightening feeling, as she had, all her life, felt absolutely comfortable and at ease with him.

'Aren't you coming in? My father has gone out to the whist drive in Mac's and I am all alone. He hesitated. 'Come on,' she said, holding him by the hand, and taking him in with her. As he sat down on his favourite armchair beside the bookcase, he thought to himself. The moment of truth has come. I cannot deceive her a second longer. I must tell her about Peggy. Please God! help me! and keep her calm, for you know the last thing on earth I want is to upset her. She was winding up the gramophone, to put on a new John McCormack record, which her father had bought for her.

'Listen to this, Hugh,' she said, bubbling over with joy, 'It's about this lovely cailín, known as "the Rose of Tralee". You'll really love it, and maybe you could learn the words and the air to it, so you can sing it to me.' He had a lovely, tenor voice, and sang in the church choir, and at all the concerts in the town hall. His heart was sinking, and his courage, faltering, as he listened to the record. He felt like some villain, ready to pounce on his victim.

Nessa sat on the floor with her head resting on his legs, and enjoyed the silvery tones of the famous singer, all the while feeling very aware of Hugh's closeness to her. When the record ended, she looked up at him with those large, innocent eyes, aglow with love and desire. He took her in his arms, and held her closely there for a few moments, his mind in turmoil, wondering how to break this sad news to her. Then he caught her by the shoulders, gently moved her back a little, and looking at her sadly and seriously said.

'Nessa! my dear, sweet Nessa! I have something to say to you?' She knew and felt instinctively that something terrible was coming, and she began to tremble. He sat her down on the sofa and held both her hands in his. 'I am finding it very difficult to begin. It has been on my mind for weeks now, but I could not muster up the courage to talk to you about it.' She could feel herself growing faint, and every vestige of colour leaving her face.

'Tell me, Hugh. Please tell me, for I must admit, I noticed a strangeness about you of late.'

'Well, the truth is, my darling, that quite by accident, I met another girl, and I have fallen in love with her in a way that I never knew before.' There was a moment of silence, while Nessa tried to register his last words in her shocked mind. Hugh continued 'Her name is Peggy O'Flaherty, and as I was walking home from school one evening, some weeks ago, she dismounted from her horse to enquire of me about a dog she mislaid, and 'twas on that evening it all began.' Nessa burst into tears, and was unable to say or do anything more than sob uncontrollably in his arms. Her whole world had collapsed around her on that lovely starry, night in December. Hugh let her cry in his arms for a long time, his own heart breaking for her, and wishing things could have been different. In vain he tried to comfort and console her.

'You'll always be my special girl, and for ever you will have a big place in my heart. Please do not upset yourself too much, and do not think badly of me, for I cannot do anything about my feelings. I have never felt this way before.' Nessa then gathered herself together, drew back from his arms, still crying, and looking like a lost, dazed child. She turned and walked towards her little bedroom beside the kitchen. At the door, she turned towards Hugh, who was standing there helplessly, and torn in two between his intense love for Peggy, and his long-standing affection and sympathy for Nessa. He was about to follow her.

'Let yourself out, Hugh. My father will soon be home, and I don't want him to see me in this state.' He kissed her on the brow, and left the cottage feeling very troubled and confused.

He walked for a long time, deep in thought, before he finally returned home. His mother and father were deep in serious conversation when he went in. Neil had told Ellen of Hugh's involvement with Peggy, and how concerned he was about the whole affair.

'The boy must be losing his mind. What business has he with that girl? Sure, they come from a completely different background and social standard, and there's no getting away from that, and how am I ever going to face Ted O'Gorman again? And my son, after doing such a dastardly thing to his daughter?'

'I am very sorry and upset about Nessa,' said Ellen, her eyes beginning to flash with indignation, 'but I know several young men who would rush at the chance of winning such a fair prize. What I cannot understand is, how you would even consider for one moment, that our fine son, the brainiest and best teacher in the parish, and the most handsome well-bred man as well, isn't good enough for Toby O'Flaherty's daughter.' Neil opened his mouth to make a comment, but Ellen continued vehemently. 'Well! I'll tell you something, Neil O'Grady. Our son is good enough for the Queen of England, let alone Peggy O'Flaherty.' Neil knew he had bitten off more than he could chew, for when Ellen got up on her high horse like this, it was very difficult to appease her.

'I know all you say is quite true, Ellen my dear, and there's no need to get upset about it. All I'm saying is, that there will be hell's bellows to mend when old Toby and Jamie hear about it.'

'There's very little they can do about it,' she retorted. 'If she loves him, and he her, they'll find a way, and personally, I'll take no nonsense from that big, fat Toby.'

'All right, my dear, let that be that, but do not expect me to get involved, because I am too much of a gentleman to cope with those ruffians.'

36

'I always knew you were a coward, Neil O'Grady, but myself and all belonging to me were in Cumann na Mban, and we'll not be intimidated by the likes of the O'Flahertys, with their high and mighty notions.'

'I wonder what Kate and Mary will have to say about all this,' Neil said, as he got up to go out.

'I'll write to them this very minute, and tell them all about it. They are sure to be pleased, and they having big ideas themselves.'

Hugh was highly amused, as he had overheard the whole conversation from outside the door. As soon as all was calm and quiet, he made his appearance, a twinkle of laughter still in his eyes.

'I gather you have heard the news, Mam.'

'Indeed I have boy, and if you are happy then I am very happy for you.'

'I love her, Mam, as I have never loved anyone before, and I cannot wait to make her my wife.'

'Does she feel the same way, Hugh?'

'Oh! Yes Mam, I know she loves me very much. We are meant for each other. Of that I am absolutely sure.' Neil was smiling to himself as he lit his pipe. 'The exuberance and enthusiasm of young love,' he was saying to himself. 'Time will tell.' As he passed Hugh on his way out he tapped him on the shoulder. 'The best of luck to you, boy. You're a brave man. We'll drink your health in Mac's.'

Hugh had brought his mother a little drop of whiskey, and he made her a glass of hot punch. She was all aglow as she sat with him, sipping with relish the warm comforting elixir, which sent feelings of hearty delight to the cockles of her heart.

'Don't you worry about old Toby, boy, or Jamie, either, for that matter. Sure, a strong well fed boy like you would floor the both of them with one punch of your fist.' Hugh laughed, for he always enjoyed his mother's fighting spirit.

37

'I hope it does not come to that, Ma, for you know I do not like violence. I'd prefer to talk things out in a rational manner.'

'That's all right son, but you're not dealing with rational people.' Then his countenance became shadowed and serious again, and he communicated to his mother how concerned he was about Nessa, and about how badly she took the news of his love for Peggy.

'The poor little thing! She must be broken-hearted; but don't worry, for we will take care of her, and time is a great healer. Someday, she'll meet a fine man.'

'I hope you're right, Ma, for she will always be dear to me.'

'What's allotted can't be blotted, son! and everything that happens to us in this life is part of God's plan for us.'

At that point, there was a loud banging on the front door. 'Who could that be at this hour of the night?' said Hugh, as he went to answer it. He opened the door, and there, standing in front of him, in a frantic and distraught state, like a man gone out of his mind, was Ted O'Gorman. He was shouting deliriously and hysterically, and his words were almost incomprehensible. When he saw Hugh standing there, he began to rant and rave louder than ever. 'You cruel bastard!' he was saying, over and over again. 'You killed my little girl. You broke her heart. May God forgive you!' Hugh, panic-stricken at this stage, pushed him aside, and ran like lightning to the cottage. He kicked the door in, and immediately he smelt the heavy odour of gas. Then he saw her, his beautiful, faithful, childhood sweetheart, lying on the floor, her face ashe white. He knelt down to give her the kiss of life; but her sweet lips were cold as ice. He was too late. She was gone.

He lifted her body into his arms, and now it was his turn to sob wildly, and wish he had never been born. He had given her the kiss of death, and he could never forgive himself. He tried to persuade himself that this was some horrible nightmare, and that soon he would wake up and see her pink cheeks and her shiny blue eyes, and when Ellen came in, she found him standing there, stroking her golden hair, and rubbing her cold lifeless hands, as though he was trying to warm them. It was indeed a sad pathetic sight to behold. 'Jesus! Mary! and Joseph!' she exclaimed. 'May God comfort us,' as she looked in shock and compassion at her only son, holding his dead love in his arms. He was as pale as death himself, and was trembling like an aspen leaf, tears streaming down his cheeks.

'Come on now, lad' she coaxed, 'she is gone to heaven and there's nothing more you can do.'

'Oh God, Ma, I killed her. I killed my own darling Nessa, and I wanted so much to explain myself more to her, and now she's gone, Ma! What will I do?' Ellen helped him lay her down on the floor.

'You musn't reproach yourself, Hugh, for you were only being truthful and honourable, and how could you help your emotions? I know it's a sad and terrible tragedy, and won't we all miss her? Wasn't she like a daughter to me, but I always thought she was too good for this old world. She's happy now, son, and put all thoughts of guilt out of your mind'. It took his mother quite a long time to get him to lay her on the floor, as the doctor was on his way to examine the body. 'Oh Nessa!' he repeated, over and over again, 'I loved you dearly and I wish it was myself that was lying there now, instead of you.'

She was buried in the Catholic cemetery, near the grotto, and Ted himself died within the year. Ellen O'Grady nursed him and cared for him until he drew his last breath.

Hugh could no longer remain in Glenbeg. The memory of Nessa, and her tragic death gave him no peace. Despite all his mother's efforts to comfort and console him, Hugh was like a lost soul. He couldn't eat or sleep, and lost interest in everything, even his class of beloved boys at the school. The light was gone from his eyes, and he went around like someone in a dazed condition.

'You'll have to pull yourself together, son, or you'll be ending up in the "quare place."'

'I can't snap out of it, Ma, not here, in these surroundings, where everything reminds me of her. I must go, Ma. I must get out of here and go to England.' Ellen was demented, for she adored the ground he walked on, and he was her only solace and comfort.

'Please don't do anything drastic like that, Hugh. Give yourself another while, and I will do all I can to help.'

'Aren't you doing that already, Ma, but I know I must get away out of the environment. Try to understand that, won't you please, Ma?'

'I understand, son, but I'll miss you sorely.'

He resigned his position in the school, and took the boat to Dagenham, where he got a job as a labourer in the Ford plant. Ellen was sad and dejected, as she had lost a foster-daughter, and now, her only son had gone to a foreign land. She prayed night and day for his return, and lived for his letters, which she kept in a box beside her bed, to read them over and over again each night, before she went to sleep.

Chapter 4

Sr Dominica O'Flaherty, that tall, swan-like figure of a woman, dismounted from Jamie's trap outside the pub in Clover Road. The neighbours, standing in the doorways, eyed her curiously, as she quickly and urgently walked, head erect, into her old home. 'Something astray now,' chuckled Michael John Flynn, as he sat on the high stool sipping his drink. 'I wonder who's for the hammer this time,' Jack Dan Murphy said, as he spat excitedly on the saw-dust floor. Maeve busied herself, polishing the glasses, while Jamie ordered Sheila to get out the best silver, and prepare a tray for her eldest sister, "the Nun". 'That's all we needed to-day,' complained Sheila, throwing her eyes up to Heaven, and running off to obey her orders.

In the study, upstairs, a large sombre room, furnished from ceiling to floor in dark oak, Toby, Jamie and Sr Dominica sat at the round table, in very serious discussion. When Sheila entered with the refreshments, the conversation ceased temporarily. Sr Dominica embraced her, and enquired from her father as to whether she was behaving herself in a proper manner, as befitted a lady of her class and social standing.

'No major problem as yet,' answered Toby, gruffly 'apart from her extravagance with my money, spending it on fancy clothes and hair-dos, not to mention that aul' shtick-lip she plasters on herself.'

'You should be more natural, Sheila, just as the Lord made you, and indeed, you would look twice as nice. I'll

41

talk to you before I leave. Thank you kindly for the tea.' Sheila stood there, awkwardly, going from one leg to another, not knowing whether to come or go. 'Off with you now, girl, and give your mother a hand with the calves,' said Jamie. She breathed a sigh of relief, and went scampering down the stairs.

She met Peggy on her way up, looking very dejected and crestfallen. Neither could she help noticing her pale, worn face, and the dullness in her usually shiny eyes.

'I hear your lover boy has gone abroad and left you in the lurch.'

'He had a very good reason for going, but he will return in a while.'

'The trio are sitting above,' warned Sheila, 'I suppose 'tis you are in the dock to-day.'

'I believe I am' answered Peggy 'but I care nothing for what they have to say, for I have my own plans for my own life, and I can assure you, they won't force me to change them one bit.'

'The best of luck to you, Peg. Rather you than I, the old man has a face on him that would turn milk sour.'

Peggy knocked boldly on the study door. 'Come in,' she was ordered. As she entered, she was greeted by stern, hostile glances from the sitting judges. She looked straight at them, her face devoid of expression, and she did not utter a word.

'What is this I hear about you,' queried Sr Dominica, in a sharp, cross tone of voice.

'I haven't the slightest idea,' retorted Peggy, coldly.

'Do you know that Ted O'Gorman, God rest his soul, called here, a few weeks before he died, and informed your brother, Jamie, of your relationship with that O'Grady boy?' Remaining calm and cool, and showing no sign of fear, Peggy replied.

'Yes! So what?'

'So what?' she almost shouted, her voice rising to a crescendo. 'Do you realise the worry and anxiety you are causing your father, with this foolish infatuation you have for that fellow?'

'His name is Hugh,' retorted Peggy cheekily.

'I'd thank you to watch your tongue, Madam,' barked Toby, 'and kindly listen attentively and respectfully to what your sister has to say to you.'

'I'll listen to my own heart, father, and I'd thank you to remember that I am over twenty-one years of age.'

'I will not tolerate another word of this impertinence,' he roared, 'sit down at once, and hold your tongue.'

'Now, Peg,' said the nun, calming down a little, 'you are well aware that there are certain social standards that a family like ours must live up to, and, unfortunately, the O'Gradys do not fit in with them. Your father has someone in mind for you, someone who will be on your own level, and will be in a position to provide for you in the manner to which you are accustomed.'

'And who might this Prince Charming be?'

'He's Willie Mullane, who owns the farm on "Beach Hill." Your father has made all the financial arrangements for your marriage to him.'

'Financial arrangements!' yelled Peggy. 'What has that got to do with love? I don't love Willie Mullane. In fact I don't even like him, and I am not mildly interested in his farm or his money.'

'If you persist in this insane attitude, arrangements will be made to send you away to France, without delay,' Sr Dominica warned.

'Do you hear that, missy,' said Toby. 'Well, heed it. I'd advise it strongly.' Peggy could feel the tears welling up in her eyes, and the cold perspiration coming on, as that nauseating feeling came over her again. Sr Dominica noticed her change of colour, being herself in the nursing

43

profession. 'Are you ill, Peggy?' To which, Peggy replied boldly.

'No, I am not ill, as such; but I am suffering from a very natural ailment. I am carrying Hugh O'Grady's child.'

This announcement came like a bombshell, and numbed them all to silence, for a short time. Then her father and brother began to rant and rave wildly, calling her a trollop, and a disgrace to the family name. Toby actually came for her, brandishing his walking stick, while Jamie swore vengeance, and vowed he would kill the blackguard, cold stone dead. Sr. Dominica, seeing that the situation was getting out of hand, calmed the men, and sent Peggy to her room out of the way while they continued their dissertation on this now, very serious, problem.

Chapter 5

Mossy Fogarty was the new postman for Glenbeg. He was the nephew of Ted O'Gorman, the son of Ted's departed sister, Nora, and he lived in the next parish with Tadg Finn, the local shopkeeper, for whom he had worked since he was a young boy. Ted left him his cottage in his will, and he also got Ted's job, for which he was admirably suited, being of an exceptionally cheerful and friendly disposition, with a kind word for everyone. He was very handsome, too, and although all the girls in the Glen adored him, he had eyes only for Mary O'Grady, the older of the two O'Grady girls. He haunted the cottage when Mary was home on holidays, and Mary herself was very fond of him too. 'Good morning, Mossy,' said Ellen O'Grady, as he cycled up the Ashe Road on his rounds. 'Have you anything for me?' Smiling from ear to ear, he got off his bike, dipped into his big canvas bag, and produced a letter. 'This has an English stamp, Mrs O'Grady, and it's definitely Hugh's handwriting.' Her eyes lit up as he handed her the letter, and she tore it open there and then, starting to read it avidly. She commented all the while to Mossy on its contents, how lonesome and depressed poor Hugh was, how he hated London, and missed the lovely, clean, fresh air of Glenbeg. Most of all how he missed herself, who, like all Irish mothers spoilt him constantly. In the last paragraph, he spoke of Peggy, and enclosed a letter which she was to have delivered into her own hands.

'You're the very man for this job,' said Ellen to Mossy. 'Would you ever take this letter, and give it to Peggy O'Flaherty, personally. Make sure you don't give it to anyone but herself. These were Hugh's instructions.'

'I'd be delighted to oblige, Mam, and don't forget to mention me to your own Mary, when you write again.'

'Of course I will, Moss. Have no fear. I know she'll go to the altar with you yet.'

'I hope you're right,' said Mossy, peddling off in the direction of Clover Road.

He was in the bar for a long time, but didn't lay eyes on Peggy, so he was wondering what he should do. Sheila was inside the counter, and seemed very friendly and nice. She chatted to him non stop, and he had a job trying to be evasive when he thought she was asking pointed questions. Should he trust Sheila, and enquire of Peggy's whereabouts? No! he had better not. You never could trust this lot. Then, to his relief, he saw her passing through the hallway which led into the kitchen. He caught her eye, and beckoned to her to come outside. He handed her Hugh's letter, and she stuck it quickly in the pocket of her dress.

'Oh! Thank God you found me,' she said, 'I wonder would you take me to Mrs. O'Grady's house, please. I need to talk to her, badly; but I don't know where the house is.'

'Sit up there on the crossbar of the bike, and I'll have you there in no time.'

Peggy carefully hoisted herself up on the bike, being careful not to hurt herself. 'Here we are now,' said Mossy, as he knocked on the brass knocker of the cottage door. When Ellen came out and saw the girl standing there with Mossy, she immediately knew who she was.

'You must be Peggy,' she said, putting her arms around her, and kissing her lovingly and affectionately. 'You're as welcome as the flowers in May. Come on in to our humble

46

home. Thanks for bringing her to me, Mossy. You're a gentleman.'

'My pleasure, Mam. If you need me later, I'll be at home for the night.'

In the kitchen of O'Grady's cottage. Peggy felt very secure in the lovely, warm, tender atmosphere of Hugh's home, so totally different from the hard, cold one of her own big, lonely mansion. She breathed a sigh of relief, and somehow felt closer to Hugh already. She was confident that here, her problem would be solved, and everything was going to be fine. Ellen sat beside her on the settee, and Peggy told her of her pregnancy with Hugh's baby, and of the nightmare she was living at home.

'They keep me under constant watch, and persecute me with base and hurtful comments. They have made it quite clear to me, that they will stop at nothing to prevent me from marrying Hugh,' Peggy said, bursting into tears.

'Hush now! Pet! and don't be upsetting yourself, for they can't go against God's will, and He will take care of us all. Neil will be here any minute now, and he will get in contact with Hugh immediately through the post office. They have ways and means, and all kinds of gadgets down there for contacting foreign parts.' Ellen was overjoyed at Peggy's great news, and held her in her arms, telling her how much she was looking forward to the birth of her grandchild, and how very happy Hugh would be. Peggy felt at ease, perfectly contented, and happier than she had been for a long time.

When Neil came home, he was amazed to see Peggy there, with Ellen fussing over her, like she was a prize hen. He hadn't seen Ellen in such good form since Hugh left home, almost three months ago.

'Neil, wait 'til I tell you the wonderful news. We're going to be grandparents. Peggy here is expecting our Hugh's baby in five months' time.' Neil too, was very happy, and kissed Peggy, warmly.

'How did you find your way here, child?'

'Never mind that,' interrupted Ellen, 'but go down to Agnes, the postmistress, and tell her to get in touch with Hugh at once. Here's his address in England. He must come home immediately to marry Peggy.'

'I'll go down, right away, and rest assured,' said he, clasping Peggy's hands warmly. 'We'll have that boy of yours home in a very short while.'

'I'll walk down along with you, Mr O'Grady, because if I'm missed out of the house, they might do something drastic, and send me away.'

'Oh! Be careful, for God's sake,' said Ellen, 'and mind yourself and your baby. We'll be looking forward to seeing you soon again.'

'Me, too,' said Peggy, and she left with Neil, who escorted her to the door of the Pub.

'I'm on my way now, straight to the post office,' said Neil, as he took Peggy's hand and kissed it. 'We should have news of Hugh for you, very soon.'

'Oh thank you, Mr O'Grady. I do look forward to that, and I appreciate your kindness, more than I can say.'

Neil turned, and walked back over the bridge. That's a nice polite lass, he thought to himself, and very grateful, too for small favours. He stopped at Macs for a quick one, and then he headed off to Agnes, to do his business.

'Good mornin' to you Neil. what brings you here, at this time of day?'

'I want to place a trunk call to Hugh, at the Ford plant in Dagenham. Here is the number, and he's on the assembly line there.' Agnes was alive with curiosity, as she put on her spectacles and studied the number on the piece of paper Neil had given her. She looked up at Neil.

'This call is going to cost you a fortune, five or six shillings maybe, if you stay on too long. Have you the money?'

'Well, I haven't it on me now,' replied Neil, 'but I'll be paid at the end of the month, and I'll fix up with you then.'

'That's all right, so,' she said, condescendingly, 'but I wouldn't do this for anyone else but yourself.'

'Ah, sure I always knew you fancied me,' he said, giving her a little slap on the bottom. She ran to the telephone, chuckling to herself, and Neil watched her while she turned the handle underneath the phone, frantically, for a long time, before she finally got through to the operator. She's like someone churning butter, Neil was thinking to himself, as he waited patiently. Eventually she called him into the little telephone box. 'Hugh is on the line now. Hurry up! Every second costs money.' Neil took the phone in his hand, and then he looked through the glass window to check if Agnes was anywhere about, eavesdropping. He couldn't see her. She was well hidden, so he spoke.

'Hello, Hugh. Peggy was up at our house today. She's expecting your child, and she's going through torture at home because of it. They're threatening to send her away, out of the country, so you had better get on the boat right away, lad.' Agnes nearly fainted with shock. There's a boyo for ya! and anyone would think butter wouldn't melt in his mouth.

'We'll see you soon so, Hugh,' said Neil, putting down the phone.

Hugh returned home one week later, on Sunday morning. Mary and Kate were home for the week-end, and Father Seamus O'Neill, the parish priest was there at Ellen's request, to make arrangements for the wedding. Ellen asked him to call to Clover Road, and talk to Toby O'Flaherty, and impress on him, what a fine upstanding lad

49

Hugh was, and how it would be totally against the law of God and man to stand in the way of this marriage, especially now with Peggy in the family way with Hugh's child, that he wanted so badly. Father Seamus was very fond of the O'Grady family, especially of Hugh. Didn't he baptise him, give him his First Holy Communion and now he was going to marry him. Hugh paced back and forth around the kitchen. On the one hand, he was excited at the prospect of making Peggy his bride, and looking forward to the birth of his baby; but on the other, he was nervous and concerned for Peggy. He wished she were here in the house with him now.

'I wonder father, should I go down myself to O'Flaherty's and ask Toby, myself, for Peggy's hand?'

'That would not be advisable,' said Mary, and Kate nodded in agreement.

'Well,' said Father Seamus, 'I think, myself, that it would be the most honourable and manly thing to do.'

'Honour means precious little to that man,' Neil said, 'a wad of notes is what talks to him.'

'He won't get much money from you, Neil O'Grady,' said Ellen, 'and you spending every penny you earn on drink and horses.'

'Let's not argue,' said Hugh, 'I'll dress up in my Sunday clothes to-morrow morning, and I'll go down to the house, as I said.'

'You do that, son' said Ellen 'for you have more spunk in you than any man I know, and 'tis bloody glad the aul' geezer should be, to hand his daughter over to you.' There was a peel of laughter.

'That's settled then,' said Neil. 'Let's all drink a toast to the prospective newly-weds.' He produced a bottle of whiskey, filled up all the glasses, and a very pleasant evening was had by all, on Hugh's first day home.

Hugh headed off at the crack of dawn, on the following morning, to see Toby O'Flaherty. Ellen made sure he was impeccably dressed, and as she brushed down the back of his suit, lost in admiration at his noble appearance, she remarked proudly.

'Boy, do you look elegant, like a real gentleman, you are. Go down there now, and give them a good eye-full, for I'm sure they think the like of us go around dressed in rags.'

'Thanks, Ma,' said Hugh, 'I feel better already.' He walked down the Ashe Road, whistling a merry tune as he went, and, feeling happier and more light-hearted than he had done for a good many months. This was the last hurdle he had to jump, and afterwards, he would have his darling Peggy all to himself. He knocked on the door of the big, gloomy house, and as soon as he did, he felt very nervous and apprehensive. The door was opened by Jamie.

'My name is Hugh O'Grady. I would like to have a word with your father, please.' Jamie's face reddened with anger, and Hugh would never forget the fire in his eyes.

'Get to hell out of here, you tramp! Haven't you done enough damage already, inflicting your bastard on this family. Leave my sister alone, and don't ever again darken this door, or I'll be up for your murder.' Hugh stood where he was, and opened his mouth to say something else; but before he had a chance to utter a syllable, Jamie punched him viciously on the nose, and he fell helplessly to the ground. He heard the sound of the big door banging, as he tried to get up, blood pouring profusely onto his freshly washed white shirt. He was stunned and shocked for several minutes, and then he got himself together, and turned for home, holding a handkerchief to his nose.

Ellen was furious at the cruel way her son was treated, and vowed vengeance on Jamie O'Flaherty. Mary and Kate were also shocked and horrified.

'Such ignorance, intolerance, and disgusting class-distinction should be stamped out, in this day and age,' said Kate.

'I detest it,' Mary avowed, 'and who in the name of God do they think they are.'

'Leave them to God,' said Neil, trying to calm Ellen, who at this stage, was like a raving lunatic. She couldn't contain her anger and indignation any longer, and she threw on her coat and hat, and ran all the way to the house of Father Seamus. Hugh didn't notice her leaving the house, because he had been in his room, cleaning himself up after his terrible ordeal. He was relieved to learn she hadn't given up the battle, because he himself was very depressed and worried, thinking he would never see Peggy again.

Father Seamus was alarmed at Ellen's state of mind, when she arrived at his home. He knew she was a fiery little woman, but he had never before seen her so wound up, and so really upset.

'Calm down, my good woman,' he said. 'There's a solution to every problem, and we'll take care of this one too.'

'There's not sense or meaning to those Flaherty's, Father, to degrade and lessen my son, in that manner, and he such a thorough gentleman.'

''Tis indeed a crying shame, Ellen, and totally unchristian behaviour.'

'Please, Father,' pleaded Ellen, 'would you go down immediately to Toby O'Flaherty, and order him, in the name of God, to allow a date to be set for the wedding, for I want my grandchild to be born legitimate.'

'I'll do that right away,' said Father Seamus, 'and let you go back to your home and relax yourself.'

'Thank you, Father. May God bless you! You are, indeed, a great friend to us.'

Brigid O'Flaherty answered the door to Father Seamus.

'Good morning, Father,' she said, her pale face blushing to crimson, because she well knew the purpose of his visit, and she was very much ashamed of her eldest son's behaviour earlier on.

'God love and bless you! Brigid. I've come to have a word with Toby. Is he at home?'

'He is indeed Father. Come on in and sit down. I'll get him for you straight away.' She led Father Seamus upstairs, to a large sitting-room, and went to get her husband. He was in the kitchen with Jamie when Brigid came in.

'Father Seamus wants to see you. He's upstairs in the sitting-room, waiting for you.'

'Ah! be damned to him! if he's coming here to tell me what to do with my daughter. I'll get rid of him quickly.'

'Don't speak with such disrespect of the holy priest, Toby,' Brigid said.

'Attend to your duties, Mam, and let me make the decisions, please,' he snarled. Then he lit his pipe and went upstairs.

As he entered the room, Father Seamus stood up, and tried to shake hands with him. He declined roughly.

'There'll be no hand-shaking at all, Father, because I know this is not going to be a very friendly discussion. So say what you came to say, and be quick about it.'

'I'll come directly to the point, Mr O'Flaherty,' replied Father Seamus. 'I have come here this morning to intercede on behalf of one of my folk, a fine, upstanding, decent boy, who wishes to take your daughter Peggy for his wife.'

'If you're referring to that young O'Grady fella, the answer is No! Do you think I have raised my daughter, and spent my good hard earned money, to throw her away to this penniless lout?'

'Your daughter loves Hugh O'Grady, and he loves her, and she would travel a long way to find a better husband. I can vouch for that.'

53

'I think, Father, with all due respect to you, that you are not qualified to advise me on the choice of a husband for my daughter. I have someone very suitable in mind for her myself, and I think I should know best.' Father Seamus was beginning to lose his patience, because he could clearly see from Toby's attitude that he was getting nowhere. He stood up and went towards the door. Then turning around he made his parting remark.

'You are a hard, stubborn man, Mr O'Flaherty, and you are setting out to destroy the happiness of two young people. I warn you though, that you will not succeed, because the very next time I see them both together, I will marry them on the spot.' Then he walked out, slamming the door behind him. This very adamant threat that Father Seamus made, seemed to intimidate Toby, somewhat; so he called the priest back. Father Seamus came into the room again, and sat down, feeling that maybe victory was in sight.

'What did you mean exactly, by your parting remark that you will marry them the next time you see them together, and on whose authority would you be acting?' shouted Toby, now almost purple in the face with anger.

'I would be honouring the wish of the couple themselves. You must remember Mr O'Flaherty, from your school catechism, that in the sacrament of matrimony, the couple themselves perform the sacrament, and that the priest is only a witness.'

Toby was very taken aback. 'I want to have a word with my eldest son,' he said, tottering downstairs to the kitchen. 'You had better come on upstairs with me lad. This damm priest is getting the better of me. I don't remember a word of that penny catechism. You might have some idea what he's on about. You were at it more recently than I.' Jamie returned upstairs with Toby, and greeted Father Seamus in a less than friendly manner. After many hours of heated discussion and argument with Toby and Jamie, Father Seamus finally, and indeed, very reluctantly, got their agreement for the wedding, and the date was fixed for May first. It was emphasised that Hugh was not to see Peggy for the two or so weeks until then.

The marriage banns were announced at first mass on the following Sunday, and from then on, preparations were in full swing in the O'Grady household. All the good neighbours rallied around as usual, offering their assistance in making the day one to be remembered. Mary and Kate were to be Peggy's bridesmaids, and Mossy Fogarty was to be Hugh's best man. Mossy was very excited at the thought of walking up the aisle with Mary. Maybe he would pop the question on that day!

Chapter 6

As the curtains of night slowly lifted over the little sleepy
village of Glenbeg, the dawn broke on the special morning
of May first, 1934. It was a glorious morning, with blue
skies and brilliant sunshine. Happy the bride that the sun
shines on said Ellen to herself. She had not been to bed at
all. She had spent the entire night cleaning and cooking,
helped by a glass of whiskey at regular intervals. She drew
the curtains on the kitchen window, threw it wide open, and
looked out to see if there was any sign of life yet. She
breathed in the fresh morning air, and relished the perfume
of the garden flowers, and the sweet aroma of the freshly cut
grass and hedges. She felt very happy, and full of joy at the
prospect of this marriage of her son to a daughter of the
gentry, for deep down in her rebellious spirit, she believed
that Hugh had won this battle, and had succeeded in
breaking through the stupid mould of social inequality and
class distinction, sentiments which she had always
abhorred.

It was not long before the cottage was alive with activity,
Mary and Kate putting the last minute touches to their
finery. Mary looked radiant in a pretty, pale blue dress,
buttoned down the front, with a large, white, picture hat,
with shoes and gloves to match. Kate wore a lemon, linen
suit, with dark brown accessories. Ellen was proud of her
two daughters, although at that moment, their presence
made her a little jittery, as she could not have another nip of

whiskey while they were around. They usually got very annoyed and irritated when they saw her, under the influence, and she didn't want to draw them on her this morning. Still, there would have been no money to fund this wedding, if they weren't so good and sensible. For that, she was very grateful, as neither Neil nor Hugh ever seemed to be able to save a shilling.

'Someone ought to waken Hugh,' said Kate, 'for he will need some time to straighten himself out after that stag party in Mac's last night. I heard him coming home in the early hours of the morning.'

'Let him rest easy awhile,' said Neil, calmly sitting at the table, eating a soft boiled egg with brown bread and jam, 'for he has a long wearisome day ahead of him, poor lad, and a longer night. I'd say young Peggy is a frisky little mare.'

'Hold your tongue, man. That's no class of talk for a man of your age, and in front of the girls, too. Have you any shame!' She was sticking a red carnation carefully into the buttonhole of Hugh's new grey pinstriped suit, which hung at the back of the door. Neil was chuckling behind her back. He enjoyed teasing her, and he loved her when she got angry.

Hugh crawled out of bed, and lit a cigarette. He was feeling jittery, partly from his nocturnal activities, and also because he was a little nervous and apprehensive. He was going to be married in two hours time, and from then on, he was to spend the remainder of his life with a lass that he had never laid eyes on, until seven months ago. He did love her very much. Of that he was absolutely sure. He was sure also that he couldn't wait to take her in his arms again and give her all the love and affection that she never got, living with a harsh, cold father like Toby O'Flaherty. Poor little Peggy, he thought. She must be feeling happy and relieved now, to know that the long nightmare in that dreary, sombre house

57

is over. Then, suddenly, the beautiful face of Nessa flashed across his mind, and he couldn't help feeling again, the same awful pangs of sorrow and remorse that had driven him away from his beloved Glenbeg.

'Nessa, my darling,' he prayed, 'you are in heaven now, and looking down on me. I know you still love me and want me to be happy. Please, take care of Peggy, the baby and me.' He shed a silent tear, and then, feeling happier and easier in himself, he dashed into the kitchen. Ellen filled the sink with hot water from her big black kettle, and he washed and shaved carefully. Then he donned his grey wedding suit, snow-white shirt, blue tie, and shiny black shoes. He turned and looked at Ellen, all dressed up in navy and white, feeling as proud as punch. He kissed her on the cheek.

'Well, Ma. Isn't it you that looks beautiful. Take care people do not mistake you for the bride.'

'She's my darling bride for the past twenty-eight years now, and 'tis younger and better-looking she's getting,' said Neil, putting his arms around her and lifting her up in the air.

'Let me down, you silly, old man, or you'll ruin my clothes.' Neil looked well, as always, and was really looking forward to a good day out with plenty to drink.

Mossy Fogarty arrived at nine-thirty, and announced that Tim Whelan's carriage was on the way up the Ashe Road, beautifully shined and polished, ready to take them all to the church. 'Have you the ring, Mossy?' enquired Ellen anxiously. He put his hand into the inside pocket of his tweed suit, and carefully produced the little, red box. 'There it is, Mam, ready for the bride's finger.' He couldn't keep his eyes off Mary. Wasn't she really pretty, and wouldn't they look well together, standing at the altar. Mary had eyes for him, too, for he was always so pleasant and good humoured, and had a very charming personality.

The carriage, bearing all the O'Grady family, and a few neighbours, stopped outside the little, limestone church at nine forty-five, in plenty of time for the ten o'clock mass. All the neighbours were assembled there to greet Hugh and rejoice with him on his big day. They were also curious to see his bride, this courageous woman who was going to make history to-day, when she married one of their own class. The little church was crowded inside, and the altar was beautifully and tastefully decorated with red tulips and yellow daffodils. The red carpet was laid from the door right up to the altar. Everyone waited in anticipation for the arrival of Peggy and her entourage of gentry. Time ticked away. Hugh looked at his watch. It was fifteen minutes after ten. He was beginning to feel a little anxious and uptight. Father Seamus came out onto the altar, with his little band of altar-boys, all the clothes and vestments spotlessly clean and starched. He threw a concerned glance in the direction of the O'Grady's who were seated in the front row. Neil left his seat, and left the Church. He looked up and down the road, but there was no sign of anyone. Ellen's heart was beating so rapidly that she thought it would stop, and Hugh was in absolute turmoil. Ten-thirty, and still no sign of the bride. Mary and Kate were mortified.

'What will the neighbours think?' they whispered to Ellen.

'Never mind what anyone thinks. What about your poor brother. My heart bleeds for him.'

People began to shuffle and cough nervously, while Father Seamus decided to recite the Joyful Mysteries of the Rosary. The Rosary ended, and the trimmings, and it was now eleven o'clock. At that stage, Hugh walked up to the altar, and whispered in the priest's ear. Immediately, Father Seamus made the announcement 'My dear brethern, I regret to inform you, that as the bride has not turned up, the ceremony is postponed for the moment.'

Shock registered on the faces of the congregation as they left the church. The O'Gradys remained seated until the church was empty, and then they went into the sacristy to Father Seamus. Neil produced a little bottle from his pocket, and gave Hugh a drink. The boy was ghastly-looking. Father Seamus conveyed his heartfelt sympathy to Hugh on his bitter disappointment and terrible embarrassment, while Ellen and the girls were numbed into silence. Neil, for once in his life, took command of the situation and gathered his family around him. 'We must all remain calm and composed now,' he advised. 'Things might not be as bad as they appear at the moment. Let's all go home, and get our heads together, and who knows what we might decide to do about this problem.'

'That is a very wise suggestion indeed, and I will be along myself in a little while, to see if there's anything I can do.' said the priest.

Brigid O'Flaherty was at her wits end. The bitterness and resentment she felt towards her husband and eldest son, knew no bounds. She never believed they could be so cruel and callous as to keep her daughter, locked away like a wild animal, in her bedroom for the past fortnight. She had hoped that they would free her, on this, her wedding day, but they did not, and she was still buried alive in that little room, at the back of the house. Brigid herself was a very kindly, timid woman; but she lived in fear of his vile temper. It hurt and affected her very deeply, to think of Peggy's terrible dilemma, and what she must be going through at this moment. She thought also of Hugh and the whole O'Grady family, their friends and neighbours, and deep down, in her heart, she was genuinely sorry for them, in their disappointment and embarrassment. She had not been permitted to visit her daughter during the past few-weeks, but she could hear her sobbing at night and feared that this horrific trauma she was enduring, would surely harm the little baby she was carrying. She looked up at the large picture of the Sacret Heart over the range, and prayed, as she had never prayed before, that somehow He would soften them, and that they would have a change of heart. Sr Dominica had told her that Peggy was to be taken to one of the Order's special homes for wayward girls, where she would have the child, and that as soon as she was well enough, she would be sent to France, under the care of Dr Ned Casey, her former fiancé. The baby would, of course, be put up for adoption. Toby had told Peggy their plans last night, and afterwards, she had attempted to run out the door past him. He apprehended her and beat her very badly. What was to become of her, thought Brigid. Oh! please Lord! help her, and find a way for her to escape. Father Seamus had called to plead with them, advising them of the wrong they were doing. Toby ordered him out of the house, and said. "Tisn't for you to tell me what's right or wrong, for I am man and master here, in my own household.'

While Brigid was storming heaven with her prayers for Peggy, Mossy Fogarty and Hugh were making their way into the yard, where young Dave was sweeping the manure into a heap. They pushed him quickly into one of the stables, and, handing him half a crown, they asked him to help them release Peggy. He agreed wholeheartedly, because he thought the world of her, and was none too happy about her cruel, severe treatment. He pointed out Peggy's bedroom window to them, and Hugh threw a fistful of small stones up at it. He had to repeat this procedure on several occasions, before eventually, Peggy's face appeared at the window. When she saw Hugh below in the yard, she got so excited that the infant in her womb stirred sharply. She opened the window and shouted.

'Get me out of here quickly, or I'll die. I can't bear it one minute longer.'

'Don't worry love! we'll have you out in quick time, but stay quiet or you'll arouse your father and brother.'

'Oh! hurry! hurry!' she begged, 'I think I'm going crazy.'

'Hush now a minute, and let us figure out the best plan of campaign.' They talked quietly together for a few minutes, and Peggy thought they would never stop. Then Dave and Hugh took hold of Mossy Fogarty's legs and hoisted him up to where he grabbed onto the chute, which ran down the wall of the house, and he scaled up the remainder of the way, like a monkey until he got a level with the window. Then he manoeuvered his body very deftly and swiftly, and swung his two legs in through the window, letting go of the chute at the same time, and landing feet first in the bedroom. Peggy's heart missed several beats while he was performing this magnificent feat. He took the sheets from Peggy's bed, and knotted them up to form a kind of rope. Peggy watched his every move and thought he was taking ages, for she was scared stiff this rescue attempt might be foiled.

'Hurry up, Mossy,' she repeated over and over again, 'if Jamie catches us, there'll be a murder committed.'

'Take it easy now, and don't panic, for we must be careful lest there be an accident. We must do this right.' Finally, he was ready, and he threw the long rope of sheet down to Hugh, holding the longer portion of it himself. Then he warned Peggy to hold on to the rope tightly, with her two hands, and lifting her gently out the window, he eased her down carefully, to the waiting arms of Hugh. Wasting no time, he then tied the sheet on to the leg of the bed, and scaled down quickly himself. They thanked Dave for his help, and breathing a large sigh of relief, they went out of the yard as quickly as their legs could carry them, and they didn't stop until they reached Hugh's house.

The O'Gradys were overjoyed to see them, and Peggy wept with happiness in Hugh's arms. She couldn't believe she was really free, free of that unhappy house and her ogre of a father, and best of all, this time, free for ever.

'Oh! Hugh,' she entreated, 'Don't let them get me, ever again, for if they do, I swear I'll kill myself.'

'Don't fret yourself one little bit, because you can rest assured, I'll never let you out of my sight again.' Ellen told Mossy Fogarty to get up on his bicycle, and go, straight away, for Father Seamus. Mossy was back again very quickly, and breathless with excitement he announced.

'The priest wants you all up at the church within the hour, and he's going to marry Hugh and Peggy quietly.'

'Praise be to the Lord,' said Ellen, 'but aren't his ways wonderful.'

'What am I going to wear?' said Peggy, as she looked down at the shabby, grubby dress she was wearing.

'We'll fix that,' Kate said, 'Come along down to the bedroom with me, and you can take your pick of clothes from my wardrobe.' Everyone freshened up a little, and when Peggy returned to the kitchen, she looked radiant, clad in a rose pink frock, which brought a warm glow to her face. Hugh went over to her, held her in his arms and kissed her.

'You surely are the most beautiful bride any man could wish for.'

'Thank you, Hugh,' said Peggy, 'And thanks a million to all of you. I am lucky to be getting such a loving family, and I have never been so happy in my life.'

Ellen cried with joy, she was so happy for Peggy, after all she had been through. She was overjoyed too for Hugh, for anyone could see how deeply he loved her, and how broken-hearted he would be if he could not make her his wife. They were married quietly, in a simple, intimate ceremony at exactly six o'clock in the evening.

Afterwards, they all returned home, and Hugh lifted his bride over the threshold of No. 9, Rosebud Cottages, and laid her down gently on the good settee with the lovely, floral chinz.

'Rest there awhile, my love,' and Ma will bring you a nice wedding supper. From this day onwards, you are going to be spoilt rotten.' He kissed her passionately, and then kissed her slightly swollen tummy, where his unborn baby was about four months old. Peggy closed her eyes, to register this happy moment in the annals of her mind and she could feel tension and anxiety easing gradually, until she became totally relaxed and content. All the family danced attendance on her, making every effort in their power, to make her feel welcome and loved.

'You are all so good,' said Peggy, 'Why, you're treating me like a queen, and this is something to which I have not been accustomed.'

'You are my sweet queen,' said Hugh 'and you had better begin to get accustomed to it.'

As the evening wore on, all the kindly neighbours of Ashe Road called, and brought wedding presents. They gave a hearty 'Céad Míle Fáilte' to the new Mrs O'Grady. Father Seamus arrived, and got a thunderous applause from all, for his courage in marrying Hugh and Peggy, in spite of the O'Flahertys. He gave a lovely speech, in which he praised Hugh and the O'Grady family, and congratulated Peggy in recognising a good man when she saw him, and going for him against all the obstacles.

'I have never had such difficulty getting any pair together,' he said, 'And I know there is no man alive that could ever again tear them apart.'

'Hear! hear!' shouted Neil, and handing Father Seamus a large tumbler full of the hot stuff, he toasted him. 'Here's to your health, Father, and may God keep you here with us in Glenbeg forever.' There was another big round of applause, and then the party got into full swing. Stories were told.

Songs were sung. Neil, well and truly inebriated, gave a magnificent rendering of Rudgard Kipling's 'If,' to the great pleasure of all. Hugh sang several times, and Peggy was fascinated by his sweet, tuneful, tenor voice. Mary and Kate danced a reel and a hornpipe, as only they could do, and Mossy played a number of waltzes and foxtrots on his accordion, as everyone danced gaily around the little kitchen. Ellen had been forced to retire shortly after midnight, as the strain of the day, combined with several drops too many, had got to her. The party continued until the early hours of the morning, and the dawn was breaking as Hugh and Peggy, wrapped tightly in the arms of each other, slept peacefully and soundly, exhausted after hours of passionate, ecstatic love.

It was afternoon the next day, when they finally arose, and Neil, in his typically witty and humorous manner, greeted them. 'Good Afternoon! Mr. and Mrs. O'Grady, I trust you enjoyed your honeymoon in Blanket Town.' Peggy was tickled pink, while Hugh felt a bit embarrassed in front of his mother and two sisters. Mary and Kate weren't taking much notice, as they were busy packing their bags for their return, later in the evening, to Dublin. They were taking Ellen and Neil with them for a few day's holiday, and also to give the young couple some time to themselves.

Hugh was glad his parents were not at home, when Jamie O'Flaherty came to the cottage that night, banging down the door in a vicious temper, and accusing Hugh and his family of kidnapping his sister, and taking her away from her own class and kind. Hugh handled him coolly and calmly, but firmly, and insisted that he leave them in peace, or he would be forced to have recourse to the law. Several other attempts were made, during the next week, to intimidate Hugh; but each situation was well taken care of, and Toby O'Flaherty soon realised that any further efforts would be a waste of time. He was seething with anger and contempt for Peggy. 'She's nothing but a trollop, and she has broken the laws of God and man,' he shouted to Brigid. 'She'll never again put a foot inside this house while I'm alive. I completely disown her, and the brat she's carrying, and not one penny of mine, will she ever see.' Poor Brigid felt very hurt and sad, and made up her mind there and then, that whatever bit of money she had herself, from rearing the calves and the turkeys, she would leave it to Peggy.

As time went by, Maeve and Sheila became frequent visitors, and they usually brought Peggy a couple of shillings which they would take from the till in the bar. Peggy was very glad of this money, as Hugh was now unemployed, and one never knew when Neil would lose his week's wages on the horses. He was completely irresponsible, but you couldn't stay angry with him for long, because he was great company around the house, always in good form, with a most hilarious sense of humour. He was very charming too, and Peggy really enjoyed listening to him, as he teased Ellen. She took him very seriously, and she was very hot-tempered. He would sit back and laugh when she got into a furious rage. He would let her rattle on for a while, and it intrigued Peggy to note how he knew exactly what to do or say, to calm her down again.

The days and weeks passed by peacefully and contentedly, for Peggy and Hugh. They grew in love for each other all the time, and he marvelled at the miraculous change that was very noticeably taking place in her lovely body. He would often joke with her about her large size. 'I'll have to have my arms extended, to get them round you soon, and I will have to kiss you from behind.' She enjoyed this, immensely, and thrived on the love and affection she received, not only from Hugh, but from Ellen and Neil also.

She was not permitted to do any housework, and Ellen insisted that she sit in the sunshine each day, with her feet up. 'Plenty of rest, fresh air and sunshine, are the best things in the world for a mother to be.' Hugh had bought her a pretty, blue, loose smock, as the summer of 1934 was particularly warm. He had got a job in the local betting office, and he had also got a small plot of ground from Fr. Seamus, in which he grew potatoes and vegetables, in his spare time. Peggy loved to walk up there with him in the cool of the evening, where they could be completely alone. She always brought her wicker basket with her, and Hugh would fill it with potatoes and fresh vegetables. These were the happiest days of Peggy's life, and she often wished then, that time would stand still, so things could never change.

August fifteenth was a big holiday in the country, and usually brought a lot of visitors to Glenbeg. On the evening of the fourteenth, Peggy was busy, shining with brasso, the knocker and letterbox on the front door of the cottage. This was the only chore Ellen would allow her do, and Ellen was always very particular about keeping them bright and shiny. She was extremely possessive about her kitchen, and was of the firm belief that two women could definitely not share the one kitchen.

Peggy looked down the Ashe Road, and thought, for a split second that she was dreaming. This couldn't possibly be, she said to herself, her eyes riveted on the tall figure of a nun walking towards her. As she came closer, she recognised her, and wiping her hands on her apron, she went to meet her. It was Sr Dominica, and to Peggy's amazement, she was smiling warmly at her. She embraced Peggy lovingly.

'You look beautiful my dear.' 'Why! you are blooming with health and happiness. It certainly suits you to be married and in the family way.'

'I feel very well, thank you, Celia, but I'm curious to find out what brings you up here. Did Father know you were coming?'

'Yes! our father knows Peggy, but why don't we go inside.'

'Oh! to be sure,' said Peggy. 'Come along, Mrs O'Grady will be delighted to meet you.' Sr Dominica was ushered into the cottage by Peggy, and she was introduced to Ellen.

'I am very glad to meet you, Sr Dominica, and you are more than welcome to our humble home. Won't you sit down there, and I'll go and fetch some tea.'

'Thank you kindly, Mrs O'Grady, but that will not be necessary.' Then there was a moment of silence, during which Ellen was thinking: She has the typical O'Flaherty air of grandeur and snobbery about her alright, the way she doesn't want to become too familiar with us poor northside folk.

'I wonder would you leave us alone for a moment, please, Mrs O'Grady' asked Sr Dominica.

'Certainly, sister,' answered Ellen, and she disappeared into the back garden. The devil mend her she said to herself, with her haughty and secretive manner. I wonder what she's up to now?

Inside the cottage, Peggy was, at this stage, feeling nervous and a trifle worried at the strange, mysterious attitude of her sister.

'Sit down, Peggy,' she said. 'I came here to bring you bad news of our mother,' and before she could say any more, Peggy said, almost hysterically, 'She's dead isn't she? Isn't that the reason you came here today?'

'Yes, my dear. She died in her sleep, last night, and your father found her early this morning.' Peggy burst into genuine tears of sorrow.

'He killed her! the brute! He worked her to death, and broke her poor heart.'

'Control yourself, at once, Peggy, and refrain from such rash, disrespectful outbursts. Try to remember the child you are carrying, and do not upset yourself any further. Our mother was a good, saintly woman, and God has taken her straight to heaven, where she is happy at last.'

'She has done her purgatory in this life anyway, living all those years under his control.'

Sr Dominica, ignoring this last remark, got up to go away. 'I must leave you now, as there are arrangements to be made, and Maeve or Sheila will let you know the details in due course.'

Her mother was buried with her own people two days later, and Peggy and Hugh attended her funeral. They were completely ignored by Toby and Jamie, while the others saluted them from a distance.

The baby was due to be born in October, but whether it was the shock of her mother's death or not, Peggy went into labour, unexpectedly, on the night of September seventh. Ellen stayed with her, helping her along. 'Take deep breaths, and go with the pain,' she advised, letting Peggy squeeze her hands tightly. Hugh ran all the way to the dispensary, urging the midwife, Julia McCarthy to come quickly. 'Take it easy, garsoon,' said Julia, 'Sure there's always plenty of time with the first.' When eventually she arrived at the cottage, her little black case in her hand, Ellen had Peggy in bed, and had several dishes of boiling water and fresh clean towels in readiness for the big event. Hugh stayed in the kitchen with Neil, waiting patiently, the cold perspiration teaming off him, as Peggy yelled. He smoked one Woodbine cigarette after another, and he was frightened out of his wits.

'Oh! Da, what's happening? Will she be alright?' Neil slapped him on the back and reassured him.

'Of course she will, for she's a fine, strapping girl, and there's no fear at all of her.'

The screams got louder, and Hugh was forced to put his fingers in his ears to block them out. He was actually beginning to feel the pain himself. Neil, seeing his distressed, worried state, came to the rescue again with his little bottle. 'Here, lad! take a swig of that, and it will give you ease. 'Tis a great pity that oul' Julia McCarthy wouldn't give poor Peggy a drop. Sure 'twould save the poor girl an amount of pain, and the baby would be here long ago.' Hugh laughed in spite of himself, and there was silence, followed after a second or two, by the loud cry of his baby.

He ran into the bedroom, as excited as a child on Christmas morning. Peggy looked pale and dishevelled, but radiantly happy, he thought, as she held the little, raw infant in her arms, wrapped in a pink, woollen blanket. Hugh bent down and kissed them both tenderly. Then he took his child in his arms and looked lovingly at her.

'Isn't she beautiful?' Peggy said in a low, weak voice.

'I can't believe she's mine,' said Hugh, 'She's the flower of Glenbeg, and she's a joy to behold.' Then he returned her carefully into Peggy's waiting arms, and stroking the damp hair from her forehead, he said. 'Take your rest now, my love, for you need it, and deserve it. You have done a wonderful job, and have given me a very precious gem that I will cherish for ever.' Peggy closed her eyes, and enjoyed the joy and happiness of that moment.

Chapter 7

'The deal is made, and the deal is fair,' declared Toby O'Flaherty, shaking the hand of Tommy O'Sullivan, the local hardware merchant, who owned the large profitable store at the East End of Clover Road. He had just finalised a grand match for his daughter, Maeve, and he was feeling very pleased with himself on that account. Tommy was a nice quiet respectable man, with plenty of money, old enough to be her father, but socially and financially, he was very acceptable to the O'Flaherty family. It didn't matter that Maeve herself found him, ugly and revolting, and hadn't the slightest interest in him, let alone love him. Toby would no longer worry about her, gadding about with every Tom, Dick and Harry, and maybe end up like Peggy. They were married within the month, and the wedding was a huge social event in Glenbeg, with the photograph of old Toby standing beside the Bride and Groom, plastered across the front page of *The Trumpet*. He gave Tommy O'Sullivan a tidy dowry with her; but sure that was a very wise investment, because Maeve would definitely, on the law of averages, outlive him, and she would inherit the store and all his money. The dowry was in fact, staying in the O'Flaherty family. Tommy was a very thrifty man, and, like Toby, thought it sacrilegious to spend the precious substance.

He was searching around for a suitable candidate for his youngest daughter, Sheila. He was very anxious to have her fixed up as soon as possible, lest she be snapped up by some poverty-stricken fellow, and they were very plentiful around Glenbeg. Sheila was his favourite, and could do no wrong in his eyes. Jamie and Sr Dominica felt the same way about her, but Dave christened her 'Sly Boots', and he was perfectly right. Sheila, who spent all her time looking after the pub now, was having a very strong affair with Edward Kelly, the editor of *The Glenbeg Trumpet*. He was a man of the world, at thirty-five years of age, and would drink Loch Erin dry. He had slept with almost every woman in Glenbeg, and outside of it, and now it was Sheila's turn. She would keep him inside the pub after closing time at night, and when he was well drunk, he would go to bed with her, and then slip out the back-door at the crack of dawn. Sheila thought he was wonderful, so swave and experienced, and dressed so glamourously. Apart from those attributes, he was nothing to look at, rather plump and low-sized, very scarce of hair, and he had a broad flat nose, on which he wore a pair of black horn-rimmed glasses.

As they sat alone in the bar one night, Sheila announced to him that she was pregnant. He dropped his glass with shock, and his face reddened up.

'What's the matter? Aren't you happy about the baby?' asked Sheila, innocently.

'Are you quite sure of this?' he questioned sharply, panic gripping him.

'Oh! yes, I'm absolutely certain. In fact I am almost three months gone now.' He didn't answer, but she noticed him clench his fists tightly, and she became afraid. 'What am I to do?' she asked him, almost in tears.

'Give me another drink,' he answered abruptly. She filled him a large gin and tonic, and he polished it off, and another, and another.

'That's the last one I'm giving you now,' warned Sheila, very concerned and apprehensive about his reaction to what she considered, good news. 'What are we going to do?' she repeated.

'We are going to sleep on it' he drooled, standing up, staggering, and then taking her by the hand, upstairs to bed. He was unable to make love to her, as he usually did, for he lapsed into a drunken stupor. Before he left, in the early hours of the morning, he kissed her and whispered, 'I'll see you to-night, and I'll tell you then of my plans for us.'

He didn't show up that night, or any other night after that, and Sheila was at her wit's end. She searched everywhere for him, but without success. She even went to the offices of *The Trumpet*, to be informed that he had not turned up there, either. She heard later, that he had left Glenbeg altogether, and by all and every account, he had other reasons, apart from Sheila, for running. It was said that he had sexually assaulted a seventeen-year old girl, whose parents were in the process of taking legal action against him. Sheila was in a state of shock and dismay. She couldn't eat or sleep, and was looking very pale and tired. What am I going to do? she thought to herself, as she felt her waist enlarging and her clothes becoming too tight for her. I could try to get rid of this baby, if I took mustard baths and plenty of castor oil. She had heard that these methods could do the trick, but, My God! that would be murder and a mortal sin, and she would burn in hell forever. She daren't tell her father or Jamie, and though Peggy would understand, she couldn't help, and anyway, she had problems of her own. The only person who could do anything for her now, was her eldest sister, the nun. She must brace herself, and go to the convent and tell her.

As she walked up the long, lonely avenue to the convent, she was trembling all over. She rang the big brass bell, and young Sr Augusta answered promptly. 'Good morning, Sheila. Come along into the parlour.'

73

'Thank you, sister.'

'Is Sister Dominica about?'

'She's in the chapel, but I'll go and get her for you.'

Isn't it well for young Sr Augusta, mused Sheila to herself; she definitely has chosen the better part; and doesn't she look cheerful and happy, without a care in the world! She looked around the scrupulously clean, neat room, with its highly polished floor, and the dazzling silver on the sideboard. She wondered about the large life-size picture of a nun, which hung on the wall, over the fireplace. She must be the foundress of the order, she thought. Hasn't she got a very stern face! Yet those eyes seem gentle and kindly.

She was roused from her ponderings by the quick footsteps coming down the corridor. There was a gentle knock on the door, then it was opened, and in came Sr Dominica, dressed in her white nursing habit. She eyed Sheila up and down, quizzically, and then pulled up a chair and sat beside her.

'This is, indeed, a pleasant surprise. It's a pity you didn't inform me you were coming. I could have arranged to take some time off.' Sheila didn't hear a word she was saying, because she could feel herself going limp with fear, and she knew she was turning forty colours. She was about to speak, when she became literally tongue-tied, and couldn't utter a syllable. Then she broke down completely, crying bitter tears.

'What on earth is the matter?' queried Sr Dominica, and she produced a large blue and white check handkerchief from her pocket. She handed it to Sheila. 'Come now, take control of yourself, wipe your eyes, and tell me all about it.' Sheila looked up sheepishly and, stuttering, she finally blurted out her story. Sr Dominica's face reddened, and she was silent for a while. Then, quite contrary to Sheila's expectations, she got up from her chair, came close to her, and took her comfortingly in her arms.

'This is indeed a serious and terrible tragedy, and I am shocked to the core.'

'I'm so sorry,' cried Sheila, breaking into tears again 'but I don't know what to do, or where to turn.'

'I know full well you were not to blame at all. Our father sheltered you far too much, and that vile villain took advantage of your innocence. We'll have to pray hard to the Lord, to find a solution to this problem, and He will take care of you in your hour of need. Go home now, Sheila, and try not to worry, but please, do not mention a word about it to Jamie or to your father. God knows what they would do at this stage. I will make certain arrangements for you, and I will call to see you in the next day or two.' She embraced Sheila, who was by now feeling a little better. She led her to the front door, and Sheila walked home, letting the gentle breeze wipe away the redness in her eyes. Sr Dominica asked for a transfer to the convent in the west of Ireland, where they took care of single, pregnant girls. She went there a month later, and Sheila followed, as soon as she was beginning to look noticeable. Toby and Jamie were told that Sr Dominica had got her a job there, and that she needed a little bit of independence; so reluctantly, he let her go. He was, by now, bedridden most of the time, and Jamie and Dave, between them, took care of him as best they could.

Sheila stayed in the convent for six months altogether, and curiously enough, she was very happy and contented there. It was far more comfortable than her own gloomy home. The sisters showed affection and kindness, and the companionship of the other girls, in similar circumstances to herself, made for a very congenial atmosphere. She became very close and friendly with a girl called Fiona, daughter of a wealthy cattle-dealer, and they spent many long, pleasant hours together, talking about their childhood, and what the future now held for them.

'If they think I am going to give my baby up for adoption, they have something else coming to them,' Fiona said to Sheila, as they sat together one night, knitting little baby clothes. 'My father gives me a generous allowance every week,' she continued 'and I am saving every penny of it, to give the baby and myself a good start in London, away from all the holier than thou, gossipers. If you would like to come with me, I'd be delighted, and we would have plenty for the two of us for a while. You can always pay me back as soon as you get a job, and get on your feet.'

'Oh! thanks a million Fiona. You are very kind indeed, and I would be very happy to go away with you. The further away we get from the insular altitude of the people here, the better.'

They both gave birth to baby boys. Sheila's little fellow was very small and delicate, but thanks to the great care he received from the good sisters, he gradually grew strong and healthy. Sr Dominica was firmly convinced it was the little drop of altar wine she put in his bottle morning and evening, that brought him around. When the time came for them to give up their babies, they both refused point blank to sign the adoption papers, and left, with their babies for London. Sr Dominica took Sheila's departure very badly, and was so upset, that she couldn't settle down again to her religious duties. She was eventually transferred back again to Glenbeg, where she was allowed home to Clover Road to nurse her father, until his death. Despite Sheila's disappearance, he left her a thousand pounds in his will. Maeve got the same amount, while Sr Dominica's order benefited to the tune of three thousand pounds. Jamie was left the remainder of his money, which was indeed a princely sum, together with the house and bar, and two large farms of land. Poor Peggy was ignored completely, and she needed it more than any of them. He was bitter and prejudiced until the very end.

PART II
1952 – 1958

Chapter 8

Alana was five years old, and already had two sisters, and a new baby brother. She was not good-looking like her two sisters, Gráinne and Deirdre. They were really pretty, but she, like her mother, had the brightest of blue grey eyes that sparkled and shone like two little stars on her small, thin face. As she skipped gaily through the porch and into the kitchen, one evening after school, she was unusually exhilarated and excited.

'Mum,' she said, breathlessly, 'Sr Bernard said I was the most clever girl in the class, and that she would very much like me to play the piano.'

'That's very good, Alana, but with your father out of work, and three other children to be taken care of, where would I get the money to pay for lessons, not to mention buying a piano? Put it out of your mind Alana, and go and mind your baby brother. I have some errands for you to do, and you can take him with you in the Pram.' Declan was three months old, and the very image of Hugh.

'We'll come too,' shouted Gráinne and Deirdre in one voice. They were four and three respectively.

'Don't get up to any mischief now, Alana,' warned Peggy, 'and take good care of your brother and sisters.'

Hugh was very seldom at home these days, as all his time was spent working his little plot of ground, to get the maximum value from it. It was of tremendous assistance, he felt, in helping to feed and nourish his growing family, and it also kept his mind occupied. When he went to bed at night, he was always so exhausted from the manual work, to which he was not accustomed, that he fell fast asleep immediately, leaving Peggy, lying there beside him, disappointed and frustrated. She became irritable and moody, because she still adored Hugh, and the only pleasure and relaxation she had in her dull, busy life, was when he was close to her in bed, making love to her. She was obsessively possessive of him, and a few months after their marriage, she began to resent Hugh's love and affection for his mother. This had caused such strain and tension in the home, that Mary and Sheila persuaded Ellen and Neil to come and live with them in Dublin. Ellen hated leaving Hugh, and Glenbeg, and Hugh himself was very lonely after his parents, especially his mother. He sadly missed her cheerful chatter, and he was sure Alana, who was two at the time, would pine away for her. Ellen and Neil came to visit, twice or three times a year, on holidays, and Alana lived for their visits.

She was an exceptionally loving, affectionate and sensitive child, and even at her tender age, she could sense a certain coldness and aloofness in her mother's attitude towards her. She very often watched, with envy, the way her mother would cuddle and show affection to the other children, especially Declan, and after a time, this built up a barrier between herself and Peggy, which was not to be let down for the rest of her life. She adored her father, and he, too had a very special place in his heart for her. He always thought of her as a real live symbol of the intense love he had for Peggy. He could clearly see though, that Peggy was very jealous of this bond of affection between Alana and himself, and this caused him immense worry and concern. He was a very quiet, peace-loving man, while Peggy was domineering, fiery, and very hot-tempered; so he was afraid to even discuss this problem with her. Instead, he lavished all his love on Alana, and this, of course, magnified the problem considerably, until it got very much out of hand. The more notice and attention Hugh gave to Alana, the more resentment and coldness Peggy built up against her. Peggy began to punish the child severely, at regular intervals, and even beat her frequently, for very small offences. Still, Hugh buried his head in the sand, hoping that the problem might go away; but unfortunately, it was there to stay.

Hugh was very devoted to the family rosary, like his mother and father before him. Every evening after supper the family would kneel on the red-flagged kitchen floor to recite it. Each of the children said a mystery, starting with Alana, then Gráinne, Deirdre and Declan. Peggy usually said the last one, and Hugh would finish with prayers for all the relations and friends, and all the special intentions.

'Mum,' said Alana, after the rosary had ended one night, 'When will Aunt Mary and Uncle Mossy be home from their honeymoon?'

'They are due home in the next day or two, and granny and grandad O'Grady are coming with them, for a holiday.'

'Oh! Goody,' yelled Alana. 'I prayed they would come soon, and my prayers were answered.'

'Indeed I'm not too happy about it,' snapped Peggy, peevishly, 'and if I once see your grandma spoiling you, or interfering when I chastise you, I am adamant to put my foot down.' Alana's heart sank, and with her eyes full of tears, she opened her school-bag, and buried her head in her books. Hugh was disgusted, and he made up his mind there and then, that he must do something about it, especially for Alana's sake. He could no longer stand by silently, and watch her being cruelly discriminated against. He didn't go to the field that night, and when the children were in bed, and Peggy and himself were alone, he sat in the kitchen in a silent, thoughtful mood. This terrible grudge that his wife bore against her own first-born daughter, was hurting him deeply. Peggy was ironing on the kitchen table, and there was a very tense silence between them.

'You're like a bear with a sore paw to-night. You'd be better off up in the field, if you are going to be such bad company. What's the matter with you, anyway?' Hugh didn't answer, as he wasn't yet quite sure where to begin. Then, her anger mounting, she left her ironing, came over to the fire to him, her hands on her hips, and in a bold, sharp tone of voice, she repeated the question. Now feeling nervous and even intimidated, Hugh could not get himself to reply.

'Have you lost your tongue, or is there some cruel, dark secret you are keeping from me?' Hugh looked up at her, straight in the face.

'No Peig. I have no secrets from you, but I do not like the manner in which you are behaving towards Alana, and I am worried to death about it.'

'Alana again, is it?' she quipped, sharply, her eyes flashing with rising rage and temper. She was just about to give off a flow of abuse, but he interrupted.

'Please, Peggy. Do let me finish what I have to say.' She sat down at that point, because she could see, by his firm tone and serious face, that he was very annoyed.

'You are behaving in a very callous, cold and cruel fashion to our daughter. She is a bright, intelligent, and a very sensitive child, and she must be feeling it. Do you realise how harmful and damaging this could be to her, and how much she craves your love and affection. Why, My God! You can't even bear to see my mother give her love. See how you dampened her spirit a while ago.' Peggy could remain silent no longer. She was furious and mad with jealousy, that Hugh should put Alana before her.

'She gets as much notice and attention from you, to suffice for the two of us, and anyway, I have more to do and think about than molly coddling your favourite darling daughter. I have two other daughters and a son to take care of, and they do not look for notice like she does.' She turned to leave the room, but Hugh pulled her back and took her in his arms. 'I'm sorry, Peggy, if I upset you, but this is something that has been troubling me for some time now.' He looked into her eyes. She was pale, thin, and tired-looking, and she had aged a lot. 'You know I love you dearly, with all my heart,' he said, feeling, at once, very sorry for her, and realising what a tough life she had, and what a good life she had sacrificed for love of him. 'All I'm asking you, darling, is to show Alana a little more kindness and affection. It would mean a lot to me, and more to her; and I feel sure you will do this for me.' He kissed her, passionately, before she could say another word, and Peggy fell into his arms, yielding to him like a flower to the sun. She loved him to the point of obsession.

St Anne's Convent National School was just about two fields away, at the back of Rosebud Cottages, and across the road from St Fintan's Church. It was there that the O'Gradys and all the other children at the north side of the Glen, received their education. There was another school at the south side, but you had to pay dearly for your education there, and it was attended by the children of the higher income classes. St Anne's was a wonderful school, run, totally, by the Sisters, and it was built by their Foundress to cater especially for the poor. Alana's happiest hours were spent there, away from her mother, who nagged her constantly more than ever, and seemed bent on making her feel really bad about herself. 'You are a wicked child Alana,' she would very often say 'You're not a bit like your sisters and brother, and you'll go to hell when you die.' This remark used to really frighten and upset Alana very much, because she had heard it so often, she was actually beginning to believe it.

In school, on the contrary, she was a star pupil, top of her class in everything, bubbling over with personality, and loved and respected by the sisters and all her school companions. Sr Bernard was the principal of St Anne's. She was an extraordinarily efficient and intelligent person, with a kind encouraging word for everyone, parents and pupils alike. She was always cheerful and bright, and took a keen personal interest in every child that passed through her hands. She was a bundle of energy, and moved so swiftly from place to place, that she was affectionately known as 'Flash'. She taught music and art, and trained the choir. Every year, at around Easter time, she would hire a bus and take a large contingent of pupils, ranging in age from four to sixteen, to Feis Maitiú in Cork city. Invariably, she had winners in every competition, and the choir always came home with the trophy. Alana entered the Feis once, but having only a very average singing voice, she won no prize. Gráinne sang as sweetly as a bird, and was always a winner. Peggy was very proud of her, and kept all her medals displayed on a tray on the sideboard, boasting constantly about them.

Alana loved Sr Bernard very dearly, and Sr Bernard, too, loved her and thought the world of her.

'When I grow up, I want to be just like you, Sister.'

'That's a lovely thing to say, Alana, and it makes me feel very proud and happy. We will work hard together towards that goal.' Sr Bernard had taken a special interest in Alana from the moment she started school, and as time went on, this interest grew into a very deep friendship. There's something about that child, she was often heard to say, I feel she is going to do great things yet. She wrote to Peggy, advising her that Alana should be taught how to play the piano, and recommended to her, an excellent teacher. Peggy, too proud to admit that she could not afford these lessons, agreed, and Alana had begun her music. She stayed on in school for hours, each evening, with Sr Bernard, and practiced the piano, under her supervision. Then when the little convent bell would ring, they would walk together up the long concrete pathway to the convent, Alana, all the while, talking openly and frankly to her about her family and parents.

'I do not love my mother, Sister, and she does not love me,' she announced one evening. Sr Bernard, very taken aback at this strange announcement, stopped and looked at her questioningly.

'Alana, my dear child, you surely don't mean what you're saying. Perhaps you are imagining all this.'

'No, Sister. I'm not imagining it, and I hate leaving here to go home to her. She loves Gráinne, Deirdre and Declan alright, but she says I am very bold and wicked.'

'That is certainly not true of you, Alana. In fact you are a very good and loving child.'

'My father thinks that too, Sister, and he really loves me, and I him, but my mother gets very cross with him sometimes, because he has no job, and she is very short of money.'

'Your father cannot help having no work, Alana. Indeed there are many more like him at present; but we'll pray that he will get work soon.' Alana was very happy with that, and prayed all the way home. She even stopped at the church and lit a candle for that intention.

Soon afterwards, Hugh got a job from the nuns, tending the boilers that heated the school and convent. Alana was delighted that her father was working in the convent for the sisters, and often boasted about it to the other children. Gráinne and Deirdre didn't fancy the idea of it at all. They were of the proud O'Flaherty breed, and considered that type of work away beneath their father's dignity. He was always black all over from the soot and grime of the boilers, and was known among the school children as 'The black

87

man'. Alana, who was totally uninhibited and had a wonderful sense of humour, got a great kick out of this, while her sisters were mortified, and resented it bitterly.

At seven years of age, Declan was a very puny and delicate boy, and Peggy gave him more care and attention than all the others put together. If the wind blew, or it rained heavily, she would not allow him outside the door, and the dispensary doctor was constantly prescribing tonics for him. He was timid and shy, and didn't mix well with the other boys at school. Hugh thought Peggy was making a 'Cissie' of him, and would have preferred to see him more rough and boisterous. 'He's a class above those thugs at the national school,' said Peggy to Hugh, as they discussed Declan's problems. 'I think I will send him to the college, where he can mix with boys of his own class and type.' Hugh was disgusted at Peggy's remark, but he had long since realised, that Peggy too, was full of snobbery, just like her family, and Hugh was very disappointed at this. Snobbery was one of Hugh's aversions, because he always believed it was gross ignorance and foolishness to think any human being could be better than the next, because of the possession of money and property.

'We couldn't possibly afford those high fees,' answered Hugh, 'And even if we could, I'm sure we would find plenty more uses for it; and furthermore, he's getting a far better education at the convent. Look how well Alana and her sisters are getting on.'

'Education isn't very important for girls,' she replied, 'but a boy needs to acquire qualifications which would enable him to provide well for a wife and family.' Hugh felt this last remark, cutting through his heart like a knife, because he was acutely aware that he was providing only a very meagre existence for his wife and family. He made no further comment, but sank away into his shell.

In due course, Peggy had her way, and Declan was sent

to College. She felt as proud as punch, as she stood at the gate and watched him walk down the Ashe Road, dressed to kill, in his grey flannel pants, blue shirt and tie, and wine coloured blazer and skull cap. He was on the junior rugby team of the College, and Peggy never ceased to boast about this. Hugh wasn't impressed.

'I never thought I would see a son of mine playing that stupid, foreign game.'

'It's a gentleman's game,' boasted Peggy, 'And I think it's grand.' Alana excelled herself at camogie, and she was captain of the school team. Hugh never failed to attend the matches. When they won, he would fill the cup with lemonade, and give all the girls a drink.

'Alana scored two goals and a point, at the match to-day,' he said to Peggy, one evening, 'She's as tough as nails, that girl is. She should have been the boy in this family.' He didn't mean any harm, when he made this comment, but Peggy tossed her head, and walked away, furiously. She didn't speak a word to him for weeks after that, and Alana was very worried about her father. These long periods of silence had become very commonplace between her parents in recent times, and Alana complained a lot about her mother to Sr Bernard.

'My father doesn't deserve to be treated with such contempt, Sister. He's a very kind gentleman, and he never raises his voice or says a cross word.'

'Don't worry, Alana! I believe they truly love each other, and they will sort things out eventually.'

January twenty-first, nineteen fifty-one, was a day the O'Grady family, and indeed, the inhabitants of Glenbeg will never forget. It was four-thirty in the afternoon, and Peggy was, as usual, preparing the evening meal. Alana was in the convent with Sr Bernard, while Gráinne and Deirdre were enjoying themselves, playing hop-scotch on the kitchen floor. Hugh was out at work, and Declan was playing a rugby match. There was a loud, strange knock on the cottage door. Who in heaven's name could that possibly be, said Peggy, puzzled, as she knew if it were Mary, Mossy, or indeed, any of the other neighbours, they would open the door and walk in. When she opened the door, she was amazed to see Brother Michael, the college principal, standing there.

'Oh! Come in, Brother. This is indeed a privilege, and a very pleasant surprise. Excuse the condition of the house.' He shook hands with her, and followed, as she led him through the porch and into the kitchen.

'Run out and play now,' she ordered the two girls, 'I want to have a chat with Brother Michael.'

'Sit down, Mrs O'Grady,' he said quietly, and then, standing in front of her, he looked at her silently for a moment, tears appearing in his eyes.

'My God!' she cried, 'There's something wrong! Something terribly wrong, isn't there?' He did not speak, but nodded his head in sad assent 'Oh, Lord! It's Declan! My darling son! Where is he! What has happened to him? He'll be alright, won't he.' She was hysterical at this stage, and Brother Michael sat beside her, held her hands tightly, and in a soft sombre voice broke the news to her.

'Declan is gone to heaven, Mrs O'Grady.'

She remembered no more, because she fainted with shock, and when she was coming round, she found herself lying in the settee, with Mary bending over her, giving her little sips of brandy. Mossy was sitting at the table, talking to Brother Michael, and the two girls had gone to the convent, to fetch Hugh and Alana.

'Declan got a kick in the head, during the game,' said Brother Michael, 'He lost consciousness, and died in the ambulance, on the way to the hospital. It is indeed a terrible tragedy.'

''Tis awful, Brother a shocking disaster, and his poor

mother will never get over it. She absolutely adored him, God help her!'

'We'll pray hard for her, and if there's anything at all we can do, please, do not hesitate to contact us.'

'Thank you kindly, Brother, I'll see you to the door.'

As Brother Michael walked down the Ashe Road, Hugh dashed past him, like a mad, demented man, almost knocking him down. He ran through the cottage door and into the kitchen. He lifted Peggy in his arms, and held her there, tightly.

'Oh, Peggy! What are we going to do! Poor little Declan!', he cried, sobbing like a child. Our only little boy! and he only twelve years old. Why wasn't I kinder to him when I had him! and he's gone now, gone forever!' They both sobbed bitterly for a long time, and then Mary decided to call the doctor to have Peggy sedated, as she was getting out of control, screaming and tearing her hair with grief.

'You'll have to try and be strong now,' Mossy advised Hugh, as soon as she finally fell asleep, 'She is going to take Declan's death very badly, and she needs your strength and support, now, more than ever, not to mention the three girls.'

'You're right Mossy' said Hugh, wiping the tears from his eyes, 'It's very difficult. He was my only son; but I'll try, yes I'll try.'

Sr Bernard and Alana were making statues with moulds and plaster, when Gráinne and Deirdre arrived with the bad news. Alana was devastated, and Sr Bernard, noticing her face becoming white as snow, held her in her arms, where she cried for a long time.

'If he hadn't been at that college, he would be alive now. Why did my mother send him there, why? why?'

'Don't say that, Alana,' said Sr Bernard, almost in tears herself. 'This is God's will. He wanted Declan for himself and he has taken him to his home in heaven.' She brought

Alana, and her two sisters to the convent, and gave them a hot, sweet drink. Then she put on her black cloak, and accompanied them home. She sympathised with Hugh. 'May God and His Blessed Mother comfort you both in your very sad bereavement. Rest assured that you will have the prayers of all the community at St. Annes.

Later on in the night, Jamie and Maeve O'Flaherty, accompanied by Sr Dominica, came to the cottage to offer their condolences. This was Jamie's first meeting with Peggy, since her marriage, seventeen years ago. They were truly sorry for her, and pledged any assistance that she needed. It was a consolation to her that they were with her, but she wished it had been under different circumstances. Jamie said he would make all the necessary arrangements for the funeral, and that she need have no worries on that score, as he would pay all the expenses. Before he left, he took a large sum of money from his wallet.

'Take this,' he said, in his gruff, abrupt voice, 'and buy yourself, and these children, something decent to wear.' As he walked out the door, he was muttering under his breath about the poor quality of her life now, and what she could have had if she had not been so stubborn and headstrong.

Declan was buried in St Gerard's cemetery, in a plot, beside the lake, where he loved to go and feed the swans. As the little white coffin, laden with fresh flowers, was being shouldered from the hearse to the grave, there wasn't a dry eye to be seen in the large crowd. At the graveside, Fr Seamus gave a very touching speech, comparing Declan to a sweet flower, picked by his Maker, in his budding years, and taken to the greenhouse of heaven, where he will blossom forth. Peggy sobbed aloud during the homily, and Hugh had to hold her in a standing position, as she was swaying with intense grief. As the gravediggers began to lower the coffin down into the ground, Peggy lost control of herself completely. She broke loose from Hugh's grip, and dashed forward, screaming 'Don't put my baby down there. Give him back to me. Oh! Declan, my darling, come back! You can't leave me, for I couldn't live without you.' Fr Seamus led her calmly back to Hugh, and beckoned to the gravediggers, who discontinued the burial, until Peggy was taken away in Hugh's arms. Ellen, Neil, and the two girls had come from Dublin for the funeral, and Ellen was almost as broken-hearted as Peggy. As they walked away from the graveside, distraught with sorrow, Neil turned to comfort her as he whispered in her ear.

'There must be some meaning for this terrible tragedy. You have always said God's ways are wonderful. Look how poor little Declan's death has brought Peggy's own family back to her after all these years.'

'Nothing could compensate a mother for the loss of her only son,' Ellen said, weeping profusely.

It took Peggy a very long time to recover, even slightly, from Declan's death. 'How is she?' enquired Fr Seamus of Hugh, when Hugh brought him some potatoes and vegetables, from the plot, about six months later.

'She cries herself to sleep every night, Father, but during the day, with the girls and myself to look after, she's not too bad.'

'Ah, poor woman! She has a heavy cross to carry, but time is a great healer, and every day she'll get a little bit better. I know you are a great source of strength and comfort to her, Hugh.'

'I do my best, Father, but there are times when she seems to want to be left alone, to weep.'

'Let her weep, my boy. Let her weep. The more she cries, the sooner she'll mend. Your mother gave me ten shillings for masses, when she was here for the funeral, and she asked me to keep an eye on her. I'll call on Sunday.'

'Thank you, Father,' said Hugh, and he made his way home.

Alana felt deeply sorry for her mother, and when she would find her alone, sobbing quietly to herself, she wanted, more than anything else, to put her arms around her to comfort her; but she couldn't, no matter how hard she tried. This barrier between them had gone too deeply, and in her subconscious mind, Alana feared rejection.

Gráinne and Deirdre were very united, but they kept to themselves, and didn't mix much with Alana.

'She's a teacher's pet and a book-worm,' Gráinne complained to Deirdre in bed, one night.

'She has no interest at all in the college boys, and doesn't care how she looks or dresses,' answered Deirdre, 'All she cares about is Dad, school, and the nuns, and I bet she thinks more of Sr Bernard than she does of Mum.' Peggy, who had overheard the girls' conversation from the kitchen, came into the bedroom, and added her opinion.

'It would be as well for her to take her bed up to the convent, for all the time she spends in this house, and I personally think its abnormal that she doesn't go to the local hops with all the other girls.'

'Of course, she's not as pretty as we are,' boasted Gráinne, 'And she's clever enough to know that she wouldn't stand a chance with the lads, while we're around.'

'She wouldn't look too bad, if she dressed herself up a bit, and put on a bit of lipstick,' Deirdre said.

'Catch Alana wearing lipstick!' Peggy interjected. 'What would her beloved Sr Bernard say?'

The results of the Leaving Certificate examination came out in August of that year. As all the pupils were assembled in the main classroom of the school, Sr Bernard read out the marks of each student for the various subjects. Alana O'Grady had scored over eighty per cent in every subject, and established a record by scoring over ninety per cent in Irish. She had won a scholarship to Carysfort College in Dublin, the training establishment for national teachers, and also a scholarship to the university in Cork, where she could enter into any faculty of her choice. She received applause from all, and the nuns were thrilled with the honour she brought to St Anne's. Sr Bernard was elated, and she glowed with delight and pride in her favourite pupil.

'I knew you would do it, Alana,' she said, excitedly, 'Didn't I always say you were a star. What will you do now? Will you go to Carysfort, or will you go to university?'

'I don't know yet, Sister,' Alana answered, thoughtfully, 'I would love to go to university, but I had better discuss it with my parents.'

'That's right, pet! Do that, and I'm sure they'll be absolutely thrilled with the good news. I'm very proud of you, Alana.'

'Thank you, Sister,' Alana answered, 'but I owe my success to the good teaching I got at St Annes.'

Alana ran all the way up to the convent to tell her father the good news. There, he was in the boiler house, as black as the hobbs of hell. His eyes lit up when he saw her, and he knew immediately, by the happiness and excitement written all over her face, that she had done well.

'Look at my results, Dad,' she said, handing him the piece of paper on which Sr Bernard had written down her marks, 'And I got two scholarships. Isn't it wonderful!' Hugh was overcome and she could see the tears of joy rolling down his black face. He took her in his arms and kissed her.

'You're a marvel, me flower! An absolute marvel. Aren't I the lucky man to have such a genius of a daughter!'

'Thanks, Dad,' she said, wiping the black marks from her own face. 'Now I had better go home and tell Mum, and Aunty Mary and Uncle Mossy.'

'Of course, darling, and don't forget to write and tell your grandma and grandad, and maybe you should call and tell

Aunt Maeve and Uncle Jamie, too. They might give you a few bob to celebrate.' Alana chuckled at that, and then ran all the way home.

Still panting and breathless, she stormed into the Kitchen to Peggy

'Mum,' she blurted out, just beginning to relate the news to her.

'I know, I know all about it,' said Peggy, 'The girls have already told me. I'm very glad for you.' This was a terrible anti-climax for Alana. Her own mother didn't appear to be very happy at all, and there was a moment of silence, during which Alana's heart sank down to her shoes. Then Peggy turned to her, a dark look on her face, which always appeared when she was about to make a serious pronouncement 'I do not want you to go to any of the colleges, Alana. You have studied now for long enough, and its time you were getting a job, so you can help to run this home. Your father's wages are very small, and I am sick and tired of trying to make ends meet. The examination for the civil service takes place in a month's time. You had better sit for that, and I'm sure you'll get it.'

Alana knew there was no point whatsoever in arguing with her mother. She was very adamant in what she said, and any way Alana was on the verge of tears. She turned and went into her bedroom, threw herself on her bed, and cried for hours. She heard her father come in, and immediately pulled herself together. She did not want him to see her crying, as she knew he would be very annoyed with Peggy, and the last thing she wanted, was an argument between them, followed by that awful silent treatment for her father. She decided to pretend it was her own decision, not to go to college, but to do the civil service examination in order to get a job quickly. She came out into the kitchen, and though feeling very sad, and bitterly disappointed, she put on a pleasant, cheerful face for Hugh. He was amazed at her decision, but he trusted her judgement fully, and was perfectly happy with it. As they knelt for the rosary, after supper, he added a special prayer of thanks to God for Alana's great success.

The only one that knew the truth about Alana's extraordinary decision, was Sr Bernard. She was flabbergasted and bitterly disappointed at her mother's harsh attitude. She was truly sorry for Alana, who had studied so hard; but charity did not allow her to say so to Alana.

'Maybe its all for the best, pet. Who knows, you may, after a while, be able to attend night classes and get your degree after all. You can rely on my help.'

'Thank you. I know that, Sister. We'll see what happens.'

Alana got fifth place in Ireland, in the clerical officers' examination, and she began work in November. She earned as much money as her father did, and handed every penny of it to Peggy, to help with the household expenses. Each evening after work, Alana took the number two bus straight to the convent, and she would stay there with Sr Bernard, helping to make the Christmas calendars, and various other jobs, until the convent bell rang at six-thirty, calling Sr Bernard to her tea. Alana then, reluctantly, returned home, hoping her father would be there, as Peggy and herself only barely communicated now, and Alana found it a terrible strain to be alone with her.

Gráinne and Deirdre went our every night to céilís, parties, and even to Mac's bar. They were always dressed in the height of style and fashion, while Alana's wardrobe was almost empty. Gráinne left school and took a job in Murphy's Local Store, serving behind the counter, and doing a little bookeeping. She was very fond of the boys and never came home until the early hours of the morning. Alana never ceased to wonder how her mother never admonished her, and seemed to turn a blind eye to the situation. She thought how different her attitude would be, if she were acting in that manner. Alana ventured to voice this opinion to Deirdre one night.

'Isn't Gráinne letting herself and the family down very badly, making herself so cheap with the boys.'

'Ah! Shut up, and don't be such a prude. She's a normal, healthy girl. You're the one that's wrong, sitting up there in the convent, with a nun evening after evening, and even at week-ends. I never heard the like of it.' Alana was hurt to the core, and tired of defending herself.

'I help Sr Bernard to make things, which are sold to raise funds for the missionary sisters in Africa, who are saving souls. Surely, there's nothing wrong with that?'

'That's nuns' work. You should be more interested in getting prettied up, and looking for a boy-friend, or else you'll end up on the shelf, like your Aunt Kate in Dublin. How would you like that?'

'I have no desire, whatsoever, to get married. I believe there's a lot more to life than that.'

'You know more than I know,' Deirdre said, in a sarcastic tone, and left the room.

Alana lay awake for hours that night, thinking about her future, and though she always knew she wanted to be a nun, like Sr Bernard, she was now more convinced than ever that the time was ripe for her to enter the convent. She was nineteen years of age, and had been working, now, for two years. Surely, now that Gráinne was working, her mother would be able to get on without her. It wouldn't be long more, until Deirdre would get a job, and then she would be quite well-off. Yes. She must apply to the order straight away. She hated the thought of leaving her father; but she knew that he would understand, as he always did, and that he would be very happy for her. She wasn't sure what her mother would say, but this time, she was not going to stop her. She would tell Sr Bernard of her decision, immediately.

Chapter 9

'I knew it, Alana. I always knew you had a vocation, and I have been praying very hard for you, of late. I am absolutely overjoyed; my prayers have been answered. You will enter our order, of course.'

'Oh! Yes, of course, Sister. Where else?'

'You have been one of us all your life, and you'll be a wonderful asset to the order, and to the good Lord who has chosen you.'

'Thank you, Sister, but how do I apply?'

'I'll have an application form for you, to-morrow, and we'll fill it up together. It's only a matter of form, but these procedures have to be gone through.' You will, of course, have to be examined in Dublin by Doctor Moore, who is responsible to our order, for making sure all who enter it are strong and healthy.'

'That shouldn't pose a problem,' said Alana, 'Sure I have never been sick a day in my life.'

Alana applied to be accepted by the order, and was sent to Dublin for her medical examination shortly afterwards. She continued to work at her job, and in the evenings when she was with Sr Bernard, they spoke non-stop about convent life. Now that Alana was about to enter, Sr Bernard made her aware of certain customs and rules that seculars would never know. Alana was fascinated, and was getting more and more impatient and anxious to get the final acceptance. Peggy was very happy about Alana's decision, as, deep down in her heart, she always knew the girl was not interested in material things like her sisters were, and she was, of course, delighted with the prestige of having a daughter a Nun. Sr Dominica too, would be very pleased. If the truth were known, Peggy really couldn't wait for Alana to go away, as she found it a terrible strain to live with her. This attachment she had to her father was a constant source of annoyance to Peggy, and she hoped that as soon as Alana would go, Hugh would devote all his love and affection on her once more, and they could have a more peaceful, trouble free relationship again. Hugh was very sad at the thought of losing Alana, and worried silently, lest her entering the convent might be a form of escape from what he realised had been a very unhappy home for her. He strongly resented Peggy's very obvious joy at her departure and detested the sarcastic remarks that Gráinne and Deirdre made, mockingly, about Alana.

The result of Alana's medical examination was finally sent to Doctor Donal Brown, the local doctor in Glenbeg. He sent for Peggy, and told her that it wasn't good.

'Alana has a shadow of tubercolosis on her left lung, and will have to go to a sanatorium for some time, perhaps six months.'

'Is it serious, doctor?'

'It could be very serious, Mrs O'Grady, but with plenty of rest, nourishment and fresh air, she should be perfect.' Alana was devastated, as this was the last thing she expected. 'Look on the bright side,' said Sr Bernard 'You're young and you'll heal quickly, after all, what's six months out of the long life you have ahead of you?' She gave Alana plenty of calendars to be making while she was in bed, and promised to call to see her once a week. Mossy and Mary brought her to the sanatorium, on the outskirts of Cork, in their new Ford Anglia, and Mary took her into one of the large stores and bought her a pretty blue nightdress and dressing gown to match. She had a lovely room with a veranda, looking out on to green fields, and she made up her mind on that first day that she was going to co-operate in every way with the doctors and nurses, in order to get strong and healthy as quickly as possible.

After six months' treatment, Alana got a clean bill of health and was discharged from the sanatorium. She was then accepted by the order, and was to enter on November ninth, just two months later. She was given a list with her letter of acceptance, of several items, which she was to bring with her. These included a black shawl, cardigan, slippers, umbrella, a pair of black outdoor and indoor shoes and a pocket watch. Alana handed the list to her mother, waiting for the long, poor-mouth litany she usually got when she needed anything that cost money. To her amazement and utter relief, Peggy's reaction was totally different. She studied the contents carefully, and then, displaying an enthusiastic interest, that Alana had never seen in her life, when the question of spending money arose, announced that she would get in touch with Sr Dominica immediately. She would know better than anyone else, where the very best quality in all those articles could be purchased. After all, we must let everyone up there in that convent see that you come from a background with a touch of class. Alana understood her keen interest at once. It was the same old story, the Flaherty's snobbery syndrome. She was about to answer that she didn't care a lot about class or granduer, but she held back, and decided to let well alone.

Alana left Glenbeg on November second, to spend her last week in Dublin with Ellen, Neil and Kate. She was more lonely than she expected to be, and as she sat in the train on her way to Dublin, she could still see her father waving to her, until he went completely out of sight. Fr Seamus had given her his blessing on the platform just before she boarded the train.

'We are all very proud of you, Alana, and none more than I, for I take full credit for your being born into this community at all.'

'Pray for me, Father, that I will persevere in my vocation.'

'I will say mass for you specially tomorrow morning, and I will remember you in every mass I say, for the rest of my life.'

'Thank you, Father, and take care of Dad for me, too.' Then throwing herself into Hugh's arms, she broke down completely.

'I love you very much, Dad'

'And I love you too, me flower.' He had put on his brave face, but Alana could see the tears in his eyes.

As the train came slowly to a halt at Kingsbridge Station in Dublin, Alana caught a glimpse of Ellen and Neil standing on the platform outside. Ellen was peering anxiously into the carriages trying to find her, but Neil was the first to see her, and he led Ellen by the hand over to meet her. They were both excited and overjoyed.

'Another Corkonian up on the single ticket,' Neil said in his own good humoured manner

'We are thrilled to bits, to have you all to ourselves for a whole week' said Ellen, smothering her with kisses, 'We intend to spoil you rotten, and nobody can say a word to us.'

Ellen really meant every word she said, because that week was the most enjoyable and memorable time in Alana's life. Kate took a week's holidays, and took Ellen, Neil and Alana to all the beautiful and historic places in Dublin. They went up Nelson's Pillar, visited Trinity College, Kilmainham Jail, Dublin Castle, Dail Eireann and many other places. They had a great day at the Zoological Gardens in the Phoenix Park, and she saw the President's House. ''Tis a big house for such a small little man!' joked

Neil, who was always the life and soul of the party. Alana liked the Botanic Gardens best of all, and was sorry it wasn't summer-time when she could see all the flowers in full bloom. They had two delightful nights at the Abbey Theatre and the Theatre Royal, and Alana was so exhilarated, that week, that Ellen thought she might change her mind.

'Maybe we could entice you to stay here with us altogether, Alana.'

'You have all been extremely good and kind to me, and I will never forget this wonderful week with you; but my life is in the convent.'

The night before she left, Neil organised a farewell party for Alana in the house, and invited all the neighbours in the small park. Kate and Alana took turns playing the piano, while everyone sang along in chorus. Those with good voices sang solo, and were a treat to listen to. Neil, nicely inebriated, gave his usual rendering of 'Love Thee Dearest, Love Thee' with his arms held around Alana. She was very touched, and Ellen and Kate were in floods of tears. The party continued until the dawn was breaking and when everyone had gone home, Ellen and Alana had a long heart-to-heart talk.

'I'm sure my poor Hugh was very lonely when you were leaving home.'

'Oh! he was indeed, Gran,' replied Alana, feeling the tears welling up in her eyes.

'He was the only one I really loved in that house, and it was heart breaking saying good-bye to him. He held me in his arms, and told me that if I wasn't happy, not to hesitate to come home.'

'He loves you very dearly, Alana, and although in appearance you may be more like the O'Flahertys, you are the only one of the three with the O'Grady manner and outlook on life.' Then Ellen hesitated and her face seemed

103

to darken. 'Are you quite sure this decision you are making is the right one, darling, because you know there is plenty of time to change your mind yet?'

'Oh No! Gran. There is no question of changing my mind. I am perfectly sure. I have always wanted to be a nun.'

'I'll miss you, my pet,' she said, beginning to cry.

'Don't cry, Gran. Sure I'm nearer to you now than I ever was. You have only to take a bus across the city to visit me, and you will come often, won't you Gran?'

'You may be sure I will, as often as they will allow me.'

'I love you, Gran,' said Alana, throwing herself into Ellen's arms.

'I love you too, my pet, and I will be thinking about you and praying for you every day.'

The next day was a typical November day, damp, dark and foggy, as Alana walked in the big gate of the novitiate on the south side of Dublin, her brown suitcase in her hand. She felt very much alone, and a trifle depressed. For the first time, since she decided to enter, she wondered anxiously, what lay ahead for her in this mysterious world behind the convent walls. There were lots of cars in the grounds, and other prospective postulants like herself, were being escorted by their parents to the convent door. She should have allowed her grandparents to come with her, but she preferred to say her good-byes in private. She very much regretted this decision now, as she felt very self-conscious and embarrassed, and wondered if the others thought she was an orphan. She rang the door bell, and a friendly, smiling sister answered.

'You are one of the new postulants, I presume.'

'Yes, Sister, I am Alana O'Grady from Glenbeg.'

'You are very welcome, and I hope you'll be very happy with us.' She was then led into a very large parlour, where the Mother General and the Mistress of Novices were waiting to greet her. Mother Teresa, the Mother General, was a tall, stately nun, with a beautiful smile and the softest, kindest pair of brown eyes Alana had ever seen. Mother Imelda, the Mistress of Novices, was, on the contrary, a small, plump, motherly little nun, and seemed very bright and cheery. Both of them kissed her on each cheek, and asked her to sit with them for a little chat.

'How do you feel, now?' asked Mother Teresa.

'A little nervous and anxious, Mother,' answered Alana.

'That's only to be expected, Alana, but I can assure you, there is no need to worry. Just put yourself into the hands of God, and take every minute as it comes,' said Mother Imelda, 'There are eleven others entering to-day, and you are the first one in, so we had better get you settled in, as I can hear a lot of activity in the hall.' Then she rang a small brass bell, and immediately, there was a gentle knock on the door. 'Come in,' said Mother Imelda, and a lovely, young novice wearing a dazzling white veil, entered the parlour. 'This is Sr Marie Clare,' said Mother Imelda, 'and she will be, what we call your angel for the first week. She will stay with you at all times, to show you what to do, and to brief you generally on our rules and customs, until you become fully acquainted with everything. From now on, you will be known as Sr O'Grady, until you become a novice after six months, God willing. God love and bless you now!'

Sr Marie Clare directed Alana into the cloister, which was a very long corridor, with large black and white tiles on the floor, and life-size statues of various saints standing in alcoves in the walls. Half-way down, there was a very wide polished, timber stair-case, and having climbed two flights of stairs, they came to another long corridor. There were doors on each side of it, with names written over each one. These were the cells, and Sr Marie Clare stopped outside the door named 'Nazareth'. She opened it, and led Alana in. It was sparsely furnished, with nothing but the bare necessities, an iron bedstead with a blue and white check bedspread, a chair, and a table with a jug and wash-basin on it. A little white linen towel hung on a rail attached to the table, and a piece of white soap rested on a small white saucer. On the chair, the postulants garb was neatly laid out. 'Take off your worldly clothes now, Sister, and get into your religious ones.' said Sr Marie Clare. Alana, noticing the cell door slightly ajar, went to close it, before undressing. Sr Marie Clare stopped her, and in a very serious tone cited one of the Order's rules. 'No one shall enter the cell of another without necessity, and if any two sisters are in a cell, the door must remain open while they remain together.' Alana, trying to understand the motive behind this strange rule, divested herself of her green coat, brown woollen dress, brown shoes, and nylon stockings, and Sr Marie Clare helped her into her habit. 'Put on this white chemise first, Sister.' Alana did as she was told, feeling highly amused at the large shapeless garment. Then came a long white drawers, red flannel petticoat, a long black serge dress, with a black cape around the shoulders, a black lace veil with a white starched rim and her own pair of black, indoor shoes. Alana then looked around for a mirror, as she was dying to see what she looked like, but there was no such thing in the cell. Sr Marie Clare, observing what she was about, warned gently: 'Vanity must be avoided, Sister! It's a deadly sin. Come along now. There's a meeting of all the newcomers in the assembly hall, just on the next floor, at six, and we must be punctual. You will meet all your colleagues and Mother Imelda will give you all a few words of advice.'

There were eleven other postulants gathered in the assembly hall, when Alana entered. Most of them were similar in age to herself; but there were two, very much older. One of them was a widow, and she sobbed bitterly for the duration of the little talk. Mother Imelda welcomed them all, once more. 'You are my children now in Christ, and I shall endeavour, to the very best of my ability, to exercise extreme care and concern for each of you, concern for your material needs, but above all, for your souls. You are like the twelve apostles, and I hope you will follow in Christ's footsteps just as they did.' She then told them, briefly, about the daily routine, and how important it was that silence be observed at all times, except during recreation periods. It was also stressed on them that decorum was vital. They should never run, and when they walked from place to place, they should do so with their eyes cast downwards, to avoid distraction. She spoke at length about 'Purity of Intention', meaning that any one of them who was here for any reason whatsoever, but to love and serve God, should get up, and leave straight away. This worried Alana a little, and she did a lot of soul-searching, in an effort to determine whether her intention was really pure. She couldn't be sure, but she decided to stay and find out. 'You will be called at five-thirty in the morning,' Mother Imelda continued, 'by one of the sisters, who will ring a small bell, and recite the words "Benedicamus Domino" outside your cell door. You will immediately answer "Deo Gratius", and then treat your bed as though it were on fire. That will be enough for you, for the moment. Your angels will now take you to the refectory for tea, and because it is your first night, you will be allowed to talk during the meal.'

Outside the door, the twelve angels waited silently and patiently, and the postulants were taken to the refectory. This was a very large room, with a long table on each side of it. The Mistress of Novices sat at the top of the table on the left side, with the postulants, while the Mother General sat at the top of the other table with the novices and professed sisters. Alana sat on the right of Mother Imelda, and she felt very tense and strained, trying to eat, and watch her words in conversation with her. A novice came around with a very large teapot and began to pour the tea. Alana put the sugar in her cup, and began to stir the tea. As she was doing so, Mother Imelda was deep in conversation with her. Alana was listening attentively to what she was saying, unconsciously stirring all the while. Mother Imelda suddenly stopped, and in a loud, rather stern voice, commented, 'What on earth are you doing Sister O'Grady? Are you churning or something?' This caused great laughter from all the others, and Alana was mortified, wishing that the ground would open and swallow her. This was her first lesson in third degree humility, and she never forgot it.

After tea, they were taken down through the cloister, and into the chapel, where they were each allocated their own prie-dieu, with three large prayer books in the ledge underneath. They were told to read the Vespers out of the red book, and if they could, they should endeavour to sing along with the community. Alana was inclined to giggle at the shrill sound of the sisters' singing voices, but she soon took control of herself. As she knelt there, her mind began to ramble back to Glenbeg, and she felt a severe pang of loneliness for her father. She prayed that her mother would be kind to him, and then asked the Lord to protect her two sisters.

Recreation followed in the very large community room, and here again there was a long table in the centre of the floor. There was a piano at the end of the room, and beside it a beautiful radiogram. There were mahogany presses from ceiling to floor on every wall, and Alana counted six sewing machines, four irons and ironing boards. Mother Imelda sat at the top of the table, presiding over the novices and postulants, and joining in very pleasant and cheerful conversation. She also kept a very watchful eye and ear on each sister present, thirty-five in all. It was very necessary for the Mistress of Novices to get to know each potential nun very intimately, and often during recreational periods, when they were relaxed and would chatter on spontaneously, she would get a feel for the type of personality each one had, and whether she could detect certain flaws or failings in anyone, which would render her unsuitable for the religious life. Many a novice and postulant was never seen again after a period of recreation, and her name was never again mentioned. At recreation one day, a postulant remarked on how happy and pleased her parents would be to have a daughter a nun, and that it was more or less for that reason she entered. There went the 'Purity of Intention', and there also went the postulant, back to her disappointed parents. As soon as the bell rang for recreation to end, everyone had to be silent immediately, even if it meant stopping in the middle of a word. The bell was always to be regarded as the voice of God, calling one to the next duty, and at the sound of it, everything was dropped, and one answered it without delay. Failure to do this, was a breach of obedience, and was taken very seriously indeed, obedience being one of the three vows which would be taken at profession.

From the recreation room, all paid their last visit to the chapel for half an hour, during which time, everyone examined their conscience, to see how they had behaved during the day, and what faults they were guilty of. After 'Examen' as this was known, everyone retired, and 'The Great Silence' was observed from that moment, until the next day. To speak a word, except in dire emergency, during that period, was a very serious offence, and one which carried a very severe penance.

In her little cell, on the first night, Alana felt very lonely. It was the first time in her life that she had slept in a bed of her own, not to mention a room of her own. She missed the chatter of her two sisters, that same silly, superficial talk about clothes, make-up, and boyfriends, which grated on her nerves then. She even missed the arguments, and the sarcastic, insulting remarks. Alone in this strange room, in deadly silence, she began to feel very anxious and apprehensive, about the life she had chosen. She wondered whether she would be suited to it, or indeed, whether her superiors would really consider that she actually had a vocation. It would be terrible to be sent home. That would be failure, and Alana never failed. What would her mother say? and what would Sr. Bernard think? She would certainly have let her down with a bang, and she would be bitterly disappointed. She hoped she would waken at the sound of the bell in the morning, and repeated the response to herself over and over again. Her heart was beating very rapidly, and try as she may, sleep would not come. Please God! let me do everything right to-morrow. The lights went out, and there was complete darkness. Alana always feared the darkness, and a little lamp had always to be kept lighting, beside her bed at home. She began to panic, and it got worse. She was losing her breath, and she was getting more and more frightened. She got out of bed, and walked around for a while, fearing that her heart was about to stop beating. Then she remembered her father's words to her, one night, when she awoke in the dark, and was almost hysterical. 'Take it easy, darlin', he had said, in his kind, gentle voice, 'There's nothing to fear. Just close your eyes, take a deep breath, and picture yourself walking in a big field in brilliant sunlight.' It worked then, so why wouldn't it work now. She went back to bed, closed her eyes, and it seemed like only minutes had elapsed, when the bell was ringing, and the sister outside her cell door was announcing 'Benedicamus Domino!' 'Deo Gratias.' Alana answered, leaping out of bed.

Sr Marie Clare arrived just as she was dressed, and as the morning was bitterly cold, she told her to wear the black shawl. They went to the chapel, where there was half an hour's meditation before mass. During this time, Alana

110

observed quite a few heads nodding, and one sister nearly fell off her chair. Breakfast was taken standing up, as it was a Penance Day. It consisted of a mug of tea and brown bread. A sister sat on a rostrum, between the two tables, reading from a spiritual book about Dom Columba Marmion, a saintly ascetic monk of the Cistercian Order. Outside the refectory, a list was pinned to the wall, telling every sister what her domestic duty was for the day. Sr O'Grady was to sweep and polish the front stairs. Others swept and polished the various corridors, polished and dusted the chapel and the parlours. Other sisters prepared the refectory for lunch, while others served hot tea and soup to poor people who came to the back door. The chores were varied every day, so that each sister had an opportunity to perform all of the various duties. Alana loved serving the food to the poor, and was frequently admonished for being too familiar with them. She could never understand this, but she musn't question it, because that would be against the rule of obedience, and would be a very bad mark against her.

Lunch consisted of a bowl of porridge or soup with a mug of tea, and was taken, standing up, and in silence. Then the postulants were taken to the cloakroom, where outdoor shoes and shawls were put on, for the walk in the very large grounds. They went in pairs, and had to recite aloud the fifteen mysteries of the rosary. It was back to the chapel after this for another 'Examen' (Examination of Conscience), and then recreation, followed by dinner. During dinner, there were some strange happenings, of which the new-comers were not made aware, and which came as a great shock to all. Some sisters left their seats, walked out to the centre of the refectory floor, went down on their knees and kissed the ground. Then, in a loud voice, they announced to all, the faults and failings of which they were guilty, and asked for forgiveness. Others performed the same ritual, but asked the community to make them aware of their faults. Their request was answered by several sisters, who stood up and replied, 'Dear sister, I observe you lacking in concern for others, or lacking in decorum or humility.' When all the faults and failings which were observed had been conveyed to them by the community, the sisters then thanked the speakers, and asked for prayers, 'to enable them to overcome their faults.' Then there were those who went on their knees, crept under the refectory table, and kissed the feet of certain sisters, admitting to the fault of pride, and praying aloud, that the Lord would make them humble. One of Alana's colleagues Sr O'Brien, who was a very spirited girl, began to shake with laughter. This nervous laughter spread to all of them, and before long, there was a general outburst, which, try as they might, they could not control. The Mistress of Novices left her seat, and in a loud, angry tone of voice, ordered those who were so amused at the sisters performing their penances, to arise and do likewise, themselves. The laughter ended, and there was shock and tension. Alana was trembling as she knelt on the floor to kiss the sisters' feet, and her voice quivered, as she spoke her faults aloud, and begged forgiveness. One of the new-comers, Sr O'Donovan, broke into tears, and refused to perform the penance. She was sent home the following day, as her humility did not measure up to that required of a potential nun.

Alana settled down very well in the novitiate, and she was truly happy. The only worry she had at all times, was the fear of being called into the office of the Mistress of Novices, and told she had no vocation. The most difficult thing of all was keeping silence, especially when the group of them were alone in the cloakroom, or in the grounds. Sr O'Brien, who was a terrible chatter-box and extremely funny, kept them all highly amused, and when she was with them, breaches of silence were the order of the day. They were admonished on several occasions on that score, and Alana never ceased to wonder how it got to the ears of Mother Imelda. The days were so full of prayer and other activities, that every minute was filled, and time passed by very swiftly. There was a weekly visit to Mother Imelda's office, when you had a heart to heart talk with her, and she told you in no uncertain fashion, what faults were observed in you, during the past week. It didn't take long for Alana to realise that she wasn't the wonderful girl she thought she was at school. There, she constantly received praise and commendation; but here at St Josephs, it was a different story. Mother Imelda somehow always managed to find the faults and failings. 'Sr O'Grady, we observe you very lacking in decorum, very untidy in your person, and guilty of having inordinate attachments to sisters. A nun must never run down the cloister, even if she is late for mass, and neither does she insert a safety pin, where a button should be. Sr O'Brien and yourself are becoming far too friendly, and are seen talking and laughing together in the grounds quite a lot. You will find some other partner in future, and you will not sit beside her at recreation or at meals. You will please rectify these faults at once, and you will declare them aloud in the refectory on Friday.'

After a month, the new postulants were permitted to write and receive letters. All were censored, of course. Alana had a long letter from her mother, complaining of how she missed her salary, and how difficult it was to meet the household expenses. Even though Gráinne was working, she spent most of her money, foolishly, on clothes and entertainment. Deirdre, who was in the civil service in Dublin, could not send any money home, as she had only enough to keep herself. Peggy sent Alana's final salary cheque, which was received after she had entered, and Mother Imelda instructed Alana to sign it and return it to her mother. She received a lovely letter from Sr. Bernard,

113

telling her of how well the Christmas calendars were selling, and hoping she was well and happy. Kate had also written, with the sad news that Ellen's mind was beginning to deteriorate. 'She rambles on about events that took place years ago, and imagines she lives in those times again. Your grandfather cannot understand it, and insists on contradicting her, and trying to bring her back to reality. She gets very cross and irritable with him, which is so sad, and so unlike her real self. I will bring her to visit you some time, when she is a little more lucid.' Alana really looked forward to that visit.

A fortnight later, one Sunday afternoon, while Alana practiced the organ for the Christmas ceremonies, she heard the loud gong bang three times. That was her call, and she answered it immediately. 'You have visitors in the parlour, Sister,' said Sister Paul, who always answered the door. Alana straightened her veil, and full of excitement and anticipation, went into the parlour. There was Ellen and Kate, sitting at a small table, near the large window, overlooking the rose garden. Ellen's eyes lit up when she saw Alana. She embraced her, holding her tightly for several minutes, and then she broke into tears.

'Oh! my poor child, what have they done to you? and why are they keeping you locked up in this lonesome place?'

'This is the novitiate, Ma,' Kate interrupted, 'and Alana is preparing to become a nun.'

'Dont you worry about me, Gran,' Alana reassured her, 'I'm perfectly content and happy, and I'm praying for you every day.'

'Your prayers have been answered, my pet, for I have bought a beautiful big house at the corner of our park, for Hugh and the children. They will be here to-morrow. Imagine that, Alana! and a lovely big garden too.' Alana was amazed, but when she looked at Kate, she got the message. It was all in Ellen's mind. 'That's fantastic, Gran.

114

They'll be thrilled. You're as good as gold.' When the visit was over, Alana returned to the chapel, feeling very sorry that her grandmother was no longer sharp as nails like she used to be. That was the last time she saw her. She died on January 21st, just five weeks later, and she was brought home to Glenbeg, where she was buried by the lake with Declan.

It was May fourteenth, the eve of Alana's reception as a novice. Out of the twelve postulants that had joined the order six months ago, ten were to be received, next morning. They had been in retreat for the past seven days, in preparation for the big day, and would come out, after the ceremony. As was the custom after the last lecture of the day, Mother Imelda gave each of them a list of religious names, from which to pick the one they wished to take for themselves. Alana chose Agnes, and marked it with a cross as she was told to do. She wondered what names the others chose, but she would have to wait until the morning to find out. They were then taken, individually, to a large wash-room upstairs, where they had their hair shaved, right through to the scalp of their heads. Alana's hair was short and straight, and this didn't bother her too much; but to some of the others, who had magnificent heads of hair, it was a very traumatic experience, and Sr O'Neill came out in tears. Her tears were very soon stopped, and she laughed heartily, as did all the others, in spite of the silence, as Sr O'Brien arrived out of the room, grinning from ear to ear, and almost shouting aloud, 'We'll all have to stay here now, whether we like it or not until our hair grows again. Sure there's not a man in the world would have us poor, plucked chickens.'

On the morning of May fifteenth, when Alana awoke, she could hear the birds chirping, she imagined, sweeter than ever. It was as though they were sharing in the immense joy she was experiencing, on the day of her reception as a novice. The ten postulants assembled after breakfast in the community room, and there, laid neatly, on the large table, were ten habits, bearing each novice's religious name. The angels were again present, and showed each postulant how to dress. Everything was much the same, except the long serge dress was more elaborate, and the cape was longer and larger. A white plated cup was put on the shaven head, and the most difficult part was fixing the white veil in the correct position over this. Each one was given a lighted candle, which they held, as they walked, in pairs, down the centre aisle of the chapel, to the exquisite strains of the organ playing such hymns as Gounod's 'Ave Maria' and 'Panis Angelicus.' The ceremony was performed by the bishop, who sat on a large, throne-like chair at the top of the aisle. He laid his hand on each sister's head, blessed her, and said: From henceforth you shall be known as Sr Agnes. The parents and relatives of the new novices were assembled in the public aisle of the chapel, at the right of the altar, and Alana caught a glimpse of Sr Dominica's tall figure as she returned to her prie-dieu. Apart from Deirdre, who resided in Dublin, she was the only representative from Alana's family, and, of course, she would never miss the opportunity of a day out.

After the ceremony, the new novices were allowed take lunch in the parlour with their relatives. Six professed sisters served at table, while Mother Teresa and Mother Imelda mingled with the guests.

'So this is Deirdre,' Mother Imelda said, as she shook Deirdre's hand in warm greeting. 'Sr Agnes has spoken of you quite a lot. You must be very proud of her now.'

'Thank you Mother. Indeed, I am, and I marvel at how really beautiful and positively good-looking, she has become.'

'As long as she is a good nun, and her soul is good-looking, we do not worry, Deirdre, my dear.'

'Of course, Mother. Sure, Alana herself was always of that same opinion anyway.' Sr Dominica couldn't wait to get a word in.

'I am extremely pleased and gratified, Mother, that Alana has chosen to follow in my footsteps. I am her mother's eldest sister, you know, and in the O'Flaherty family, there were always, going back for generations, vocations to the religious life.' She was about to expand on the family background, when Mother Imelda interrupted.

'Sr Agnes is following in the footsteps of Christ, Sister, like yourself. I'm sorry her parents couldn't be here, but I'm sure you will tell them how happy she is with us, here at St Joseph's.' Then Mother Imelda moved on to the next guest, leaving Sr Dominica very abruptly. Deirdre and Alana looked at each other in amazement. That put her in her place, Alana thought to herself, as she was sure Deirdre did also.

As the afternoon was warm and sunny, everyone retired to the grounds, where they were able to converse in private with their relatives. Alana and her guests chose a lovely spot in the garden, beside the lily-pond, where they sat together on a white, wrought iron, garden seat. Deirdre was wound up with chatter, as she proudly told Alana about this wonderful boy-friend she had, who worked in the office with her.

'He's a hunk, and a really nice, decent fellow, and it's a very serious affair. I'll bring him to visit you soon, and I know you'll love him.'

'I would very much like to meet him, and I look forward to your next visit.'

'Your Aunt Maeve and Uncle Jamie sent you these letters' said Sr Dominica, ceremoniously handing Alana two white envelopes. 'They regret they couldn't attend personally, because they are both extremely busy at the moment.'

'Thank them for me, please. I cannot read them now, until Mother Imelda has read them first. Anyway, I will write to them both.'

'Did you know,' asked Sr Dominica, 'that your Aunt Sheila has been in contact with me. She is very happily married in London, and has a teenage daughter now, also. She called her son Pat, and he is at university. Fiona, her daughter, is still in school, and very clever, I believe. They are all coming home very soon, to live at Clover Road, and Sheila will take over the pub.'

'I'm delighted to hear that.' said Alana, 'I didn't know Sheila very well, but Mum always talked of her kindness to her.' Alana was overjoyed to learn from Deirdre, that her Aunt Mary and Uncle Mossy had a daughter, who is the very image of poor Grandma O'Grady. 'They must be thrilled to bits,' Alana said, 'I must ask Mother Imelda to let me have a little gift, to send to the baby.' The time went by so quickly, that Alana was very surprised when she heard the little chapel bell ring for vespers. On the first stroke of it, she bade them farewell and headed straight for the chapel.

There was great celebration in St Joseph's for the remainder of the evening. As the new novices entered the refectory for dinner, they were given loud applause by all the community. Ten places were reserved for them at the top of Mother General's table, and beside each place was a large white box. Alana opened the box, bearing the name Sr Agnes, and inside were greeting cards and letters of congratulation from all the community in Glenbeg, and from school friends and former fellow workers in the civil service. There was a lovely letter from Fr. Seamus, and he also sent a book about the life of the foundress of the Order, which was read aloud in the refectory. Sr O'Brien, now Sr Barbara, monopolised the conversation during dinner, and Mother Teresa was in floods of laughter at her witty remarks. She was the most drole person Alana had ever known, and even when she was trying to be serious, she was funny, and had the art of making everyone laugh. 'You had better talk and laugh as much as you can, now,' remarked Mother Teresa to her, 'because from to-morrow morning onwards, you will really have to tow the line once more.'

The new postulants were excused from any further prayers or religious duties after dinner, and were ordered to retire to their cells. It was felt that the strain of the eight-day retreat, and the excitement of the day was tiring for them, and that they needed to rest and compose themselves. Alana was glad of the peace and quiet of her little cell, and alone there, her mind wandered back to the events of the day. She was very happy, and enjoyed a certain sense of security at having being received as a novice. The only shadow on the most beautiful day, Alana thought, was Sr Dominica's boastful conversation about religious traditions in the O'Flaherty family. There wasn't a word about her father or the O'Grady family, and the fine traditions of love and charity that Alana had always admired and tried to imitate. She wondered how a nun, like Sr Dominica, who was twenty-five years professed, could still harbour such sentiments of class distinction, and how she couldn't miss the opportunity of bringing them to bear, even on the religious life. Alana didn't want to mar the memory of her very special day with these thoughts; so she did what her father would have advised her to do, leave her to God.

After breakfast next morning, Alana was delighted to see from the notice board outside the refectory, that her duty for the coming week was that of sacristan. This was, she felt, a great privilege, and something she always looked forward to doing. She was totally responsible for taking care of the priest's vestments, arranging the different colours that were worn on feast days, penance days, extra special days, and then the ordinary days. She had to make sure the altar was always appropriately decorated, that the linen was spot-lessly clean, and that everything was present and correct for every ceremony. She lit the candles before mass and benediction, and made certain the altar boys were clean and tidy at all times, and knew their duties. It happened on her third day as sacristan, that Tommy O'Shea, a blonde, cherub-like little altar boy, had a nasty fall as he was bringing the cruets to the priest, during mass. There was a loud crash, as he fell, breaking glass and sending water and wine all over the altar steps. The poor little lad got a terrible fright, and became completely disorientated, but Alana acted quietly and quickly, and the mass continued with the minimum disruption. Later, in the sacristy, as Alana held the little distressed Tommy in her arms, and tried to comfort him, Mother Imelda walked into the sacristy.

'Tommy isn't injured? Is he Sister!'

'No, Mother. He's perfectly alright, but just a little upset.' She glared at Alana in a very serious, angry manner, and then departed very abruptly, without uttering another word. Alana was very puzzled and troubled by Mother Imelda's attitude towards her, and wondered what on earth she was guilty of. She had, she thought, acted very calmly and efficiently, when the accident happened, and, in fact, she was feeling very proud of herself on that account. There must be something radically wrong, she was saying to herself, as she hung the vestments and tidied up the sacristy.

As Alana walked down the cloister, towards the refectory, she got a gentle tap on the shoulder. It was Mother Imelda. 'I want to see you in my office, immediately after breakfast please, Sister.'

'Yes, Mother,' answered Alana, her heart sinking with fear of what was to come. I am definitely going to be sent home, though I don't know what I've done, but what else could this be about? Her face was like thunder when she came to the sacristy, and now I am summoned to her office. She couldn't eat breakfast, and thought it would never end, so she could find out what her fate was to be.

She knocked on the door of the office of the Mistress of Novices. 'Come in, Sister,' answered Mother Imelda, in a stern tone. Alana opened the door, her whole being now trembling, and she walked towards the large table, where Mother Imelda sat, her eyes cast downwards. As Alana approached, she looked up at her, a mixture of anger and concern in her expression. 'Sit down please, sister.' Alana sat down, and at this stage, her lips were dry with fear and apprehension. 'I have called you here this morning, Sister, to reprimand you for a very serious breach of the spirit of chastity, which I observed you committing as I entered the sacristy, after Mass.' Alana was numb, and reduced to silence for a second Why! she never committed such a breach in her life.

'In what way, Mother, did I commit this offence?' she stammered.

'You were cuddling and caressing young Tommy O'Shea.'

'But Mother,' interrupted Alana,

'Sr Agnes!' interjected Mother Imelda, 'Please! Do not speak until I have finished what I have to say.'

'I'm sorry, Mother,' Alana replied, now almost in tears.

She opened the drawer in her desk, and took out the Rule Book, reading from it, aloud: 'Nobody shall touch another, even by way of jest, except in a gesture of welcome or farewell, when anyone is coming from, or going to a distance. That's our rule, Sister, plain and clear, and you broke it this morning. You were satisfying your own base desires, when you were performing that action, and I take a very serious view of it.' She then got up, went to the press at the end of the room, and took from it, what looked like a piece of thick chain, with sharp spikes on it. She handed it

121

to Alana. 'For your penance, you will wear this chain around your knee, until you are told remove it.' Alana took the chain, and feeling relief that she was allowed to continue in her religious vocation, replied, 'Thank you, Mother. I am sorry, Mother.' She then went on her knees to beg forgiveness for her fault. 'God love and bless you now, Sister,' said Mother Imelda, laying her hands on Alana's head. Alana then left the room, walking backwards out the door, as was the custom.

Chapter 10

On the morning of November first, just six months after their reception, the ten novices stood in line, outside the office of the Mistress of Novices, awaiting their turn to enter and bid farewell to Mother Imelda, before departing for six months to various other convents of the order. This was to be a test of their ability to get on with other professed sisters in a community, to adjust to a different daily routine, and to perform in a satisfactory manner, whatever duty was allocated to them, while always remembering to fit in all their spiritual duties in the course of a busy day. 'You are going to Hampshire in England Sr Agnes, and I know you will be a credit to your training, here at St. Joseph's.' Alana began to cry, as she felt lonely at the idea of going so far away from her new family, and from the happiness and great security she had felt there. 'There's no need to be upset Sister. I know you will be grand. You are a very good sister.' Then Mother Imelda kissed her on both cheeks, and Alana left the office, cherishing in her heart the words of praise she had received for the first time since she entered, one year ago, and deriving great consolation from them.

The convent in Hampshire was very small, with a community of four, including the Reverend Mother. It had been a large, private house, purchased by the Order and converted into a convent, with a small school attached. It was situated by the side of the street, and had no garden whatsoever, and the Catholic church was right beside it. The school was a private one, not recognised by the state, and great efforts were being made, to raise sufficient funds, to adequately equip the school, thus bringing it up to the standard required by the English government for recognition. It was Alana's job to teach in class, and also to organise plays and concerts in the Parish Hall, as part of the fund-raising drive. This was a challenge that Alana loved and needed, and from day one at St Ita's Convent, Hampshire, Alana devoted her heart and soul to it.

Alana enjoyed the comparative freedom of her new home, and before long, she had so many projects in hand, that the day wasn't long enough for her. She always made sure to observe her spiritual exercises, except once, when she completely forgot her examination of conscience. She confessed this to Mother Maria, and promised to perform adequate penance, to punish herself for this serious omission. Mother Maria was very fond of Alana, and was herself, a very kind, saintly nun.

'These things happen to the best of us, Sr Agnes, and I know it was a genuine act of forgetfulness; but there is something else I would like to say to you,' she added, her countenance becoming more stern.

'What is it, Mother,' Alana questioned, rather anxiously.

'Well!' said Mother Maria, slowly and deliberately, 'I met Monsignor O'Hara one morning, last week, and he asked me who was the new, little nun we had. He said he observed you swinging from the church bell, as you were ringing the Angelus one evening, and he added: "Why! Mother, she's not like a nun at all."' Alana became pale, and felt ashamed and worried, but in her gentle, understanding manner, Mother Maria commented 'Don't look worried, Sister. I know you are young, and it's difficult to put an old head on young shoulders; but I wouldn't like anyone to make a remark like that about you again, so please mind your decorum from now on.'

'I will indeed, Mother,' and kneeling on the ground,

Alana begged forgiveness for this fault. Mother Maria laid her hands on Alana's head as was customary, and said 'God Bless you, Sr Agnes! and may he spare you your very cheerful and generous disposition.'

For the next few weeks, Alana endeavoured to walk slowly, from place to place, eyes cast downwards, as she was taught to do in the novitiate. Then, as the week of her play and concert in the town hall approached, she found herself lapsing into her old ways, and rushing madly from place to place again. She had really bitten off more than she could chew, what with teaching class until three thirty in the afternoon, getting her spiritual duties done, and then spending the evenings and nights putting the final touches to the children's performances, every second counted. Two elderly sisters were always very careful to move out of her way, when they saw her approach, and constantly complained to Mother Maria: 'She is like a young filly, and her thorough disrespect for the habit she's wearing, should be severely chastised.'

It happened, one evening, as Alana was taking the stairs two steps at a time, on her way to the little chapel, that, as she rounded a corner on the staircase, her gold pocket watch, which hung from a chain attached to the belt of her habit, flew out and hit against the banister, breaking the glass. She reported the incident to Mother Maria, who sent the watch to be repaired. She got it back soon afterwards, and within a week the same thing occurred, and the watch had to be repaired once again. Three times, Alana had the same accident with the watch, in the same place, and in the very same manner. On the third occasion, Mother Maria was annoyed 'This will have to end, Sister! We are a very poor community here, and I cannot afford the expense of having your watch repaired once a week.' Then she went to the drawer in her desk, and took from it another larger, gold pocket-watch.

'Now, Sister, take this and wear it, until you are ready to return to the novitiate. Be extremely careful of it, as it is of very sentimental value to me. I will have your own one repaired, and I will return it to you before you leave.'

'I am very sorry for this inconvenience and breach of the spirit of poverty, Mother, and I will do my best to avoid a recurrence of it.'

'I sincerely hope so, Sister, because if it happens again, I will have to enter it as a bad mark against you, in the otherwise excellent report of you I am sending to St. Joseph's.'

On St. Patrick's Day, the fruits of Alana's hard work were to be reaped. On that day, there were two performances of her play and concert in the Parish Hall, one in the afternoon, and one at night. The play, which was written by Alana herself, was her own version of the life-story of St Patrick, and was both interesting and amusing. It followed a very lively, entertaining concert of solo singers, comedy acts, Irish step-dancing and beautiful renditions of Percy French songs by the choir. Alana herself accompanied on the piano, all the singers and dancers. It was a phenomenal success, and the hall which seated eight hundred, was packed to capacity for both sessions. The Monsignor and the sisters had places of honour in the front row, and Alana worked hard behind the scenes, making sure everything ran smoothly. She presented Mother Maria with almost two hundred pounds towards the school fund, and was very highly commended for her wonderful work.

Alana was rewarded by getting the next day off, and was exempted from all duties, except, of course, the spiritual ones. She spent the day writing letters, because, due to her busy schedule, she had a lot of unanswered correspondence. Her letter to Sr Bernard was a very long one, and Alana gave her a detailed account of the play and concert. She knew Sr Bernard would be delighted with her great success, and more especially she would be proud that Alana was following in her own footsteps. It was six in the evening before Alana realised it, and she was late for vespers. She dashed to the chapel, and at the very same place on the stairs, Mother Maria's gold watch hit the banister. To Alana's unbelievable horror and dismay, the face was completely cracked. This was the last straw, and she was in dire trouble. As she knelt in the chapel, she couldn't pray. All she could think about was the broken watch, and how she was going to avoid having to break the news to Mother Maria. She must never know, Alana thought, or otherwise, I am in very serious trouble. I could even be sent home. She was to return to the novitiate in May, and she fervently hoped that somehow a solution might manifest itself before then.

Sr Dympna, the cook was taken ill, and had to go to hospital, and Alana was ordered to go to the kitchen in her absence.

'But Mother! I have never, in my whole life, done any kind of cooking. I couldn't even boil an egg.'

'You'll soon learn, Sister, and what better time than now, with only three of us in the house. Sr Monica has gone to Hammersmith to make her Lenten Retreat. I'll give you the ingredients for the meals, and show you what to do.' Alana didn't earn any words of praise for her culinary efforts; but the sisters didn't suffer from either hunger or food-poisoning. Mother Maria was lucky though, to escape injury, the evening the chips were cooked for dinner. Alana sat on the left of the Reverend Mother at the table on that evening, while Sr. Agatha sat on her right. As soon as grace was recited, they began to tackle the meal of fried fish, peas and chips. It was a penance day, and there was silence. As they stuck their forks, with great difficulty into the incinerated potato chips, they began to fly all over the table in every direction, and one chip hit Mother Maria's glasses. She remained perfectly composed and serious, while Alana thought she would choke with repressed laughter.

As they left the refectory, Mother Maria tapped Alana on the shoulder.

'Bring me my watch please, Sister.'

'I'll drop it in to you later, Mother,' answered Alana, her laughter turning very quickly to worry. She did not return it the next day, and a week later, the same request was made of her by Mother Maria, to which Alana gave the same answer. Another few weeks elapsed, and it was Easter Saturday. Alana was decorating the altar in readiness for the big feast day. The little chapel was just like a room, with a small altar top, and six prie-dieus for the sisters. It was right next door to Mother Maria's office. Mother Maria put her head out of her office door as Alana was passing by.

'Sr Agnes, will you please return my watch to me right now.'

'Of course Mother,' said Alana, 'I will go to my cell and get it immediately.'

As she walked upstairs she was in a state of panic. The moment she dreaded had come, and no solution had been found. Her mind was in turmoil, and all kinds of thoughts were flashing through it. She picked up the broken watch from the table near her bed, and then suddenly it came to her. Before she could give herself time to think any further, she dashed down the corridor to the little room, where the altar carpets were stored. The carpet on the altar steps was to be changed to red for Easter. She picked up the little pile of red carpet, and walked towards the top of the stairs. Then she threw herself on top of the carpet, and rolled with it, down the stairs, the watch in her hand, until she landed with a loud thud, outside Mother Maria's door. Mother Maria quickly opened the door, and terrified out of her wits, went to where Alana lay in a heap on the floor, her eyes closed, in feigned injury.

'Oh! my poor child, are you hurt, Sister.'

'Oh my back,' groaned Alana. Mother Maria rang her little brass bell, calling Sr Dympna to come quickly, as Sr Agnes was hurt. They both bent down to examine her, and then Alana, who had deliberately dropped the watch, cried 'Oh Mother! look at the watch, I've broken it.'

'Never mind the watch, Sister, as long as you are alright, yourself.' Alana got herself up slowly. 'I'm just a little shaken, Mother.' Mother Maria ordered Sr Dympna to help Alana to her room, and a cup of hot, sweet tea and two asprin were sent to her shortly afterwards. Alana felt ashamed and sorry for giving Mother Maria such a shock; but at the same time, she felt very relieved that this problem which had been worrying her for some time, was now finally solved.

On May second, Alana's term at St Ita's in Hampshire came to an end. Feeling very lonely, she bade farewell to Mother Maria and the other sisters.

'We'll all miss your very nice, cheerful presence, Sister. You made us feel young again for a little while.'

'I'll invite you to my profession, next year, Mother.'

'I'll be honoured to attend, Sister, but you have a long, hard year to complete, before that big day. We'll all pray hard for you, and we will never forget you.'

'Thank you, Mother, and I really appreciate your patience and kindness to me during the past six months.'

Back in Dublin, in St Joseph's, with her nine colleagues the tough, spiritual year began for Alana. It was a rigorous, soul searching year, and was definitely intended to separate the girls from the women, but Alana and the nine novices soldiered on until the end. They were professed on May second 1953, and to the magnificent strains of the choir, singing 'Veni Sponsa Christi' (Come, Spouse of Christ), they took the three vows of poverty, chastity and obedience, for a period of three years. Peggy, Hugh, Gráinne and

Deirdre came to Dublin for the important event, and, of course, Sr Dominica, accompanied this time by Maeve. Mossy and Mary brought baby Elaine with them, and Alana marvelled at her likeness to her grandmother. Kate came with Neil, and Alana couldn't believe how feeble he had become. He hardly knew her and wasn't the same man at all since Ellen's death. 'That's not my Alana,' he said, as Kate tried to help him recognise her. 'I am, indeed your very own Alana,' she said, holding his hand tightly, tears beginning to appear in her eyes. Mary, wishing to alleviate the sad moment, brought Elaine over to him, and put her in his arms, and he was quite happy holding her there, for the remainder of the evening, as he sat in the shade of a small summer house in the garden. Hugh stayed with him, and Alana was glad of that, because she had noticed him very quiet and strained, as he usually was, in the presence of the O'Flahertys. She hadn't a chance to talk much to him, since they just met after the ceremony, in the morning, and she earnestly wished the others would leave, so that she could have some time alone with him and her mother and sisters. She thought her mother looked tired and worn, but she was elegantly dressed in navy and white, and apart from an odd remark here and there to Alana, she spent the evening in deep conversation with her two sisters, seated on a bench; a good distance away from the O'Grady clan, who sat together on little, white garden chairs around the summer house, where Neil had fallen fast asleep.

'Mum seems to have deserted us,' said Alana.

'Ah! blood is thicker than water, darlin'. They're as thick as thieves.' Alana was sorry for her father, as she knew he was feeling humiliated by their upper crust attitude towards him. Gráinne and Deirdre were bored to distraction, and Alana caught a glimpse of them sneaking away from the O'Flahertys, and hiding behind a clump of trees, where they smoked cigarettes. It was definitely not their scene at all, and it was very difficult listening to Sr Dominica boasting about Sheila's son and daughter. Pat qualified as a veterinary surgeon, and Fiona had begun her first year at university, studying Law.

'They are surely two chips off the O'Flaherty block,' sneeered Gráinne.

'You're dead right there,' agreed Deirdre, 'and I hear they refuse to serve behind the bar. They think its beneath their dignity.'

'They didn't even admire our little beauty,' Mossy added, holding Elaine up in his arms. She looked very pretty in a little pink, frilly dress, and Mossy took a photograph of Alana, holding her in her arms.

'The elite are coming to join us,' whispered Kate, as Sr Dominica, Maeve and Peggy came towards the group. 'We must be leaving now' announced Sr. Dominica, as Maeve and herself formally shook hands with everyone. 'We are delighted to see you so happy Alana and we hope you will live up to your high vocation.'

'I'll do my best' answered Alana, 'Thank you so much for coming.'

'We enjoyed the day immensely,' replied Maeve, 'and we wish you continued success.' Peggy walked with them to the front gate, and everyone breathed a sigh of relief when they were gone. When Peggy returned, she expressed great displeasure at the cold, disrespectful manner in which Gráinne and Deirdre behaved towards their aunts. 'You left me down, very badly,' she said, fire beginning to appear in her eyes. Kate, sensing the approach of a row, decided it was time to take Neil home, and she was joined by Mossy and Mary, who were staying in Dublin for a few days. 'Let's go to the parlour and have some tea,' said Alana, leading her parents and sisters through the rose garden, with its magnificent display of colourful roses, and under the trellised archway, out on to the front garden. Peggy

131

straightened Hugh's tie, and warned Deirdre and Gráinne to be on their best behaviour, as Alana rang the hall-door bell. Sr Paul answered the door. 'Oh! it's you, Sr. Agnes!' she remarked, and pointing to Hugh, she said 'And this is definitely your father. He's the very image of you.' Alana then introduced Peggy and the girls.

'I'm so happy to meet you all, and I hope you had a lovely day.'

'We thoroughly enjoyed ourselves,' answered Peggy, in an accent that was definitely not her usual Cork one. Sr. Paul then ushered them into the small parlour, where the table was beautifully set.

'Give me a few minutes,' she said 'and I'll bring you a nice supper. You must be famished.'

'Thank you kindly Sister,' said Hugh, opening the door for her, as she went out.

Alana was relieved to have her family to herself at last, and eagerly enquired about her friends and neighbours in Glenbeg.

'You wouldn't know the cottage, if you saw it now,' Peggy said, 'I had it all decorated, and bought some lovely new furniture with the money your Uncle Jamie gave me.'

'That's nice,' answered Alana, feeling a little sorry for her father who, she knew, would have loved to have been able to provide the funds himself.

'How are they all at St. Anne's Dad?' enquired Alana, endeavouring to change the subject, and make her father feel important.

'They're all in great form, and wild with excitement about your profession. I was warned to bring back every detail of the big day.' There was a gentle knock on the door, 'This must be Sr Paul,' said Alana, going to open it for her. To her utter surprise and amazement, she was looking not at Sr Paul, but at the beaming face of SrBernard.

'Sr Bernard! What a pleasant surprise. Where on earth did you come from?'

'Alana, my dear—or should I call you Sister Agnes, you look radiant.' They greeted in the order's traditional manner, and then Alana led Sr Bernard into where the family were seated at the table. Hugh pulled out a chair for her,

'We are delighted to see you, Sister,' he said.

'I'm sure your presence has put the final, perfect touch to a wonderful day for Alana', added Peggy.

'I would have liked to have been here for the actual ceremony, but that was not possible. However, this is the next best thing,and I will be able to spend a few days here with her.'

'That's wonderful' said Alana, now aglow with joy and excitement.

'What do you think of your sister now?' asked Sr Bernard, addressing Gráinne and Deirdre, and looking with real pride at Alana. The girls, who up to now were virtually silent, perked up immediately. 'I think she's a heroine,' said Gráinne. 'I certainly could never do what she did, one day is enough for me,' was Deirdre's reply. Sr Bernard then opened her black handbag, and taking from it a brown official looking envelope, handed it to Hugh. 'This is a present for you,' she said. Hugh, looking puzzled and mystified, tore it open, and began to read, all eyes focused on him. When he had finished reading, he looked up, and Alana will never forget the happiness on his countenance, as he proudly announced that, thanks to Sr Bernard and the community, he had been selected from hundreds of applicants for the post of school inspector. Alana hugged him and expressed her joy and congratulations to him. Peggy and the girls were absolutely overjoyed.

'I don't know how to thank you, Sister' he said to Sr Bernard, tears in his eyes.

'You really deserve it, Hugh,' she said, 'I'm delighted to be the bearer of such good news, and I suppose it's the Lord's way of rewarding you both for giving him your daughter so generously.' When Sr Paul arrived with the trolley full of goodies, everyone was in high spirits, and enjoyed the most wonderful celebration supper.

The O' Gradys returned to Glenbeg the following day, and though Alana was very lonely, she was consoled by her father's change in fortune, and by the fact that he would, at last, be able to provide a decent living for his family. She knew that this was his greatest wish in life, and she was very happy for him. Sr Bernard stayed at St Joseph's for the next few days, and Alana was allowed go with her to Bray on a picnic, one day. Sr Paul packed them a delicious basket, and in a secluded spot, on the Sugar Loaf mountain, they sat together and enjoyed a delectable day of prayer, intimate conversation, and beautiful food.

Chapter 11

On June eighteenth, Alana left St Joseph's Novitiate as a professed sister, and her destination was St Oliver's Convent in the centre of the city, not very far from where her grandfather and Aunt Kate lived. There was a very large school attached to this convent, and Alana was to teach there as a junior assistant mistress, until it was decided where and when she would go to become a fully-trained teacher. Alana settled in very quickly to the busy daily routine at St Oliver's, and it soon became patently obvious to all, that she was a born teacher. The girls in the sixth standard that she taught, were all from the working classes, and that especially endeared them to Alana's heart. Sr Anne, the principal Sister of the school, never ceased to wonder at the great discipline Alana had in her classroom, without even raising her voice, and the magnificent manner in which Alana had handled a problem child, who had been a constant source of annoyance and class disruption to previous teachers. She had warned Alana about her from the very first day, but Alana saw this as a challenge, and was adamant to overcome it. Sheila Murray was really a problem, and could upset a barrack of soldiers. She couldn't sit still at all, and couldn't concentrate on anything for longer than a minute or two. She would leave her seat and distract other children, drop pencil boxes, spill ink and talk and laugh aloud. Alana didn't chastise or rebuke her, but on the contrary, kept her fully occupied at all times, giving her responsibility for various little tasks, encouraging her all the while with words of praise and kindness, and eventually establishing such a friendly relationship with her, that she became a model pupil, striving always to please Alana and thus earn more praise and love. Her parents called to thank Alana for the great work she had done with her. 'She is a new girl Sister, and no longer gives us an ounce of bother. You have given her great confidence in herself, and she idolises you.' Alana was very happy about this, and became very fond of Sheila, who, eventually, was one of her best pupils.

As the months went by, Alana grew to dislike Mother Frances more and more, every day. It was the first time in her religious life that she had felt like this about any sister, but there was nothing at all she liked about the Reverend Mother at St Oliver's. She was an elderly nun, with a very pale complexion, who never smiled, and always spoke in a whining tone of voice, which irritated Alana. She hadn't heard any comments about her from the other sisters, and she wondered whether she was the only one who harboured these feelings. Sr Patrick the housekeeper, who was a little younger than Mother Frances, seemed to have an inordinate attachment to her, always getting in to the community room for recreation before everyone else, so as to get the top seat beside her. She filled her hot water bottle every night, and diligently brought it to her cell, and wherever Mother Frances was, Sr Patrick was never too far away. Alana became worried and troubled about the hostile feelings she bore towards both these nuns, and after a time, she decided to confide in Sr Anne. They were out for a walk one Sunday afternoon, and during the course of the conversation, Alana got the ideal opportunity. It was the month of October, and she was just four months at St Oliver's.

'We are going to be very busy from now until Christmas,' Sr Anne remarked 'with the annual sale of work at the end

136

of November, and the Christmas examination papers to be prepared and corrected.'

'It's nice to have plenty to do,' answered Alana, eagerly, 'and I was actually thinking of doing a Christmas play with the children, if Mother Frances would get me the costumes.'

'You had better forget that idea, Sr Agnes. Mother isn't mildly interested on what goes on at the school.'

'Why is that Sister?' Alana questioned in astonishment. Sister Anne paused for a while, and then she answered 'Well, Sister, our Reverend Mother comes from a very wealthy family background, and brought a very large dowry with her to the Order. She has spent all of her religious life up to now as bursar in St Josephs and never has any dealings with the poor. She is at St Oliver's only three years, and I'm afraid she is making it quite obvious that she doesn't like it, and her attitude towards the children of the less privileged, unfortunately leaves a lot to be desired. I don't mean to be uncharitable, or to pre-judge her, Sister, but I think it is my duty to inform you.' Alana, now understanding her own feelings for Mother Frances, replied, 'I'm very glad you have told me, Sister, because I must admit that I do not like her at all, and this has been worrying me quite a lot, of late. As a matter of fact, I intended to talk to you about it today.'

'Well, don't worry, Sister, because the community at large feels just the same way as you do, with the exception, of course, of Sr Patrick, which I am sure you have noticed.'

'Indeed, I have, Sister, and I find the situation between them most disturbing.'

'You must not be troubled or disturbed, and in spite of your feelings for Mother Frances, you must obey and respect her at all times.'

'Of course, Sister,' replied Alana, 'and I am very grateful to you for informing me of these facts.' They were, by now, just a few minutes from the convent, and as they were about to open the front door, Sr Anne stopped and gave Alana one final word of warning. 'You must never discuss anything I have told you, and be very careful never to discuss much at all in the presence of Sr Patrick, as she brings back every little story to Mother Frances.' Alana was totally disedified, and felt sad and very disappointed that this kind of conduct should go on behind convent walls.

As Alana walked out of the refectory after supper, on the evening of October twenty-third, she received a gentle tap on the shoulder, and Mother Frances whispered.

'I would like to see you in my office please, sister.'

'I'll come straight away,' Alana replied, following Mother Frances upstairs, past the community room, and into her office just beside it. Inside, Alana could hardly believe her eyes. Mother Frances was actually smiling.

'Sit down please, sister'.

'Thank you, Mother,' said Alana, as she pulled up a chair beside her desk.

'I have just had a telephone call from your Mother. She told me your sister Deirdre is to be married here, in Dublin, to-morrow.' Alana was extremely surprised at this news, and was about to ask a few questions, when Mother Frances interrupted. 'Your parents, and your sister Gráinne are coming up for the wedding, and I have instructed Sr Patrick to give the wedding breakfast here, in the parlour.'

'Oh! Mother, that's just wonderful, and so very kind of you. I am very grateful indeed, as I am sure my family are.'

'They will be here at the convent at about two o'clock, to-morrow, and if you mention it to Sr Anne, I am sure she will let you off school for the afternoon.'

'Thank you, Mother. I'll certainly do that,' said Alana, getting up to leave the room.

'You must have got a little bit of a shock, Sister, at the suddenness of this event. I think you ought to go to bed now. You can get the remainder of your prayers there, and I

will send Sr Patrick up later on with some hot milk for you.'
Alana thanked Mother Frances graciously, and left the
room. She was very happy to experience this very kind side
of the Reverend Mother, and delighted at the prospect of
meeting her family again, so soon after her profession. She
wondered what Deirdre's husband-to-be would be like.
Deirdre had promised to bring him to visit her, several
times, but she had never done so. It will be interesting to
know what her mother thinks of him, Alana thought; but no
doubt he has measured up to her standards, or else she
would not be coming all the way from Glenbeg for the
wedding.

The table in the Parlour was beautifully laid out. Indeed,
Alana had never seen anything like it in her life. There was
a large three-tier wedding-cake in the centre, silver trays of
turkey and ham, dishes of sprouts, cauliflower, and roast
and boiled potatoes, and little silver jugs of cranberry sauce
and parsley sauce. The sideboard was laden with all kinds
of desserts, fruit of every description, trifle, meringues, jelly
and apple pie. Little vases of colourful flowers were placed
here and there, along the table, and larger vases, at various
points around the room. Alana was most pleasantly
astounded when she walked in. Sr Patrick and Sr Joan had
even given Hugh a glass of whiskey, and he was smiling
from ear to ear. Deirdre wore a long white dress, and a veil,
with a tiara type head-dress.

'This is Tommy.'

'At long last,' said Alana shaking his hand.

'Thank you, Sister. I have heard quite a lot about you,
and I'm sorry I didn't get to know you before becoming
your brother-in-law.'

'Never mind,' said Alana 'as long as Deirdre knows you,
that's all that matters.'

'You look beautiful, Deirdre,' said Alana, kissing her
sister.

'Thank you, Alana,' she replied quietly.

Tommy was a middle-sized man, with dark, straight hair, and very brown eyes. He spoke very well, and when they sat to partake of the excellent meal, Alana noticed how courteously he made sure everyone was seated, before he sat himself. She thought he was a good bit older than Deirdre, maybe about thirty-five years of age. Deirdre looked pale, and didn't seem to have much to say, and Alana thought she detected tears in her eyes. Gráinne was the life and soul of the party, and she really looked very beautiful in a long mauve dress and wide picture hat to match.

'Your hat has gone to your head,' Hugh said to her as she babbled on, non-stop, laughing at jokes she told, which sometimes didn't even make much sense.

'She's tipsy,' whispered Peggy to Hugh, 'I saw a small bottle of whiskey in her bag.'

'She'll be all right as soon as she has eaten,' Hugh assured her.

'We had better get started,' said Alana taking her cue, 'or this lovely food will be cold.' She stood up, and recited aloud the grace before meals, and then everyone began to eat. Sr Patrick and Sr Joan left then, shortly after Alana arrived, as the sisters felt that it should be a private family party.

Alana acted as hostess, carving the meat, and putting it on the plates. She passed around the vegetables and potatoes, and everyone helped themselves. Deirdre and Tommy sat at the top of the table, with Peggy seated beside Deirdre, and Hugh beside Tommy. Alana thought her mother looked elegant, in a wine coloured suit with pink accessories, but she seemed very tense, and wasn't eating very much.

'Where are you going for your honeymoon?' enquired Alana.

'We are sailing out from Dun Laoghaire to-night, and then we will go on to London,' said Deirdre.

'There's no place like London,' Tommy added, 'and I know every street and alley-way there.'

'I think it's the last place God made!' Hugh said; 'I worked there for a few months, and hated every minute of it.' Peggy didn't make any comment, but looked anxiously at Deirdre, who had her eyes cast downwards onto her plate.

'What's the matter, Deirdre' Alana enquired, tenderly. Deirdre looked up, and tears were streaming down her cheeks.

'She's just a bit lonely,' said Peggy, handing her a handkerchief. 'Wipe your eyes now, and don't be such a baby. Remember this is your wedding day.'

'It feels like a funeral to me!' Gráinne said, 'I never saw such long faces.'

'There's no need for such sarcastic comments,' Peggy said angrily, 'Please try to remember where you are, and behave accordingly.'

Alana served up the desserts, and then the tea and coffee, but she sensed that there was something wrong, and she felt very uneasy. When the meal was over, Hugh stood up and said a few words. He thanked the sisters for their kindness and generosity in providing such a splendid meal, and wished the bride and groom, joy and happiness. 'This is the second little bird that has left our nest,' he said; 'I hope she will be as happy as we all can see the first one is, and I hope that they will both love each other as much as Peggy and myself do.' There was a great clap, and then Alana added a few words, after which Tommy spoke, expressing his gratitude to all concerned, and pledging that he would take great care of Deirdre.

Everyone dispersed for a while, after the meal. Peggy

141

went with Deirdre to a smaller parlour, to help her change into her going-away outfit. Tommy and Gráinne decided to go out for a walk, and Alana was delighted to be left alone with Hugh.

'There's something wrong, isn't there Dad?' Hugh hesitated. 'You must tell me. Please, don't hide anything from me.'

'I was warned not to tell you, Alana, but since you asked me, I can't lie to you.' Alana braced herself for the worst, as Hugh continued 'Deirdre is expecting a baby in five months' time.'

'What's so terrible about that?' said Alana, 'She is married now, and sure a child is a great gift from God.'

'I know that, darlin, but the problem is that Deirdre didn't want to marry Tommy.'

'Oh!' said Alana, her heart bleeding for her sister, 'That is very serious, and I fully understand poor Deirdre's tears. I bet Mum insisted, and had her way.'

'It's even worse than that Alana,' Hugh said, lowering his voice, and almost in tears. 'Not alone did your mother insist on the marriage, but she insisted that the wedding should be in Dublin, and that Deirdre should wear white, and wait for this! She forced both of them to resign their jobs in the Customs and emigrate to England.' Alana was deeply shocked. Would her mother stop at nothing, to keep up appearances? What was going to become of Deirdre, away from home in a foreign country, with a man she didn't love, and bringing a baby into the world, without family or friend to console and help her? 'Why did you allow this, Dad? It is a very serious matter, and you should definitely have strongly opposed mum, in this extremely wrong and cruel decision.' Hugh got up and walked towards the window. He stood there, silently, for a while, and Alana knew he was in tears. She felt her own heart breaking for him also, and she knew, deep down, what a difficult, determined and obstinate woman her mother was. After a few seconds, he turned and faced her again 'Alana, my darlin, I tried as hard as I could. I even asked Mary and Mossy to intervene, but it was no use. She told us it was her decision, and it was final. Don't you know, Alana, how much I love my daughters. I am heart-broken, and don't know what to do.' Alana went to him, and taking him by the hand, led him back again to his chair. 'Don't upset yourself now Dad. I'll pray very hard, and get the prayers of the community, and please God! she will be alright.' Alana didn't feel very confident about this, but she had to be strong for her father, as she knew how deeply he was hurting.

The remainder of the evening was 'hell on earth' for Alana. She was trying to be cheerful, and felt the strain of holding a conversation almost unbearable. She couldn't look her mother straight in the face, and the more she looked at Deirdre, the more she saw the sadness and desolation she was feeling. It was a tragedy and there was nothing she could do about it, but join in a big charade of pretence, because that was the way her mother wanted it. May God forgive her, she said to herself, wishing the taxi would come to take them away, so she could be alone in her absolute misery. She almost broke down completely, when she finally said good-bye to them, on that dark, dreary October evening, and the taxi doors were hardly closed, when she was in her cell, sobbing wildly, until she thought her heart would break. She didn't even go to the chapel, and hadn't finished her prayers, but she didn't seem to care any more. All she could think about was Deirdre, on her way to London, her little pale face, and the dark look in her eyes, and her poor father on his way home to Glenbeg, with the woman who had caused all this heartbreak.

She couldn't sleep a wink, and as she lay on her bed, tossing and turning, and listening to the wind howling outside her window, she worried about Deirdre out there in the middle of the ocean, the ship rolling, and she, probably feeling ill and lonely. Alana became ill herself during the night, and afterwards she was so weak, that she was frightened, and wondered how she was going to cope with the busy day ahead of her. During tea-break at school, the next day, Sr Anne remarked on how pale and tired she looked; so Alana decided to confide in her.

''Tis indeed a very sad story Sister, and I fully understand how you must feel, but this is your first big test of the strength of your own vocation. Put your trust in God, and leave Deirdre to Him. Work is your greatest therapy, Sister, and the best thing for you is to put your whole heart into it now, and continue the great job you are doing for the Lord.'

'Your right, Sister,' answered Alana, 'I'll do as you advise. It is the best way. Thank you for your help Sister. I feel a little better already.'

'That's the spirit,' said Sr. Anne, 'and now, let's get back to class.'

For the next month, Alana worked very hard in preparation for the Christmas sale of work, but Deirdre was always there in the back of her mind. She tried not to worry, and she threw herself more than ever into her work. Then one evening, at vespers, she was called to the telephone. It was Kate at the other end of the line. 'Your Grandfather is dying Alana, and will not live the night. I would very much like if you could be with him at the end.' Reluctantly, Mother Frances allowed her to go to the house, and Neil breathed his last breath at three o'clock next morning, with Kate and Alana by his bedside. He had been unconscious for hours before, but as he died, Alana felt him squeeze tightly on her hand. He too, was buried in Glenbeg with Ellen and Declan.

Chapter 12

Business was booming in the very large school hall on Saturday night, the second and last night of the sale of work. Almost every item in each stall had been sold. It was getting late, and Alana was feeling very pleased with herself, as she bargained with the customers to try and sell her last few bits and pieces. There was a crowd gathered around her stall, and as she held her own little auction, she was amazed at the feverish way people tried to outbid each other, completely inflating the price of the goods. She thought she heard a voice calling 'Alana!' but she knew that could not be, as nobody here knew her by that name. She had had far less sleep than she was accustomed to, for the past few weeks, and she thought that she might be suffering from hallucinations of some sort. Then she heard it again, loud and clear, and looking out beyond the crowd, she could hardly believe her eyes. It was her sister, Deirdre, standing there, large as life, looking paler and more miserable than ever. 'My God! it's really you, Deirdre! Where in heaven's name have you come from? And how did you find me here?' Alana could actually feel her whole body trembling, with both surprise and shock, as she waited for the reply.

'I called to the convent,' said Deirdre, 'and the Reverend Mother told me where to find you.'

'Just sit down here and wait for a moment,' said Alana,

leading Deirdre to a chair behind the stall. Then she took the box of money, her night's takings and brought it across the hall to Sr Anne 'I have sold everything, Sr, but I havn't time to count the money, as my sister Deirdre has arrived unexpectedly and I must go and talk to her.'

'That's fine, Sister,' answered Sister Anne, 'I hope everything is alright with her now. Don't hesitate to talk to me if there's a problem.'

'Thank you' Alana replied, as she quickly returned to Deirdre. ''Tis very crowded here,' Alana said, 'Why don't we go up to my classroom, and we can be alone.'

As they sat there together, Deirdre poured out her heart to Alana, crying bitterly as she spoke. 'I want to die! I want to die!' she repeated over and over again, as she told of her horrific ordeal from the night, just one month ago, since she left on the boat for London. 'I hate him, and he hates me. He told me so, going over on the boat. He said he never wanted to marry me, and that he would get his revenge on my mother, for forcing him into the marriage, and for leaving his job and his country.' She began to cry hysterically, and Alana was worried, lest she might be losing her sanity. She put her arms around her, and tried to comfort her. 'Calm yourself now, Deirdre, and we'll get help for you. Everything is going to be alright. I'll see to that; but you must try and take control of yourself, or you'll injure the little baby you are carrying.'

'I don't care about the baby,' she continued, 'after what I went through in London on my own, I'll never be the same again.'

'On your own?' Alana said in amazement.

'But where was Tommy?'

'He booked us into a cheap hostel the night we arrived, and when I woke up next morning, he was gone, and I haven't seen him since.'

146

'Oh! you poor child,' said Alana 'Whatever did you do then?'

'I told the manager of the hostel, and he gave me a job as chambermaid, and a free room in the hostel, until I had enough money earned to come home. I arrived this evening, and went straight to Auntie Kate.' Alana was devastated, and she was unable to speak for a few minutes. She was almost in tears herself, as the awful facts she had just heard, began to sink into her mind.

'What will you do now?' Alana enquired, regaining her calm.

'I don't know,' she said 'but you could help me if you were to leave the convent.'

'What! me give up my religious vocation. Surely you don't mean that?'

'I need you now, more than anybody else, and charity begins at home. Please help me, Alana, or I'll do something drastic. Come home. Please do.' Alana was totally confused and very upset.

'I cannot leave now. I have just taken vows for three years.'

'You can get a dispensation from them' answered Deirdre, 'I know a Dominican priest down the road, and I'll send him up to the convent to you, to-morrow.' Alana was so tired, that she didn't argue any further, and hoped that maybe she would forget the idea after a good night's rest.

Deirdre didn't forget the idea, and didn't change her mind. Next day, after lunch, as Alana was at recreation, her gong rang, and she excused herself from the community room to answer it. 'There's a priest in the parlour to see you,' said Sr. Joan. Alana hesitated for a minute, wondering whether she should go straight in, or whether she should think about things for a while.

'Would you mind, please, Sister, telling Father that I'll

be with him in a short time. Maybe you would give him some refreshments, while he's waiting.'

'Certainly, Sister,' answered Sr Joan, looking curiously at Alana.

Alana went to her cell, and sat there trying to gather her thoughts together. She was perfectly happy in the religious life, and all her superiors were happy with her. She had, just a little over six months ago, taken vows for three years, and now there was a priest in the parlour, sent by Deirdre, to get her a dispensation from these vows. She didn't want this dispensation; so why was she going to talk to this priest? On the other hand, Deirdre was in trouble, and was completely dependent on her, to help her through the difficult time ahead. She had threatened to do something drastic if Alana didn't come out, and Deirdre's own mother, who should be her tower of strength, was going to be her biggest problem. How could she persevere in her religious vocation, and concentrate on her prayers and other duties now, with the worry of Deirdre on her mind. Yes. She must leave. She must tell this priest to go ahead and arrange for a dispensation for her. Her mind was made up, and she went back to the parlour.

She was greeted by an old, white-haired priest, who was very kind and fatherly. As she entered the room, he left his chair and walked over to meet her. Shaking her hand warmly he asked.

'You are Sr Agnes?'

'That's right, Father. Thank you so much for coming to see me, and I am sorry for keeping you waiting.'

'That's all right, my child, and now let's sit down, and have a little chat.' They both sat down facing each other, and as he looked at her, straight in the face, Alana felt he was searching her soul, and became a little nervous.

'I am Father Dermot Hogan,' he began 'and your sister,

Deirdre, asked me to call here to see you. She said you want to be released from your vows, and want to go back into the world.'

'That's correct, Father. I cannot go on any longer. Can you arrange for a dispensation for me?'

'Before we come to that, Sister, can I ask you for what reason you wish to abandon the religious life?' Alana was very surprised at this question, as she presumed that Deirdre had already put him in the picture.

'Has Deirdre not told you, Father?'

'No Sister, she just said that you were professed a little over six months ago, and that you had become very unhappy and wanted to leave.' Alana thought for a second. Maybe she should go along with this story or otherwise he would realise she had a vocation, and persuade her to stay.

'That's more or less the reason Father. You see I have never seen the world at all, as I was always with the nuns, and now, I feel I should go back there and see a bit of life, otherwise I'll never know, Father, will I?'

'Did that thought ever strike you, before you took your vows, Sister?'

'No, Father. It never entered my head.'

'How old are you, Sister?'

'I'm twenty-two Father.'

'And you have never had any experience of life.'

'No, Father, I was never interested. I spent all my time with my friend, Sr Bernard, and I automatically assumed I should be a nun, like her.'

'I see,' said Father Dermot, thinking very hard. Then after a long pause he said.

'I suppose your decision is final. You are absolutely sure of what you are doing.'

'I am perfectly sure, Father, and I won't change my mind,' Alana replied, adamantly.

149

'That's settled then. You had better go and send the Reverend Mother here to see me, and I will break the news to her. She will have to take it from here.'

'Thank you, Father,' said Alana, kneeling down and asking for his blessing.

'May God bless you, now, Sister, and may His Holy Spirit direct you. I will remember you in my masses.'

Mother Frances was in the chapel when Alana came over to her and whispered in her ear .

'Fr Dermot Hogan wishes to see you in the parlour now, Mother.'

'What on earth does he want to see me for?' she moaned, slowly getting out of her prie-dieu, genuflecting, and then leaving the chapel. Alana stayed on for vespers, but her mind was in turmoil. She dreaded meeting Mother Frances after the terrible shock she was about to get. She was bad enough when there was nothing wrong; but this news would drive her completely crazy. Alana felt like running away immediately, and avoiding any further ado, but of course she daren't do so, as she would be breaking her vows, and living in mortal sin. She must go through this awkward and very embarrassing period, until she got her dispensation from Rome.

Supper was almost over, when Mother Frances came into the refectory. It was the season of Advent, which was one of penance, so the meal was eaten in silence. Alana quietly studied the expression on the face of the Reverend Mother, to see if she could detect any kind of reaction. She couldn't, though she did observe little pink blotches on her usually ashen complexion. As soon as Alana stepped outside the refectory door, she was summoned to the Reverend Mother's office, where Mother Frances interrogated her in great depth about her reason for wishing to leave the order. 'In all my years in the religious life,' she said, 'I have never come across a young, professed sister, who, up to last night, appeared perfectly happy and bubbling over with real enthusiasm, now, all of a sudden, almost on a whim, decides to walk away from it all.' She paused for a minute, and Alana felt very humiliated. 'Has this sudden decision of yours anything to do with your sister? Sr. Anne told me she called to see you last night.' Mother Frances was now coming too near the truth, so Alana thought her best form of defence was attack. She braced herself, and then in a bold tone of voice, replied.

'I am no longer happy in the religious life, Mother, and it has nothing, whatsoever, to do with my sister. I want to leave, and that's final, and I do not wish to discuss the matter any further with you.' She then turned to leave the room, but Mother Frances called her back.

'Just one moment, please Sister Agnes.' Alana stopped and turned around. 'I will telephone Mother Teresa immediately, and let her know of your decision. I will let you know presently, what her instructions are.'

'I will be in my cell if you need me.' Alana replied, leaving the room.

Later that night, Alana was sent back to the novitiate, where Mother Teresa waited for her in the parlour. She greeted Alana very affectionately, and Alana felt like throwing herself into her arms, bursting into tears and admitting the truth, but she dare not, for Deirdre's sake.

'What's this I hear about you, Sister Agnes?' Mother Teresa commented, 'Aren't you the little renegade!'

'I'm sorry, Mother,' answered Alana, sheepishly, 'but I want to go home.' Mother Teresa didn't take her seriously at all.

'You have been working too hard, Sister, and you are overtired, and when that happens, the mind begins to play tricks on us. You will remain here with us, at St Joseph's for a while, and have a good rest. You will retire early, each night, and your breakfast will be brought to your room, each morning. You may do anything you please, all day long, but you will, of course, get your prayers. We will pray together for one hour each day, that the Lord will remove this temptation from you, and help you back to yourself again. You have a true vocation, Sr Agnes, and we have great plans for you for the future.' Alana found it impossible to disagree with Mother Teresa, she was such a kind, saintly person, and she was being so decent and nice to her. She promised to do exactly as she was told, but deep down, she was adamant that she would return to the world, to look after Deirdre, even though it meant giving up the life in which she was so happy, and for which she was perfectly suited.

During the next three months, Alana was treated like a queen at St Joseph's. Every effort was made to ensure that she was perfectly rested and totally free of any possible anxiety. Full breakfast was brought to her by Sr Paul, each morning, and she even got the morning newspapers on her tray. She was allowed absolute freedom to persue any activity she wished. The only thing she was asked to do, was to spend an hour, each day, with Mother Teresa, praying before the Blessed Sacrament. 'During this hour, Sr Agnes, we will pray together, that the Lord will take away from you this terrible temptation. You will listen attentively for His voice, and He will tell you to carry on, in the path He has chosen for you. He wants you, Sister, and He has chosen you from thousands to be his Spouse. Open your heart and soul to Him, and He will give you the grace you need to continue. After each visit, we will talk together for a while, and you will try to tell me what the Lord said to you.' Alana knelt there with Mother Teresa each day; but her thoughts were only with Deirdre, and her mind was so solidly made up to leave, that she did not pray, but wished that her superiors would accept her decision soon, and set her free. She gave the same answer each day to Mother Teresa.

'There is no change, Mother. I have lost my vocation and I am leaving.' Mother Teresa was very kind and patient, and Alana was feeling ashamed. She honestly wished she could change her mind and remain. That was what she really wanted; but Deirdre was her problem, and she was going to take care of her.

Deirdre, who telephoned Alana every night, was growing very impatient. 'They are doing their utmost to hold on to you in there,' she constantly said, 'For God's sake, don't let them brain-wash you. Be firm, and tell them straight and plain that you want your dispensation without delay.' She's right, Alana thought to herself. I cannot allow them to prolong this agony any longer. I must be more adamant, and insist that the wheels be set in motion, immediately. She wrote a long letter to her father, telling him of her intentions, and warning him not to mention a word to her mother for the moment. The letter was sent to Mary, with an enclosure for her, telling her to give her father's letter to him, on his way home from work, and to see to it, that he read it in her house, before going home.

Mary followed Alana's instructions to the letter, and waited patiently for Hugh to pass by on his way home from work.

'What are you doing standing there, on this damp, foggy evening?' Hugh said, 'You'll catch your death of cold, girl.'

'I was waiting for you. I have a letter from Alana for you, and she warned me to make sure you read it here, in our house.' Hugh looked puzzled.

'What is she up to now' he said, as he went into the cottage with Mary. She handed him Alana's letter, and he read it carefully.

'Trouble!' he said, as soon as he had finished, and then he stuffed it into his pocket.

'Have a drink,' said Mary.

'No, thanks all the same,' he said, and he was gone.

Hugh, who could never keep a secret from Peggy, began to act very nervously as soon as he went into the cottage.

'How's Alana?' he enquired of Peggy, 'Have you heard from her recently?'

'Not for a while now,' answered Peggy, 'I suppose she is very busy.'

'Ah! she's very happy, I'm sure,' he repeated three or four times, until Peggy began to wonder.

'What's this sudden concern for Alana all about?'

'Ah! nothing at all,' he assured her, 'Sure, I think about her all the time.' Hugh could contain himself no longer, so he went into Gráinne's room, where she was getting ready to go out. He showed her the letter, and she read it through. 'She's getting sense,' said Gráinne 'but you are not doing such a good job at keeping her secret. Anybody listening to you, would know there was something amiss.' He thought he heard Peggy coming to the door, so he stuffed the letter into his pocket, and went back to the kitchen, where he began to protest again, about how happy Alana must be, and how proud he was of her. Peggy thought he must have taken a few drinks, so she took no notice of him, until she heard him say, 'I would be very surprised if she ever left the convent.' Then she became very suspicious, and began to seriously question him.

'Are you trying to tell me something, Hugh?' He did not reply. 'If you are,' she said, becoming slightly irritated, 'you had better come right out with it.' Hugh knew the game was over, but he could not break the news to her himself. He went to Gráinne's room, and standing at the door he said, 'Come out here, please, Gráinne, and tell your Mother.' She shook her head, and threw her eyes up to heaven, and gestured her firm refusal to him. Then she sat on her bed, with her hands in her ears, to block out what she knew was going to be a terrible scene. Hugh walked over to Peggy and silently handed her Alana's letter. When she finished

154

reading it, sl.. sat down, and flew into a wild rage. 'My God Almighty!' she shrieked, 'this is disastrous—this is the last straw. That girl is a lunatic. What does she think she's doing. She cannot be allowed to do this dreadful thing. What will people think. We'll be disgraced. She must be stopped, and I'll see to it that she is.' Hugh was about to comment.

'If she's unhappy . . .

'Shut your mouth, you idiot,' she roared. 'I'll telephone Sr Dominica, right away. She will know what to do, and how to put a stop to her gallop.' Hugh did not dare to say another word, as she put on her coat, and ran to the post office.

Meanwhile, at St Joseph's, Alana had made it perfectly clear to her superiors that they were wasting their time trying to entice her to stay, and telling them she wanted her dispensation as quickly as possible. Mother Teresa changed her tune completely at that stage, and Alana saw the side of her which was very frightening indeed. Her face became transformed, and with a voice like thunder, she warned: 'I am speaking to you in my capacity as Mother General of this order, and endowed with the power of the Holy Spirit. I warn you, Sister Agnes, that if you throw away your vocation, you will rue the day.' Alana was terrified, and really worried and upset by her remarks, but she timidly replied, 'I'm sorry, Mother, but I must go.'

Alana was then taken to the palace of the Archbishop of Dublin, Dr John Charles McQuaid, where she signed some papers, which he sent to Rome. 'Your dispensation should be back in two weeks,' he said, abruptly. Alana thanked him, and he gave her his blessing. There was no turning back now. She had voluntarily signed a formal request of the Pope of Rome, to dispense her from her vows, and by a stroke of the pen, she had thrown away her own happiness to help her sister. It was an awesome experience, and in her cell that night, she felt frightened, confused, and very sad at the absolute finality of it.

Her Mother wrote her a long letter, expressing her disgust and disappointment at Alana's rash decision, and telling her that she was disgracing herself and her family. You must be taking leave of your senses, it read and I can assure you that I would rather you would throw yourself into the Liffey, than to do what you are doing. These were harsh, cruel words, and they sent goose-pimples out through Alana's body. What her mother would do or say, when she saw Deirdre arriving home with her, didn't bear thinking about. Sr Bernard's letter was very sad. She told Alana that it was the worst news she had ever in her life heard, and that she felt so unhappy about it that she had cried in bed every night since she heard it. She begged Alana to think again. 'You and I know, Alana, that all your life, you have worked towards becoming a nun, and now you are deserting the life you have always so eagerly desired on a foolish impulse.' Alana was in tears as she read Sr Bernard's letter, and wished with all her heart that she could have spared her loyal, good friend, this terrible disappointment. Both these letters had left Alana in a very distressed state of mind, but then one night, she was called to the telephone. When she heard her father's cheerful voice at the other end of the line, she was overjoyed 'I'm delighted to hear you are coming home again to me, me flower! I can't wait to have you back. You're as welcome as the flowers in May.' Her father's kind words were a source of great joy and consolation to Alana, and were a big boost to her low morale. She learnt later, that he was sent to the telephone by Sr Dominica, and was instructed to stress on Alana that her desire to abandon the religious life was a temptation from the devil, and that she should have the courage and strength to fight it, and remain in the order. Gráinne was present with him in the telephone box that night, and she couldn't believe her ears when she heard him say the exact opposite.

On the morning of February fifth 1958, Alana attended mass in the convent chapel as usual. Then, after breakfast, she was instructed to go to the parlour, where Mother Teresa and Mother Imelda awaited her. On the floor, Alana saw a large open case, packed neatly with new clothes, and hanging on the back of a chair was a navy wool coat and scarf, and a blue dress.

'Your dispensation arrived yesterday,' said Mother Teresa, solemnly, 'and we have arranged for you to leave this morning.' Mother Imelda then handed Alana the clothes she was to wear, and pointing to a screen in the corner of the room, she said. 'Go in there, please, Sister. Take off your habit, and put on this outfit.'

'Thank you, Mother' said Alana, taking the clothes and retiring behind the screen. When she was fully dressed, she came out, and Mother Teresa handed her two envelopes, one of them very bulky.

'Take these, sister. There is a cheque for one hundred pounds in one, and the other contains fifty pounds in cash. This should keep you until you get your job back.' Alana was overcome.

'Thank you very much indeed, Mother I am most grateful.'

'That is the least we could do for you' replied Mother Teresa.

'You worked very hard while you were with us.' There was a ring on the front door.

'That will be the taxi', said Mother Imelda. There was a very emotional few minutes between Alana and her superiors, as farewells were said. They both went with Alana to the taxi, and just as it began to move away, Mother Imelda ran after it. The driver saw her, and stopped the car. Alana rolled down the window.

'Your ring, Sister. You forgot to take off your ring,' she said breathlessly. Alana took the gold ring from her finger, and handed it to Mother Imelda. Then the taxi drove off, and twenty minutes later, stopped outside Kate's house. Deirdre and Kate came down the garden path to meet her. 'Thank God, you're here at last,' said Deirdre, hugging her. Kate kissed her warmly. 'You look very well, and glamorous too,' she said 'except for your hair. We'll have to do something with that before you go home to Glenbeg or your mother will disown you altogether!'

Chapter 13

The atmosphere in No. 9, Rosebud Cottages was so heavy, that Gráinne was on the verge of 'cracking up'. Her mother was in a constant state of fury at the idea of Alana leaving the convent, and she and her father were forced to listen to her rantings and ravings at breakfast, dinner and supper. How her father endured it, Gráinne could never understand. He's not a man at all, she thought to herself, for if he was, he would have her murdered. The breaking point came for Gráinne at breakfast, one morning, when Peggy was in particularly foul humour. Gráinne sat at the table, trying to eat her breakfast, while her mother sat in front of her, launching a vicious verbal attack on Alana. 'That girl is bringing shame and disgrace on this family, and she doesn't care. She was always strong-willed and defiant, but I never thought she would go so far as to defy the Lord. May God forgive her! How am I going to face the neighbours? I'll never again be able to walk the roads. If she left the country for all our sakes, but no! She will come parading back here as though she has done nothing wrong. My God! I often wish she was never born.' Gráinne could take no more. She got up from the table, and all the pent up tension that was simmering inside her head, came to the boil, as she screamed at the top of her voice. 'Shut up! Shut up! You're driving me insane. I cannot stand it any longer.' And she grabbed her coat from the nail at the back of the kitchen door, and went out, slamming the front door behind her.

Peggy was shocked at Grainne's outburst, and realising she had gone too far, became sorry and frustrated. She clenched her fists, and began to bang the table, and then, putting her head down on the table, she dissolved into tears. She remained in that position for quite some time, until suddenly, she thought she heard a noise coming from the porch. She got up and went out to investigate. There, on the floor, was a white envelope. She picked it up and saw that it bore Alana's handwriting, and was addressed to herself. Maybe she has changed her mind, she thought, tearing it open, and beginning to read.

6th, February, 1958

Dear Mum,

I left the convent yesterday, after receiving my dispensation from Rome, and I came straight to Auntie Kate, where I will remain for the moment. The reason for this is that Deirdre is also here with me, and is afraid to come home, knowing that it was your urgent wish that she stay in England.

She was deserted by Tommy after one night, and has suffered quite a lot, as you can imagine, all alone in a strange country, and in her condition. She is very troubled and upset, and I fear for the child she is carrying, and due to be born in April. It is my intention to take care of her and of the baby when it is born.

We would both love to come home to Glenbeg, but unless we do so with your approval, it would be better if we did not. I have one hundred and fifty pounds, which I received from Mother Teresa before I left, and this should keep both of us until I get my job back, that is, of course, if you do not want us home.

We await hearing from you, and I sincerely hope, for Deirdre's sake, that you will be sensible about this, and realise that you are her mother, and that she is carrying your grandchild.

That's all for now!

Love, Alana.

She has some nerve, thought Peggy, as she finished reading. What am I going to hear next? Now I have double trouble, two daughters wanting to come home to this village, one an ex-nun, and the other a deserted wife, married four months, and eight months pregnant. Then she asks me to be sensible. I think she is having some sort of brain-storm. Peggy's temper was mounting again, the more she read the letter, and the more she allowed her thoughts to run away with her. She went back into the kitchen, and made herself a hot cup of tea. As she sipped it slowly, she was planning a suitable reply to Alana's letter. She could definitely not allow them to return to Glenbeg. After all, apart from what the neighbours would say, she had her own family to consider. Jamie and Sr Dominica were very good to her, and Sheila and herself were on the best of terms, even visiting each other frequently. She couldn't possibly let these latest dreadful bombshells ruin everything again. Sheila was lucky. Her husband, George, was English, very refined and well-spoken, and as sensible as a rock. He was an accountant, and had already got himself a good position with one of the large firms in Cork. Their son, Pat, had qualified as a vet, and Fiona was now attending university where she studied law. They definitely had the blue blood of the O'Flahertys running through their veins, but unfortunately, her three daughters took after the O'Gradys. True, they were kind and good-natured; but they had no real ambition, and no desire at all to be anything but ordinary commonplace people. Alana was the only one that showed some promise, but now she had ruined herself. Hugh had a good position, and handed her all his salary, but refused to socialise with the right people, preferring to spend his leisure hours, sipping pints with the villagers. Gráinne was very involved with Eoin O'Dowd, a handsome boy, and a radio-officer. The O'Dowds were a very fine family. The father was a sergeant in the guards, and the mother was a teacher. If they were to hear of these scandals in the family, they might be wary of their son becoming tied up with the O'Grady's and Gráinne would be heart-broken. Peggy herself would be extremely upset, as she was cultivating their relationship, and putting on a great show of grandeur for Eoin. There was no way Alana and Deirdre were going to spoil this.

She went to the drawer of the dresser, took out her notepaper and began to pen a reply to Alana's letter. She informed her, in no uncertain terms, that there was no question of their returning to Glenbeg. 'If Deirdre and yourself have made a mess of your lives,' she wrote, 'You had better pick up the threads, elsewhere, far away from this village, and let the rest of us live in peace, without the shame of your misdeeds bringing disrepute on us.' She wrote on in that vein for several pages, and when she had the letter completed, she felt great relief, having got rid of all the bitterness she felt towards them. She put Alana's and her own letter on the mantelpiece, and busied herself preparing a meal for Hugh. To-day was his half-day, and they usually went to Cork in the bus to do some shopping. She would post the letter there, because she did not trust Agnes the Postmistress at all.

Hugh could read Peggy like a book. As soon as he came into the kitchen and looked at her, he knew she was excited about something or other. She had that fiery sparkle in her eyes, which he knew so well.

'So! any news?' he said, kissing her on the forehead. She went to the mantelpiece and handed him Alana's letter.

162

'Read that,' she said, in a peculiar tone of voice. Hugh took the letter, sat in his armchair, and began to read. Peggy stood over him, anxiously awaiting his reaction. 'Well! What do you think of that?' she asked, her hands on her hips, a posture she usually adapted, when her mood was bold and vindictive. Hugh certainly knew what she thought, and he also knew that there was a very serious difference of opinion in the offing. He was aware that the atmosphere was highly explosive, and that he had to watch his words very carefully. He did not reply for a minute or two, and Peggy got impatient with the delay.

'Come on,' she said, 'tell me what you think.' Hugh took a deep breath.

'Sit down,' he said 'and let us talk this matter over calmly and rationally, without raising our voices.' She sat down on the edge of the chair, not at all in a relaxed posture, and with her eyes firmly fixed on him, she waited for his comments. After some deliberation, Hugh asked.

'What do you think, yourself, Peggy?' She immediately got up, went again to the mantlepiece, and taking from it her own letter to Alana, she gave it to him.

'That is what I think,' she replied, boldly. 'Read it for yourself.'

As Hugh read the letter, his heart sank, and his feelings went from deep pity for his two daughters and an urgent desire to comfort and help them, to anger at Peggy's harsh attitude towards them. He must take a firm stand on this issue; otherwise he would lose his two daughters for ever, and at the same time, he must remain calm, or he might lose Peggy. He handed the letter back to her. 'Come on, now' he said, gently holding her by the hand, and bringing her down, to sit beside him.

'You surely couldn't mean everything you have written there.'

'I mean every word of it,' she answered, 'and you can't

have much respect for Gráinne and myself, not to mention yourself, if you don't go along with it.'

'Peggy, my dear,' he said, 'There is nothing in this wide world that I would not do for you, and I have always done things your way; but please, do not ask me to turn my back on my children.'

'They are no longer children,' she went on, 'but grown up women, and they didn't consider you or me, when they brought this trouble and disgrace on themselves. They can get out of it now, in the same way that they got into it, and that's my final decision.'

'If my family had adopted that attitude, when you and I were in trouble, what would have become of us?'

'We wouldn't have got married,' she answered, 'and the way things have turned out, I'm not so sure that it would have been such a bad thing.' These words pierced Hugh's heart, and cut him to the quick, and he didn't say another word.

Peggy got up, stamped across the room to the cooker, took Hugh's dinner from the oven, and put it down on the table with a bang. Then she got her coat and handbag, and said sharply, 'I'm going to Cork.' Out the door she rushed, slamming it hard. Hugh felt slightly relieved that she had gone, as he never before needed so badly to be alone with his thoughts. After turning the problem over and over again in his mind, he realised that the only just solution, as far as he was concerned, was to have the girls home and with Peggy's consent. The only way to do that, was to bring them home, and he reckoned that there was a fair chance that she would then accept them. She wasn't really that hard-hearted. Her bark was worse that her bite. He got up and ate his dinner. He noticed Peggy's letter still on the table. Thankfully, she had not taken it with her to post it.

Before he left the cottage, he wrote a note, and left it on the dresser for her.

'Dear Peggy,

I have gone to Dublin to bring the girls home. We should be here to-morrow night. This will give you plenty of time to reconsider your decision. I hope and pray that you will welcome us home. If you do, I will never forget it, and it will make me very happy. If you do not, I will understand, but things could never again be the same between us. I love you, Peggy, and what I am doing is for both of us. You will realise that yourself some day.'

Mossy drove Hugh to Dublin that evening, and it was after midnight, when they arrived at Kate's house. They had knocked three times on the door, before they finally heard Alana's voice.

'Who's there?' she asked.

'It's only myself and your father are here.' The girls got into their dressing-gowns, and came quickly downstairs.

'Is there something wrong, Dad?' said Alana.

'No, me darlin', everything is fine. We have come to bring you both back to Glenbeg.' They looked at each other in delight and amazement.

'Does Mum agree to this?' asked Deirdre.

'She will,' answered Hugh, 'Just take her easy, and everything will work out alright.'

'I'm going to miss them,' said Kate.

'Not for long,' Mossy told her, 'I'll bring Mary and Elaine up to you, next week, and they can stay for as long as they wish.' Kate was delighted to hear this, and went into the kitchen to make a pot of tea. 'Poke up the fire, Alana,' she said, as they all sat round the dying embers, in the large sitting room, ''Tisn't every night we have visitors after midnight.'

Mossy let Hugh and the two girls out of the car outside their own cottage the next evening.

'I won't go in,' he said, 'This is a family affair, and it's better that way'.

'Thanks a million for everything,' said Hugh.

'Wish us luck,' Alana said, as they walked towards the door.

'You'll be OK,' said Mossy, 'If things go wrong, you know where to come.'

Peggy and Gráinne were sitting by a blazing fire when Hugh and the girls walked in. Gráinne was first to get up and greet them warmly. 'God, it's great to be home,' said Deirdre. Peggy looked at her, and Hugh could detect a softness in her eyes. 'Come over here,' she said to her, 'and put your feet up. That long journey couldn't have been good for you, in your condition.' Deirdre threw herself into her mother's arms, and burst into tears. Hugh and Alana were still standing in the same position, and Hugh anxiously awaited Peggy's reaction to her. As soon as Deirdre was seated, and Peggy had settled a little stool for her feet, she turned to Alana, 'Welcome home,' she said, and Hugh breathed a sigh of relief. He knew how much it had cost Peggy to say this, so he went to her, and kissing her tenderly, he whispered, 'Thank you, darling.' Alana then opened a little black purse, which she took from her pocket, and produced a thick wad of notes, which she handed to Peggy. 'There is one hundred and fifty pounds there, Mum,' she said, 'It will be a help to you until I get my job back.' Peggy's eyes lit up, and her attitude to Alana changed dramatically. 'Thank you very much, Alana' she said. 'You are very good. This is, indeed, a very pleasant surprise.' Hugh was smiling as he thought to himself. Money makes the mare go, especially the O'Flaherty mares.

For the next few weeks, Alana enjoyed the comparative freedom of living in the world again, and of not having to answer bells or gongs. Peggy could not understand the way she walked out among her neighbours, as though nothing had happened; but Alana enjoyed this more than anything else. Some of them thought she would never be real again, after being in the nuns, and almost approached her with reverence. Molly Murphy, an elderly widow, who lived in number five, was fascinated with her.

'Did they really shave off all your hair'? she asked.

'Oh, yes, indeed,' answered Alana. 'Do you know Molly, that I used to wash my head with a face-cloth, every morning, it was so bald.'

'Praise be to God!' said Molly, 'but how did you get it to grow again?'

As Alana walked down Ashe Road one evening, on her way to Clover Road to visit her Aunt Sheila, Biddy Leary and Mamie Cronin, whom she barely knew to see, went out of their way to give her a royal salute, almost genuflecting in front of her. As soon as she had passed by she overheard Biddy remark to Mamie, 'That's the eldest girl of the O'Grady's. She's the one that came out of the nuns.' Alana was highly amused as she continued her journey.

She had got a temporary teaching post in the national school, and after giving her mother some money each week, she spent the remainder, buying baby clothes and other bits and pieces that Deirdre needed for her confinement. She went to lunch to Clover Road every day, and she was developing a great relationship with Aunt Sheila. Alana thought she was the best and most decent one of the O'Flaherty's, and she was very considerate and understanding. Pat and Fiona were also very fond of Alana, but she was always a little nervous when Jamie was there. He had that abrupt manner of his father, and she thought he didn't like to see her there. 'Don't take any notice of him,' Sheila said. 'That's just his way; but he is really very kind and good, and often enquires about you.' Alana was always at ease with Sheila's husband, George. He was a great character, and he thought the world of Alana. He taught her to drive, and promised to arrange finance for her, so she could buy a small car for herself.

Alana's period of temporary teaching came to an end, after four weeks, and she didn't know what to do with herself. Her mother refused to allow her help around the house, so she was bored to distraction. She spent most of her time at the convent with Sr Bernard, and that wasn't much help to her either, because ever since she left the convent, Sr Bernard couldn't conceal her utter disappointment at Alana's decision. As they sat together one evening, making copies of a piece of music for the choir's forthcoming competition at Feis Maitiú in Cork, Alana noticed Sr Bernard's face redden, as it usually did when she was angry or upset. She put down her pen.

'Alana,' she said 'the more I think of it, the more I realise what a dreadful mistake you have made.' Alana was stunned.

'What brought this outburst on, Sister?'

'Look at you here with me. You have no interest whatsoever in this world, and I know that.' Then she stopped, and a peculiar expression came over her face. 'I also know,' she continued, 'why you left us, and it had nothing whatsoever to do with being unhappy or losing your vocation.' Alana grew pale, as she asked, 'How can you be so sure of this?'

'Your Mother told me it was for Deirdre you came out. I was horrified, and I'll never forgive them for bringing her near you at all, so soon after your profession.'

'If my mother hadn't forced her to marry, and sent her to England, things might have been different,' said Alana 'but there's nothing we can do about it now, but accept it.'

'Tell me the truth,' said Sr Bernard, 'are you happy, now?' Alana answered

'I am not happy, Sister, and I do now realise what a

terrible mistake I have made. However, with Deirdre and the baby to support and take care of, I do not have much choice.'

Alana was called back to her job in the civil service, ten days later, and this was a great relief to her. She knew she was getting on Peggy's nerves at home, and that it was only a matter of time, before a big row would erupt. She decided to take George's advice and buy herself a Morris Minor car. He was true to his promise, and arranged the loan for her. When she brought the new car home, there was great excitement. Hugh and the girls were delighted, and she took them for a drive around the glen.

'You're a great driver,' Hugh commented proudly.

'You must teach me to drive,' said Gráinne.

'I'll teach the three of you,' answered Alana, 'and you can borrow the car anytime you want to.'

'That's a very generous offer,' said Hugh, 'but I'm thinking I would never manage all that complicated foot-work.'

'I'd say Mum would be a good driver' remarked Deirdre, 'although, for some reason, she didn't appear over enthusiastic about the car.'

'If she is half as good a driver as she was a horsewoman, she'll pass us all out,' Hugh said.

At supper the car was the main topic of conversation.

'I can't wait for Eoin to call and see it,' Gráinne said, excitedly.

'Can he drive?' asked Alana.

'Oh, yes. His father has a car, but only lends it to him on the very rare occasion.'

'Why don't the two of you go off to Cork in it, tonight,' said Alana.

'Do you mean that?'

'Of course,' answered Alana. Gráinne was over the moon.

169

'Isn't it wonderful, Mum. Can you believe we have a car of our own.' Peggy didn't reply, but turned to Alana.

'This car is going to cost quite a lot of money to pay for and to run. I hope you will be able to pay for it, and that it won't affect your weekly allowance to me.'

'You'll get your money Mum,' Alana replied, tensely, and there wasn't another word about the new car.

Deirdre went into labour on the night of the twenty-first of March, and Alana drove her immediately to the hospital in Cork, and decided to stay there for the night, in order to be near her. She gave birth to a baby boy, the following morning, and as Alana looked with loving admiration on the tiny infant, she couldn't help thinking that this little fellow had altered the whole course of her life. Deirdre named him Neil, after her grandfather, and Alana was very pleased about that. Hugh was thrilled to have a baby in the house again. 'A home without a cradle by the fire is very empty,' he would say; but Peggy moaned, non-stop, about the injustice of raising a child without a father, and about the cramped and crowded conditions under which they were living. Deirdre grumbled a lot also, about Tommy getting away scot free, and herself being stuck with his baby. Alana didn't take much notice of this at first, hoping it was just the after-effects of the birth, and that when she was properly rested, all would be well. As time went by Deirdre became more and more disgusted. 'I have no feeling for this baby,' she announced one night, 'and I'm sorry I didn't put him up for adoption.'

'Don't let me ever again hear you speak like that about your son,' Hugh said, sternly. 'You should be down on your two knees thanking God for giving you such a beautiful baby.' Alana was horrified.

'Surely, Deirdre,' she said, 'You cannot possibly mean what you have just said.'

'I mean every word of it,' replied Deirdre. 'I was never

170

cut out for this motherhood caper.' This last remark was too much for Peggy.

'You should have thought of that, when you were breaking the sixth commandment with that Tommy O'Brien fellow,' she snapped 'but you have made your bed, and you must lie in it now.'

'I'm going out,' said Deirdre, grabbing her coat, 'and I may not come back.' Alana ran after her.

'Please, Deirdre, don't do anything foolish. This is just a phase, and you'll get over it. I'll help you.'

'Drive me down to Mac's bar,' she said 'I need a drink. You can pick me up in an hour.' Alana did as Deirdre asked her for peace sake, but Deirdre refused to come home with her an hour later, and Alana had to almost lift her into the car, when she finally came out of the pub at closing time.

Deirdre went from bad to worse, and caused havoc in the family. Nobody could do anything about her, and everyone's nerves were frayed for fear she would come to any harm. Peggy took care of Neil during the day, while Deirdre slept off her drinking orgies, and Alana took over, as soon as she came home from work in the evenings. There were nights when Deirdre didn't come home at all, and it was widely known that she was having an affair with Johnny Burke, a married man with three children of his own. She was the talk of the glen and Peggy was so ashamed, that she refused to go outside the house any more. Hugh worried silently and, although he put on a brave face, he looked like an old man.

There was a loud knock on the cottage door, one night, and when Hugh answered, he was confronted by a distraught Mrs Burke.

'I want to see your daughter, Deirdre' she shouted.

'Come inside, Mrs Burke,' said Hugh 'and we will talk things over quietly.' She came into the kitchen, where Alana was bathing Neil in front of the fire. Peggy was dozing on the armchair, and Gráinne was deeply engrossed in a book.

'Where is she the dirty bitch?' Mrs Burke said. Peggy sat up.

'If you are referring to my daughter, Deirdre, she's out.'

'Oh, she's out, is she, and she's with my husband, throwing back gins and tonic at his expense, and the expense of my poor children.' She began to cry.

'Don't upset yourself, Mrs Burke. That won't solve anything,' said Hugh. 'Look at her own little baby in the bath, there. Don't you think we are heart-broken too.'

'He was a very good husband and father,' she continued, 'until your trollop of a daughter crossed his path. May God forgive her.'

'Excuse me now, Mrs Burke,' said Peggy, fire now in her eyes, 'but if you came here to insult me and mine, you had better be going the way you came. Your husband is just as much at fault as our daughter, and we could just as easily call him filthy names, but we are not ignorant people, so we don't resort to that kind of thing.' Mrs Burke was about to pour out another violent stream of abuse, when Hugh interrupted her.

'My good woman,' he said, leading her to the door 'the best thing to do is go home to your children, and we will do all in our power to get our daughter back on the right path, and to get your husband home to you.'

'The sooner the better,' she replied, as Hugh led her out through the door.

'What in God's name, are we going to do?' said Peggy, when she had gone.

'There isn't much we can do,' answered Alana, 'except hope and pray that Deirdre will see the light'.

'You are a lot to blame for this, Alana,' said Peggy. 'You should have stayed in the convent and prayed there, instead of coming out disgracing us all, and then insisting on

172

bringing Deirdre home. She should have been made to stand on her own two feet, as I said, and then she would have to take care of herself and her child.' Hugh felt sorry for Alana.

'Ah, Now, Peggy, her intentions were good, and she acted out of kindness and pity.'

'You have to be cruel to be kind,' retorted Peggy, sharply, 'and look what her good intentions have done now.'

'Mum is always right,' interjected Gráinne, 'and it's a pity she's not heeded more.' Alana's heart sank, and she didn't say another word. She brought Neil down with her to her bedroom, and she lay there in tears, for hours afterwards. There was certainly a lot of truth in what her mother had said. She felt sorry and guilty, long before her mother had voiced her opinion, sorry for throwing away her religious vocation, to live in a miserable world, in which she was very unhappy, and guilty for causing so many people so much pain by her action, and for the terrible consequences she was now witnessing. She remembered vividly Mother Teresa's words to her: You'll rue the day. It had come to pass. She did rue the day, and this was only the beginning. If only she could have one more talk with Deirdre, and tell her how much she cared about her and Neil, and how she would solve any problem that troubled her, no matter how bad it was; but Deirdre had not returned home for the past five nights, and there wasn't a trace of her or Johnny Burke in Glenbeg. She heard her father go down to bed. He was a very early riser, and he didn't believe in burning the candle at both ends. Her mother was still working around the kitchen, and Gráinne was out enjoying herself with Eoin O'Dowd. What a terrible pity, she thought, that she didn't have a normal relationship with her mother. She badly needed someone to talk to, but her mother and herself never saw eye to eye about anything, and anyway she was attaching the blame for everything on her. She had never felt as lonely and desolate as this in the convent. If she was ever troubled or upset about anything there, she had only to go to the Reverend Mother's office and talk things over. She felt really alone, and a dark cloud of depression descended on her. There was not one ray of hope on the horizon, and her life stretched out before her, like a dark, foggy road, in which she was completely lost. She slept fitfully, and during these short intervals of sleep, she dreamt that she was still wearing her religious habit, and was walking down the long cloister at St Joseph's .

Neil cried, and this brought Alana back to reality. She got up immediately, and took him into the kitchen to feed him.

'Look what you're reduced to now,' said Peggy sarcastically. 'You certainly have literally gone from the sublime to the ridiculous, giving up your high calling, where you were admired and respected, and reducing yourself to the level of a skivvy for your depraved sister.' Alana looked at her mother, her eyes filling up, and in a calm deliberate tone of voice, she replied.

'I have never considered myself to be either above, or beneath anybody else, and I didn't enter the convent, to be admired or respected, but to do God's work, and I consider what I am doing now, to be an act of charity, and if that means I am a skivvy then so be it. Who am I anyway, that I shouldn't be a skivvy, any more than anybody else. I'm not an O'Flaherty, you know. I'm an O'Grady.' Peggy was livid.

'You're a fool Alana,' she said.

'Ah, but this world won't be long teaching you a thing or too?' Then she went into her bedroom, and Alana and Neil were alone again.

Chapter 14

'Remember now, your name is Murray,' warned Johnny Burke, as Deirdre and himself rang the bell on the reception counter of a tatty hotel in East London. A fat, middle-aged woman came out of a small door behind the counter, and looking suspiciously over her glasses at them, asked.

'You're looking for accommodation, I presume.'

'That's correct,' replied Johnny.

'Double or single?'

'Double.'

'How long are you planning on staying?'

'A week or two, maybe less.'

'Have you money?'

'Sure, we have,' answered Johnny, 'How much do you want?'

'Fifty quid,' she answered. Then Johnny took from his inside pocket, a large black wallet, and Deirdre, never in her life, saw so many notes. He counted out fifty pounds.

'There you are now,' he said. She checked the money, and opened up a shabby red book.

'Your name, please.'

'Mr and Mrs Pat Murray.'

'You're Irish?'

'We are that.'

'What part of Ireland?' she enquired.

'South West,' replied Johnny. She handed them a large key.

'Room seven,' she said, 'upstairs, and the seventh door on the left.'

The room was small, but clean and comfortable, with the bare necessities: a double bed, large wardrobe with small dressing table attached. Deirdre threw herself onto the bed, and fixed herself into a very alluring position.

'Where did you get all that money, Johnny Burke?' she enquired.

'Don't be so nosy, now' he replied, looking down at her with a mischievous smile. He was good looking enough, very tall and well built, his auburn hair slightly receding from his forehead; but he was forty years of age or more.

'I'm going to take my little honey suckle shopping tomorrow, and I'm going to dress her up like the Queen of England.' Deirdre jumped up in the bed with excitement, threw her arms around his neck, and kissed him several times. He took her in his strong arms, laid her down gently on the bed and slowly undressed her. As she lay there, naked, in front of him, he began to take off his clothes, all the while, looking passionately at her lovely, young body.

'You're beautiful and I adore you,' he whispered, as he lay down beside her, gently arousing her passion to a state of frenzy.

'Oh! Johnny, my darling, I love you,' she whispered, as their bodies united and they lay there as one, their strong desires perfectly satisfied. They slept for a while, and made love again and again, until they were absolutely exhausted. They didn't awaken until almost midday, and when Johnny got out of bed, and looked through the window, it was snowing heavily, and the roof tops were covered in a thick, white blanket.

'We're going to have a white Christmas, I think,' he said dressing himself quickly, because the room was very cold. Deirdre was sitting up in bed, the blankets pulled right up around her and she was shivering.

'Johnny,' she said, 'You won't ever leave me, will you?'
He came over to her, and caressing her lovingly, he replied:

'Put that thought out of your little head. You know how much I love you. My God! I never knew the meaning of love until I met you.'

'But what about your wife?'

'Don't even mention that aul' frigid hatchet face. She made my life a misery for the past fifteen years. There's as much love in her as there is in a dead duck.'

'She probably has the guards out looking for us now, and if they find us you'll have to go back to her, and I will kill myself.'

'Hush now!' he said, 'they won't find us, and even if they do, they'll never be able to tear me away from you.'

'What of the children? Don't you miss them?'

'I do love them dearly, but for the moment, they are better off with their mother. I'll find a way of getting in touch with them, when we get fixed up here. Get yourself dressed now, because you and I are going to do our Christmas shopping, and that's all that matters right now.'

Deirdre was elated, and she bathed and dressed quickly, feeling very happy and secure with Johnny. He was a strong, burly man, but he was as gentle as a lamb, and very kind and generous. Her family at home, especially Neil and Alana, flashed across her mind momentarily, but she did not want to spoil this beautiful day with such thoughts, so she dispelled them rapidly. She knew Alana would take care of Neil, and she herself had no time at all for babies, so he was better off without her, and she reckoned she had done him a big favour.

Johnny ordered a taxi to take them to Oxford Street, and while they waited in the hotel bar, he gave her a large brandy.

'Drink this down,' he said. 'It will warm you up and raise the cockles of your heart.'

'Your taxi is here, Mr Murray,' announced the porter. Johnny, not recognising the name, didn't respond, until he was tapped on the shoulder. 'Your taxi, Mr. Murray.'

'Oh! yes,' he said, becoming slightly flustered. He handed the porter half a crown and then, taking Deirdre by the hand, they went out to the taxi.

'Where to?' asked the driver in his cockney accent.

'Oxford Street, please,' answered Johnny.

'I hope you have plenty of dough,' the driver said, 'Cos that's quite a distance, and will cost a few quid.'

'Drive on,' ordered Johnny, 'You'll be paid every copper of your fare.' Deirdre was in high spirits 'This is really living,' she exclaimed excitedly, as she moved closer to Johnny and looked up at him with those big blue eyes. Johnny stroked her hair, and was so pleased with her reaction, that he went a little further. 'Driver,' he said, 'Take us on a tour of the city. I want my new bride to see everything.' Then he winked at Deirdre, as the driver drove on, giving them a running commentary as he went. Deirdre was fascinated at everything she saw, especially the coloured lights, Christmas decorations and big Christmas trees. They went past Buckingham Palace, and the taxi driver stopped the car, so they could see the changing of the guard. Although Deirdre enjoyed seeing all the historical buildings, and loved Trafalgar Square, she could hardly believe her eyes, when they turned into Picadilly Circus, and she saw the big flashing neon signs, and the huge stores, beautifully decorated and full of magnificent things. She had never experienced anything like this before. 'Am I dreaming?' she asked aloud 'or is all this really happening to me?. Gee! It's like fairyland, with all the lights and glitter. I want to stay here, forever.' Johnny was smiling as the taxi stopped outside Debenhams. 'We're here, my sweet,' he said and he caught her by the hand and brought her out. He paid the driver, and gave him a generous tip.

'This is my card. Just telephone if you need me again.'

'Good luck to you,' Johnny said, and they both went into the store. Deirdre wanted everything she saw, and Johnny satisfied her every whim. She was in and out of fitting rooms for hours, trying on coats, dresses, skirts, and hats of every description, while Johnny gave his approval or otherwise, when she paraded out, and admired herself in the large mirror. She finally came out of the shop wearing a royal blue, wool dress, a full length, fur coat, with fur boots and a fur hat to match.

'You'll be broke,' she said to Johnny.

'Don't worry, my dote,' he replied, 'There's plenty more, where this came from, and sure, 'tis worth every pound to see you looking so happy and so elegant.' She smiled her coy smile, and kissed him gratefully.

'I love you Johnny Burke.'

There seemed to be no end to Johnny's money as they wined and dined and went to all the shows and clubs in London, during the following week. Whenever they passed a shop, and Deirdre admired anything in the window, he bought it for her, immediately. The one thing Deirdre could not understand though, was why such a rich man as Johnny should choose to stay at the small shabby hotel. When she asked him one night, he answered: 'It's best that we stay in a place like this, just in case they're looking for us. I have paid off that landlady, and she knows exactly what to say, if there are any enquiries. Trust me.' She did trust him, and she loved him, this gentle, generous giant of a man, who pandered to her every fancy, and made mad, passionate love to her several times in the course of the night. He bought a large Christmas tree, decorated it with fairy lights, tinsel of all colours, balloons, and many other little Christmas baubles and novelties and stood it in the corner of the bedroom, beside the window. When they returned home in the early hours of Christmas morning, laden with bags and parcels full of goodies, the taxi driver had to make three trips upstairs to land all the stuff into the little bedroom. Johnny and Deirdre were nicely inebriated, and sang 'Silent Night' in a less than silent manner, as they staggered hand in hand across the hall and upstairs. Johnny stopped at the bedroom door. 'You stay outside,' he ordered Deirdre, 'until I tell you to come in.' Then he went inside, plugged in the Christmas tree, making the room come alive with the flashing, coloured lights. He then took a small package, wrapped in red paper, tied with a gold bow from his inside pocket, and placed it in a prominent position, beside the angel, at the top of the tree.

'Come in now,' he shouted.

'What's all the big mystery about?' she commented, letting out a shriek of delight when she saw the glittering tree. 'Oh! this is so exciting, Johnny, You think of everything,' and she hugged him affectionately. He rooted through the parcels and took out a bottle of champagne. 'Whoever finds a small, red parcel on the tree gets the first glass,' he said. 'I'll give you two minutes.' Deirdre, frantic with excitement, searched the tree, knocking off little balls and balloons as she did so, and then, finally, found it.

'Here it is!' she yelled.

'Open it, its my Christmas present to you.' She unwrapped the fancy paper, and uncovered a white, heart shaped box. She opened the box, and inside, set in red velvet, was the most exquisite gold ring with a huge cluster of diamonds. Deirdre's mouth and eyes opened wide, and she was speechless for a second. 'Oh! Johnny,' she exclaimed, 'This is absolutely divine.' She put it on her finger, admiring it for a long time. Then she came to him, and kissed him passionately, expressing her gratitude as she did so. He popped the champagne and poured out two glasses.

'Happy Christmas, my beauty,' he said.

180

'I'll drink to that,' she replied, and they sat on the bed, and polished off the bottle of champagne.

They fell into bed sometime later, and Johnny immediately lapsed into a drunken stupor. Deirdre lay beside him, frustrated and lonely, her whole body alive with desire for him. She closed her eyes and tried to sleep, but the passion and excitement she felt didn't allow her any rest. She turned in to him, and roused him, but despite all her wild endeavours, she could not bring him to the passionate stage at which she herself was. She needed to feel his body submerge itself in hers. She moaned and groaned in extreme longing. He worked hard to satisfy her, the perspiration teaming from his brow, but to no avail. An hour or more went by, Deirdre urging him on, proclaiming aloud, her great love for him, and then Johnny ceased to try further, and fell back on the pillow. Deirdre got out of bed, went to the bathroom, and decided a shower might ease the way she felt. She stayed there for a long time, enjoying the warm, comforting spray of the water, and turning her face up to it, to savour, fully, its soothing sensation. When she eventually came back into the bedroom, clad in the white satin nightress and gown that Johnny had bought her, she went to the bed where he still lay motionless. 'How do I look Johnny?' she asked, and there was no reaction whatsoever. She bent over and kissed him, and his lips were cold. 'Oh my God,' she thought, 'What's the matter with him?' She slapped him on the face, stroked his hair, and then she noticed his extreme pallur. 'Jesus Christ,' she said, her heart thumping rapidly, 'He's dead. He can't be,' she said, as she tried to pull him up, screaming 'Johnny, wake up, please, wake up. You cannot leave me.' She got worse and worse, until eventually, she went into a state of complete hysteria.

The landlady heard the rumpus, and came into the bedroom. Deirdre had gone completely out of her mind, as

181

she pulled the bedclothes from the bed, and threw them on top of the Christmas tree. Mrs Edwards slapped her on the face.

'Calm yourself, child, and tell me what happened?'

'He's dead. My Johnny is dead, and I'm all alone.' Mrs Edwards looked at Johnny lying on the bed, stark naked, pale and lifeless, and she immediately knew Deirdre was speaking the truth. She took Johnny's pulse, and there was none there. Then she took Deirdre downstairs, and gave her a stiff brandy.

'This will help you,' she said. 'We'll have to call the police.' Deirdre sobbed loudly. 'I didn't hurt him. I loved him, I adored him. He was the best thing that ever happened to me, and now he's gone, dead. Oh! God, my Johnny, he's dead, he's dead, and I'll never see him again.' Mrs Edwards tried to comfort her, but Deirdre wasn't listening. She wanted to go up to the bedroom, and stay there with him, and it took all the landlady's effort to keep her downstairs.

The police arrived, and took photographs of the room, and all the other routine investigations that are carried out in such cases. They rang for an ambulance, and Johnny's body was taken to the morgue. Then they came downstairs into the living room, where Mrs Edwards sat with Deirdre who was now a little calmer. 'We have locked the room,' the older of the two said, 'and we have taken the key. We also want the master key, as nobody is to go in there, until our investigations are completed.' Then looking at Deirdre he enquired.

'Are you his wife?' Deirdre hesitated, and then she replied.

'No, Sir.' Mrs Edwards looked shocked, and tried to vindicate herself, bringing in the red book in which Johnny had signed them in as man and wife.

'Would you mind leaving us for a while,' the policeman asked her.

'Certainly,' she replied, and she left the room.

Deirdre was frightened almost to death, as he shot questions at her.

'What is your name?'

'Deirdre O'Grady.'

'Are you married?'

'Yes, sir, but my husband disappeared after one night.'

'What is your address in Ireland?'

'No. 9 Rosebud Cottages, Glenbeg.'

'Was the dead man married?'

'Yes sir.'

'What is his real name?'

'Johnny Burke, sir.'

They wrote down all this information and then, walked towards the window, where they conferred together for a while. Deirdre gathered that the older of the two was Inspector Stevens, and it was he who asked the questions, while the other man did the writing. They came back to her, and Inspector Stevens asked.

'Were you aware that Mr Burke had almost eight hundred pounds in a canvas bag in his suitcase?'

'No, sir,' replied Deirdre, 'but I did notice that he was spending quite a lot of money?'

'Have you any idea where he came by all this money?'

'I have not, sir! But I asked him, and he told me not to be curious.'

'I'm afraid we will have to take you down to the station for further questioning,' Inspector Stevens said. Deirdre was terrified.

'I didn't murder him,' she cried. 'I didn't do anything wrong.'

'We are not accusing you of anything. This is routine.'

She was taken away in the police car, and having been read her rights, she was fiercely interrogated for several hours, until it became patently clear to the inspector that Deirdre was telling the truth. He looked at his watch. 'It is seven-ten in the morning, now,' he said. 'We will go back to the hotel to fetch your belongings. Meanwhile, you will remain here, until we can arrange to send you home to your parents in Ireland.' He gave her a cup of hot tea, and brought her to a cosy little cell, where she fell into a sound sleep.

Later on in the evening, Deirdre was driven in the police-car to Paddington Station. The Inspector sat in the back seat of the car with her, and warned her in a kindly manner.

'Your place is at home, looking after your baby, and that's where you should stay. You are not educated or experienced in the ways of this world and the people in it.'

'But what's going to happen to Johnny?' she enquired, beginning to cry.

'His body will be returned in due course to his wife for burial. His death has saved him a lot of trouble I can assure you.' Deirdre couldn't understand this last remark, so she questioned further.

'What does that mean?'

'That's not for you to worry about,' he answered, abruptly, 'just remember my advice to you, because you may not be so lucky next time.' She was put on the boat train at Paddington, and the Inspector handed her a sealed brown envelope. 'The people on the ship are aware that you are travelling, and you will be taken care of. Just hand this letter in at the ticket office.' Deirdre thanked Inspector Stevens, and boarded the train.

As the train rolled across England on its way to Fishguard, she re-lived in her mind, the short but sweet two months she had spent with Johnny, and the tears rolled down her cheeks at the thought of him lying dead in a morgue. She hated the idea of going further and further away from where he was, and dreaded facing her mother. She could never again go outside the house now, because Mrs Burke would murder her. She could imagine all the gossip and consternation that was going on in Glenbeg, and she thought that she would be better off to hitch a lift to Dublin as soon as she got off the boat in Cork.

The crossing was very rough, with a storm force-ten gale blowing up at sea. The ship heaved and rolled, and Deirdre was very ill. She sat, curled up on a pullman seat, grateful for one thing at least, and that was the big, warm, fur coat Johnny had bought her. She needed a brandy to settle her stomach, but she hadn't one penny in her pocket. If Johnny were here, she thought, he would take care of me, and I could have as many drinks as I needed. She cried for him until she thought her heart would break, and she felt her body becoming weaker and weaker. She didn't remember another thing, until the pungent aroma of smelling salts pierced her nostrils, and when she finally came round, she was lying on a bed in a small cabin, the ship's doctor leaning over her.

'You'll be all right now. Just lie there and take it easy. You had a little weakness, but it's all over now. I'll have a pot of hot, tea sent to you.'

'Thank you, doctor,' she murmured, closing her eyes again.

She was called by a stewardess at about ten-thirty, next morning, half an hour before the ship was due to dock. She struggled out of bed, feeling so low that she didn't care what became of her, or indeed, whether she lived or died. She made an effort to freshen herself up, put on her fur coat and hat, and left the cabin. She went out on deck to breathe in some fresh air, and as she leant over the railings, looking at the familiar landmarks of her native shore, the stark, grim realisation of the terrible mess she was in, hit her very forcefully, and she was almost numb with anxiety and worry. What was ahead of her in about five minutes' time, when she walked off the comparative security of the ship, and how was she going to live through the shame and disgrace that she had brought on herself and her family? She caught sight of her father and Alana standing on the quayside, huddled together under her father's big, black umbrella. At least she had someone to turn to, and that was a relief to her; but how was she going to face them, after all she had put them through?

She walked down the gangway, holding her head down, and as she came near them, she looked up; but they didn't appear to recognise her.

'It's me, Dad,' she said standing in front of him. His eyes lit up.

'My poor child, I didn't know you in all that finery.' He took her in his arms, his eyes filling up with tears. 'I'm so happy you are home, pet. I thought you were gone forever, and that I would never again lay eyes on you.'

'I'm sorry, Dad,' she cried.

'Whisht now! We'll get over everything together.' She turned to Alana.

'Please forgive me,' she said.

'Not to worry,' answered Alana, 'Sure, there is nobody perfect, and don't we all make mistakes.'

'I don't deserve to have such a wonderful father and sister,' Deirdre said, as she sat in the back seat of Alana's car, on her way home to Glenbeg.

Alana was very tense, and didn't speak much, as she drove the car out of the city traffic; but Hugh never stopped talking to Deirdre about Neil.

'You won't know him when you see him. He's a bonnie lad, and as cute as a fox. He is the life and soul of the house.'

'What about Mum?' enquired Deirdre, 'How is she taking all this?'

'Ah! She'll come round,' Hugh assured her. Then Alana interrupted:

'Dad, I think we ought to put Deirdre fully in the picture about everything, before she goes home.' Hugh didn't answer, but Deirdre replied.

'Please do, Alana. I would hate to walk in unprepared.'

'I suppose you are not aware,' continued Alana, 'that Johnny Burke stole over one thousand pounds from Agnes O'Dwyer, the postmistress, on the night you and he left.' Deirdre was shocked to the core.

'But how did he get away without being caught?' she questioned.

'He gagged Agnes and tied her hands and feet, and she wasn't discovered until next morning.'

'My God!' Deirdre exclaimed 'that's why the police took me in for questioning.'

'The guards and the English police have been looking for him this past two months.' Alana said, 'and the whole, terrible affair made front page news on *The Trumpet*. Your own name was mentioned as having gone away with him.'

'Sweet Jesus!' exclaimed Deirdre, 'Most of this stolen money was spent on me. Look at this fur outfit, that must have cost a fortune, not to mention the cases full of other exclusive and expensive clothes.' Then she showed them the massive ring on her finger. 'This was the latest purchase. Can you imagine what that cost?' Alana and Hugh were silent, and Deirdre began to panic. 'Don't take me home. I couldn't face it,' she said to Alana. 'Just drop me off at the railway station and if you could lend me a few pounds, I'll get the train to Dublin, and make my own way from there. I'll pay you back as soon as I get a job.' Hugh turned back to her and took her by the hand.

'Now, now,' he said, 'Don't be talking nonsense. We're taking you home. You'll be safer with those who love and care for you. Your mother will have a lot to say no doubt,

187

but just listen to her, and as soon as she gets it off her chest, all will be forgotten. You know her. She shouts a lot, but other than that she's as good as gold.' Deirdre calmed down a little, but she was still very apprehensive and ill at ease.

'I suppose Molly Burke is out for my blood,' Deirdre said.

'She is very angry and upset to say the least,' answered Alana, 'We had several visits from her, and I can assure you, we had our hands full, trying to placate her.'

'She must be at her wits end altogether, now that Johnny is dead,' said Deirdre, fear gripping her again. 'My God, I am to blame for all this. I'll never live it down.' She broke down, and cried aloud, 'I never thought things would come to such a bad end.'

'Stop fretting now,' Hugh advised, 'and just take everything as it comes and try to make the best of it. Time is a great healer.'

As they passed the little parish church, Deirdre blessed herself, and whispered a prayer for help, and coming along by Mac's bar, she knew that what would be a great help to her would be a large brandy. She daren't go in there though, for fear she would be lynched.

'Now is the hour,' said Alana, as she stopped the car outside the cottage. 'Let you and Deirdre go in first' she told Hugh, 'and I will follow with the cases.'

Hugh walked ahead of Deirdre, through the porch and into the kitchen. 'We're back,' he said, rubbing his hands nervously in front of the fire. Peggy was at the sink, and had her back to them, while Neil was in his pram, in a little alcove by the fire, propped up on pillows, and wide awake. Deirdre stood there, in the middle of the kitchen, looking nervously from one to the other, and not knowing what to do or say. Hugh beckoned to her to go to her mother, and she did.

'I'm so sorry, Mum,' she mumbled. Peggy turned round

quickly. Her face was pale as death, and her eyes were hopping out of her head.

'So, well you might be sorry,' she said angrily, 'and the terrible tragedy you are responsible for. May God forgive you, for not alone did you degrade yourself and mess up your own life, but you have made Minnie Burke a widow, and her children orphans, as well as bringing shame and humiliation on them and on your own family. Look at your infant son in the corner. What do you think people will say to him in years to come. I'll tell you what they'll say. "His mother ran away with a married man, who committed robbery to keep her in style and grandeur, and then died in her bed".' Alana came in with the cases and put them down on the floor.

'Don't be too hard on her, Mum. She has suffered too.'

'Suffered! is it?' she shouted. 'Look at her, dressed up to the nines, with her funny hair style.' Her voice was getting louder. ''Tis sack cloth and ashes you should be wearing, after the wicked sins you have committed. Only for your poor little baby there in the corner, and your father and Alana, I can assure you, I would not have you inside my door, and before you sit down in this house, go to your room and take those clothes off you. They belong to Agnes O'Dwyer, and 'tis down to her they will be sent, together with anything else that was purchased with her money. At least that will be some small form of restitution.'

Deirdre was glad of an excuse to leave the kitchen, and she went to her bedroom, and changed into a pair of slacks and a sweater. Alana brought her a cup of tea.

'Drink this, and rest there for a while until she cools down. I suppose we had better bring all these clothes down to Agnes.' Deirdre took the ring from her finger.

'Don't forget this,' she said, 'It is probably more valuable than all the rest put together.'

For the next few weeks, Deirdre obeyed her mother's

189

every command and listened to her lectures, rebukes and criticisms without a murmur. She never left the house, and even though she could still feel no motherly love for Neil, she tended and cared for him as best she could. It was an extremely difficult time for her, and she wept many a silent tear for Johnny, and wondered what would eventually become of her. She certainly had no intention of spending the remainder of her life in this one-horse town, among hostile neighbours, and under her mother's thumb. She would not remain sane at all, but for her father and Alana. They tried their best to make her miserable existence a little more tolerable. Her father brought her a small brandy from Mac's every night, and Alana kept her supplied with cigarettes. Mossy and Mary invited her to their house for a game of cards on a few occasions, and she could let her hair down and talk freely to them. They were like a breath of fresh air, they were so kind and understanding, and very broadminded. She hadn't seen Gráinne since she came home, as Gráinne had got a better job as receptionist to a doctor in Cork, and had taken a flat there. She was engaged to Eoin O'Dowd, and according to Mary, she seldom came home to Glenbeg, and when she did, she stayed at O'-Dowd's house. She had become very high and mighty Mossy thought, and was half ashamed of her humble home. Of course, she was the jewel in Peggy's crown, and she couldn't wait for her to be married into the O'Dowd's.

Johnny's body was brought back to Glenbeg on January tenth, and he was buried in the parish cemetery. Alana took Deirdre and Neil to Clover Road, while the family attended the funeral. She was very upset that day, and Sheila bent over backwards to comfort and console her.

'Don't feel guilty,' she said, 'Remember, you gave Johnny over two months of happiness, more than his wife gave him in all the years of their marriage'

'But he stole all that money for me,' cried Deirdre.

'You were not to know that, and anyway, most of it was returned. We mustn't judge the poor man. Just let him rest in peace, and you must get on with your life.'

Minnie Burke's two brothers came home from America to attend the funeral, and afterwards they brought their sister and the children back with them. It was a consolation to the O'Gradys that Minnie was well taken care of, and they were also releived at her departure, as it made life less awkward for them in Glenbeg.

Chapter 15

The drawing room over the pub in Clover Road was now a very pleasant and relaxing room, since Sheila had decorated and refurnished it. The soft, peach-colour, wool carpet with the cream, three-piece suite, and peach scatter cushions, were very soothing and cheerful. Two large, wicker rocking-chairs stood in the alcoves beside the two big windows and it was in one of them that Sheila sat one Saturday afternoon, reading a spicy novel. She took off her glasses and put down the book on the small table in front of her. 'Fiona!' she called, 'Please turn down the volume on that record player. It is impossible to concentrate with that noisy music blaring in my ear.' Fiona was in her glory, bopping to the loud sound of Bill Haley's 'Rock around the Clock.'

'But Mum!' she argued,' ''Tis absolutely crazy stuff, and it's meant to be played loudly.'

'Your father has as much sense as yourself, spending his hard-earned money on that thing. Sure the old gramophone there on the sideboard is good enough.'

'You're old-fashioned, Mam, you must move with the times.'

'You had better be moving now, and go and relieve your Uncle Jamie in the bar. I'll take over from you as soon as your father comes home, and has eaten his dinner.'

'Where is dad, anyway?' Fiona asked.

'He went to Cork to a meeting in the home of one of his clients, who has some financial problem or other to be sorted out.' Fiona put away her records carefully, and went downstairs to the bar. She had qualified as a solicitor, and her father was arranging a position for her with a reputable law firm in Cork.

Sheila was looking through the window, amused at the various people going into Pat's surgery next door, with small animals to be treated. The widow Malone was wheeling Percival, her pet marmalade cat in a large plaid luggage trolley.If anything happened to Percival, poor Alice would lose her life. He had a better life than lots of human beings, and Pat was constantly warning her that he would get a heart attack from over feeding. Little Christy Sullivan had a white rabbit in a cage, and Des Forde looked more than a little concerned, as he carried Inky, his kerry blue bitch in his arms, holding a large, white hankerchief to her leg. There was no shortage of business for Pat this evening, and Sheila would hear about all the ailments and operations at dinner. George was late, and she wondered what on earth could be keeping him. He was usually very punctual, and now, at six-thirty, he was half an hour late. She went to the kitchen to put the final touches to the evening meal, and as she came to the end of the stairs, she saw Alana coming through the front door, looking perplexed and worried. 'Come on in to the kitchen,' said Sheila, 'You are just in time for dinner.' Alana followed her through a small door on the left of the stairs, and into the long kitchen.

'Whatever it is, it smells good,' said Alana.

'You'll be able to savour it shortly, just as soon as George comes. He's very late already, though I shouldn't imagine he'll be much longer. We have time for a quick drink.'

'I'll just have a cup of tea,' Alana said. Sheila gave her a mug of strong tea, while she poured herself a glass of cool, white wine from the fridge. They both sat on high stools at the counter.

'Deirdre wasn't around to-day, was she?' enquired Alana, rather anxiously.

'I haven't seen her for days,' replied Sheila, 'Is she misbehaving again?' Alana thought for a moment, as she sipped her tea.

'Well, she has begun to spend a lot of time out of the house again, though quite honestly, the way mum is carrying on at the moment, I find it hard to blame her.'

'What's the matter with her now?' asked Sheila.

'Oh', answered Alana, 'She's making Deirdre and myself feel like second-class citizens, talking non-stop about Gráinne, and the wonderful man she has chosen. She tells us that Gráinne, is the only one of us with her feet on the ground, and that she will never again see a poor day. On and on she goes, until you feel like screaming.'

'I can well imagine,' said Sheila, 'Your mother is full of that nonsense.'

'Of course, you know' Alana said, 'that Gráinne is going to Rome to be married.'

'Oh, yes, indeed, sure that's all Peggy talks about these days. But tell me about Deirdre.'

'Well,' continued Alana, 'She has been out almost every night for the past few weeks, and on several occasions she didn't return until the early hours of the morning. She left home about ten o'clock this morning, supposedly to meet an old school pal, but she hasn't returned yet.' Sheila looked at the clock on the wall.

'My goodness,' she exclaimed, 'It's seven-thirty, where on earth is George?' She was really worried looking.

'He was probably delayed,' Alana consoled her, 'I'll pour you another drink, and he'll be here before you have finished it.'

Pat came in from surgery.

'Hi Alana,' he said, cheerfully, 'it's unusual to see you around at this time.'

194

'How's business?' enquired Alana.

'Very brisk indeed,' he replied, as he sat down to read *The Trumpet*.

Pat was a darling boy, very much like his grandfather O'Flaherty in appearance, being of the small, stocky breed, but he definitely had the cheerful personality of his father. Sheila finished her second drink, and there was still no sign of George. Alana could see her becoming very anxious, and Alana herself was feeling very uptight. She had forgotten about Deirdre in her concern for Sheila. Pat put down the newspaper, and came over to the counter to the two women.

'What's the matter, Mam?' he said, 'Fretting about Dad, as usual?' Turning to Alana, he remarked jovially, 'She's a terrible worrier, where Dad is concerned. If he's not home on the dot, she begins to imagine all sorts of queer things.'

'He has never been as late as this,' said Sheila, 'he must have had some sort of accident.'

'Don't be silly, Mam,' Pat said, 'Let's start dinner without him.'

'Run out and fetch Fiona,' said Sheila, as she began to serve up the dinner. Fiona dashed into the kitchen in top gear, and breathless. 'Lovely to see you Alana, but I haven't a minute to spare. The bar is crowded and I must dash back' Sheila served Fiona's dinner first.

'Are we eating without Dad?' she said.

'I'm afraid so,' wailed Sheila mournfully. 'He hasn't come home yet, and if we wait any longer, the meal will be ruined.'

The meal was delicious, consisting of tender roast pork and apple sauce, creamed carrots with fresh, green peas, and big flowery potatoes in their jackets. 'That was lovely, Mam,' said Fiona, excusing herself and returning to the bar. Sheila hadn't eaten a bite, and as the clock struck nine, she began to cry. Pat himself was now beginning to worry. 'Let's call Eric Jackson, his client in Cork, and he'll be able to tell us what time he left him, or even if he's still there.' Pat rang the operator, and spoke to Eric, as Sheila stood beside him, anxiously awaiting the news. Pat put down the phone, turned around slowly, and looking extremely worried, announced that his father had not been to the house at all, nor had he an appointment with him. Sheila lost control of herself completely at that stage.

'Ring the guards, quickly,' she urged. 'He must be in some sort of trouble and is running away. We must find him, and tell him that I'll sort it out for him.'

'You're jumping to all sorts of conclusions, Mam,' said Pat, 'You'll find there's a perfectly logical explanation for this. Now try and be calm, and I'll go and make a few enquiries. Alana will stay here with you, until I return.'

'Can you wait ten minutes or so?' asked Alana, 'I would like to go home and tell Mum where I am, and I'm also anxious to know if Deirdre came back.'

'Take your time, Alana,' Pat replied, 'there's no great hurry.'

Alana sat into her car, and drove quickly home. As she stopped the car outside the cottage, she could see Peggy and Hugh sitting in the porch, and Neil was on her father's knee. As soon as the little fellow saw Alana, his hands and legs began to move frantically with excitement. Alana picked him up in her arms, and cuddled him affectionately.

'Any sign of Deirdre?' asked Peggy.

'None at all. I thought she might be home by now.' Then she told her parents about Sheila's dilemma, and how George hadn't returned home. Peggy's face assumed a strange sort of knowing look, and Alana knew she was thinking along the same lines as herself; but none of them mentioned a word of their thoughts to the other.

'Go back and stay with your aunt,' said Peggy, 'because she's very highly-strung, and not at all as tough as I am.'

She handed Neil back to her father, and left again for Clover Road.

'Any news?' she asked, as she entered the kitchen.

'Nothing!' answered Pat, looking anxiously at his mother, who was by now, beside herself with grief and worry. 'I wont be too long,' he said, as he left to visit George's best friend, to try and find out if he knew whether he was in any trouble, and where he might be. It had been decided not to inform the guards until they had made their own enquiries.

'Did Deirdre come back?' Sheila asked.

'No, not a trace of her,' replied Alana, 'Mum and yourself are in the same predicament now.' Alana had great pity for Sheila. She had always been so kind and understanding to everyone; but Alana had always believed George to be a rock of sense and reliability, and he was the last person in the world, she thought, would have behaved in this manner.

'Do you think he'll come home?' cried Sheila.

'We'll only have to wait and see,' Alana answered, not wanting to give her false hope. Pat returned no wiser than he was before he left. As soon as he walked in the door, Sheila jumped up.

'Tell me you found him, Pat. Oh, please, tell me.' Pat dug his hands into his pockets, and cast his eyes down.

'No Mam, I'm afraid I cannot tell you anything. I have made enquiries all over the village, and nobody has seen hide nor sight of Dad. It's as though he disappeared into thin air.' Sheila buried her face in her hands and sobbed. Pat went over and sat beside her. 'One thing is sure, anyway, Mam, and that is he didn't have an accident. The guards have confirmed that, so where there's life, there's hope. The guards are now searching for him, and they will keep in constant touch with us' Sheila continued to sob, and Pat appeared very distressed.

'The best thing to do now, Sheila, is to go to bed,' said

Alana, and please God there'll be news soon.' Pat made her a steaming hot brandy punch, and when she seemed a little easier, Alana took her leave of them. When she arrived home in the early hours of the morning, her heart was heavy and she was at a very low ebb. Is there any luck or grace in this family at all, since I left the convent, she thought, and she remembered again Mother Teresa's words: 'You'll rue the day.'

Alana's worst suspicions and fears were confirmed some days later, when Sheila received a post card from George in a sealed envelope. It was posted from Dublin, on the same date that he left home, and it read: 'I have done what I thought was best for everyone. I have gone to Australia with Deirdre, to make a new life for us and the baby to be born. Please forgive me and try to understand that I had no other choice. I will always cherish you and our children, and believe me, it's easier for all of you this way. I will write soon again'—George. Sheila read and re-read the card until its contents finally sank into her brain. There was nobody in the house except Jamie, and when he heard her screams of anguish from the Bar, he dropped everything, and ran into the kitchen. She had gone completely berserk, breaking cups and glasses on the floor, and shouting at the top of her voice. 'She's a tramp and a thief! She has ruined my life, stolen the only man I have ever loved. Oh! God! what did I ever do to deserve this trial and heartbreak.' Jamie tried to calm her, but she became worse, declaring that she would drown herself in the Cush. Jamie telephoned for the family doctor, asking him to come quickly to the house, and explaining briefly, her sad plight. Doctor Brian Kearney was with her in a matter of minutes, and he had to give her an injection to sedate her completely. Jamie and himself then carried her upstairs and put her to bed. 'She should sleep now for several hours. I'll call around again later on in the evening.' Then handing Jamie a little bottle of blue tablets, he said, 'Keep an eye on her, and should she awaken before I return, give her two of those. She has received a very severe shock to her system, so make sure to keep her warm.' Jamie thanked the doctor, and saw him out. He closed the bar on his way back, and sat beside Sheila's bed, his heart breaking for her.

Alana was the first to hear the terrible news officially. Pat telephoned her at the office, next morning, and asked her to meet him for a cup of coffee, in a small restaurant near her office in Cork. Alana was there before Pat, and when he sat to the table, she knew what he was going to tell her. She was, none the less, very shocked and upset, and Pat himself could hardly hold back the tears.

'How is Mam?' enquired Alana.

'She's still sedated,' Pat replied, 'but to tell you the truth, I cannot see her recovering from this, for quite some time, if ever.'

'I will do all in my power to help her,' Alana promised, 'because she was always good and kind to us all, especially to Deirdre. My God! Its a terrible tragedy!'

'Fiona is very cut up about it' Pat said. 'You know how she idolised Dad, and he her.'

'I know,' said Alana 'but it's just as well she is starting work next week, and moving to a flat in Cork. That will help her somewhat.'

'What about yourself?' asked Alana, 'How do you feel?' He thought for a minute before replying.

'I have turned the facts over in my mind again and again, and although I feel very sad and lonely, and very concerned for Mam, I have come to the conclusion that what Dad did, when he discovered Deirdre was pregnant, was really the only thing he could do in the circumstances, and will be easier for us all in the long run.'

'Thats very magnanimous of you indeed, Pat.'

'That is not to say that I condone his illicit relationship,

199

but he made a mistake, and in one way, he is paying for it too. We must keep the whole affair a dead secret though, and think up some plausible excuse for his absence, otherwise his going will have been in vain.'

'We'll figure something out,' said Alana, as they left the restaurant.

'Dont forget to call on Mam,' Pat said.

'Dont worry,' Alana replied, 'I wont neglect her.'

Hugh was distraught and very heartbroken when Alana broke the news to him; but, as usual, Peggy was furious, more furious than she had ever been, if that was possible. Alana didn't tell her, until Neil was fast asleep in bed, because he was a clever child, and she did not want him upset.

'Try not to shout so loudly,' Alana implored, 'You'll disturb poor Neil.' But Peggy couldn't help herself.

'This is the last straw,' she said. 'The girl must be possessed by a devil. Imagine, three men in the space of two years, one of them dead, and his family uprooted to foreign parts; and now her own aunt's husband, who will probably come to a bad end too, not to mention poor Sheila, and her two lovely decent respectable children. I never again in this life want to lay eyes on that girl, and at this moment, I honestly wish she were dead.'

'Oh, don't say that Peggy,' said Hugh, anguish in his voice.

'I'll say it again and again,' she answered boldly, 'because I really mean it. Imagine what the O'Dowds would say if they heard it, and poor Gráinne just two weeks away from her marriage in Rome.'

'The O'Dowds are the least of my problems,' Alana said, 'my main concern now is Sheila, and I'm going down to her right now. I may be late,' and looking sympathetically at her father, Alana left the house.

She sat by Sheila's bedside for hours that night, and even

succeeded in getting her to sit up and eat poached egg on toast. She was most edified at the brave way in which Pat and Fiona behaved; but what she admired in them most of all, was the complete absence of any bitterness in them, either towards Deirdre or their father. She promised Fiona that she would take care of Sheila, while Fiona was in Cork, and assured her that she would drive her home to see her mother any time she wished. Jamie, of course, was very disturbed and worried and went around the house biting his nails, and giving out under his breath. Although he never addressed Alana one way or the other, she knew that he appreciated her concern and care for Sheila. Apart from Peggy, the only other bitter person in this sad affair was Sr Dominica. She was allowed to visit Sheila for an hour each afternoon, and during that time she was more of an upsetting influence than a comfort to her sister. She bluntly condemned George and Deirdre in a most unchristian manner, prophecying damnation on their souls. Maeve was an angel of mercy and it was she more than anyone, who eased Sheila's anguish with her calm, cheerful manner.

Alana herself was hurting deeply inside, hurting mainly for Sheila and the children, and for her father who adored Deirdre, and who was failing before her eyes, from sheer grief and loneliness, and the constant nagging of Peggy, her cruel heartless criticisms of his seed and breed. Only for the hours she spent in the office, Alana would have cracked up completely. She needed to confide in someone, to get the huge burden she was carrying, off her chest. That someone was a great friend of hers who worked in the same office with her. She was a widow, about the same age as her mother; but she was the kindest and most gentle person Alana had ever known. Mrs Buckley was also very fond of Alana, and always gave her good, sound advice. Sr Bernard was still a great help to Alana also, but the mention of Deirdre's name was like a red rag to a bull; so Alana found it impossible to talk about her anymore. As soon as Gráinne was married, Peggy was relieved, and began to be a little more pleasant to live with, and Alana was very happy, especially for her father's sake. Mrs Buckley had been advising her for some time, to take a holiday; but while her mother was in such foul fighting form, she was loath to leave her father alone with her. Now that her humour had changed for the better, she thought the time was opportune. She had a hundred pounds or more in the bank, and what better way to use it, she thought, than to take Sheila and Neil away for a few weeks. Sheila was reluctant to go at first, but eventually, Alana persuaded her that a change of environment, and plenty of fresh air would do her a power of good.

They set off in Alana's car, and drove to the west of Ireland, where they stayed in a small hotel in Salthill. Even though it was late in September, the weather was very kind to them, and they enjoyed long walks on the beach, and beautiful drives in the very rugged but scenic roads of Connemara. Neil loved the sand and the water, and Alana felt that he, more than anyone else, was helping Sheila to overcome her great sorrow. She even rode on a merry-go-round with him on a few occasions, and it made Alana very happy to see her enjoying herself and laughing at his antics. When Neil was asleep each night, Alana and Sheila would sit in the hotel bar, and enjoy the music and the company of the other guests. Alana always made sure Sheila had a few drinks, so that she would talk more freely, and get any fears or anxieties off her chest. Alana was a great believer in talking things out and getting rid of them.

'You know, Alana,' she said one night. 'George married me when Pat was nine months old, and he has always loved him like his very own; but I do think that he would have loved a son of his very own; and that maybe that was why he did what he did.'

'Don't think like that' said Alana 'George is a man, and he fell by the wayside like any man could, but unfortunately, because of Deirdre's pregnancy, there was no turning back for him. His leaving was because, of a mistake, and had nothing whatsoever to do with you. I bet he is suffering more than you are, because added to loneliness, he has the feeling of guilt which is the worst feeling of all.' Sheila cried for a while, and Alana didn't try to stop her. Then she dried her eyes, and said.

'I suppose you are right, Alana, and I should be grateful for twenty-three very happy years,'

'That's the spirit,' Alana said, adding 'And grateful also that Pat and Fiona have done so well for themselves.'

'He was an excellent father to them' Sheila said 'and I can only hope and pray that, someday, he might come home again to me.'

PART III
1962 – 1966

Chapter 16

Gráinne was very lonely, and bored to distraction since Eoin went back to sea. The O'Dowd's residence was situated in a very isolated spot at the top of Beach Hill, on the eastern side of the glen, and people seldom passed that way. She was married seven months now, and very disappointed that she was not pregnant. At least a baby would keep her occupied, and she would feel closer to Eoin, but she must wait until his ship returned before she could try again, and that was a long way off. Although Mr and Mrs O'Dowd were very good and kind to her, she had nothing much in common with them and she found it impossible to feel at home there. She dreaded Saturday night, when the friends would gather for the weekly game of whist, and she always retired to the solitude of her bedroom, where she would write a long letter to Eoin. If she were given some housework or other chores to do, the day would pass by more quickly; but Mrs O'Dowd had her own routine, and her own special way for doing everything. She spent every morning hoovering and sweeping imaginary dust while Gráinne moved from place to place out of her way. This house is like a glassy palace she thought to herself, and she regretted that she hadn't kept her own small, untidy flat in Cork.

Conor O'Dowd, Eoin's father, was a tall, well-built man, and although his hair was grey, it was very plentiful, and he still looked young and handsome. Gráinne could see that he loved Maura, as much, if not more, than he did on the day they were married. Gráinne was very fond of him, and looked forward to the nights when he was at home, because he always made a fuss of her, and insisted that she join them in a hot claret before retiring. His conversation was very stimulating, and Deirdre enjoyed his amusing and interesting stories about the characters he encountered during his time as a guard on the streets of Dublin. He was telling one such tale just before bedtime, on a very bad night, towards the end of January, when the door-bell rang.

'Who could that be on such a bad night, and at such a late hour?' he said, as he got up to answer it.

'Maybe 'tis Eoin surprising us,' Gráinne remarked hopefully.

'Nonsense, child,' retorted Mrs O'Dowd, 'Sure he won't be back for several months yet.' She hardly had the words out of her mouth, when Mr O'Dowd ushered Alana into the dining room. Gráinne was very surprised to see her, and a little embarrassed too, at her shabby attire.

'What in heaven's name brings you here at this hour?' she enquired.

'Uncle Jamie was found dead in his bed an hour ago,' she said. 'Sheila found him, and the doctor says he had been dead for several hours, so Mum sent me to bring you home.'

'We are so deeply sorry,' Conor said, 'I knew your uncle well, and he was a very genuine man.' Gráinne was shocked, but deep down she was grateful for the opportunity to return home for a while.

'I'll grab a few bits and pieces,' she said, in an almost excited tone of voice, and she went upstairs.

'Sit down and have a little drink, Alana,' said Mrs O'Dowd, 'This must have come as an awful shock to you.'

'Thank you, Mrs O'Dowd,' she said 'he will be a sad loss to all of us.' She had just finished her drink, and was feeling all the better for it, when Gráinne came back, dressed in a

208

navy gaberdeen coat with a hood on it, and a small travel bag in her hand, and ready to go.

They drove to Clover Road, where all the family was gathered, and Sr Dominica was alone in Jamie's bedroom, washing him, and laying him out in the brown habit. The bar was closed and there was a black crepe on the door, with a card pinned on to it, notifying the neighbours of the death of the owner. Maeve and her husband, Tommy O'Sullivan were in the kitchen, and Maeve, calm and practical as always, had boiled too large hams to make sandwiches for the wake. Tommy carved the meat into thin slices for her, and she put it between the bread, and laid the sandwiches neatly on large trays. Upstairs in the drawing room Sheila was sitting on the sofa with Pat and his fiancée, Clodagh Breen sitting on either side of her, as she wept non-stop. Peggy was serving drinks to the handful of people that had already arrived to pay their respects, and Hugh sat quietly by the window, trying to amuse Neil, who was beginning to get cross and contrary, as it was long past his bed-time. Fiona was fascinated with him.

'He's a darling,' she remarked to Hugh, 'and so intelligent for his age.'

'He's all that,' replied Hugh, thrilled with the opportunity of relating at length to Fiona, several incidents confirming her observation about the intelligence of his beloved grandson.

The wake continued throughout the night, with friends and neighbours from every corner of Glenbeg assembling in the house, drinking and eating, and proclaiming the praises of poor Jamie. Alana and Hugh left early in the night, as Neil had fallen asleep, and any way Alana couldn't bear the atmosphere of drink and tobacco smoke that pervaded the whole house.

'I think all that drinking is very disrespectful to the dead,' Alana remarked to her father.

'Ah! they mean well, a chroí,' he said, 'and I don't think Jamie would mind seeing them enjoying themselves. In spite of everything, he was a good natured fellow.'

The funeral took place two days later, and afterwards the family were called together in the drawing room, where Jamie's will was read by the family solicitor. Peggy was not summoned, as there was no mention of her in the will. This was one of those occasions when Alana felt very sorry for her, and very annoyed by the fact that even to death, the old, stupid class distinction had remained. The pub and house was left to Sheila with a sum of three thousand pounds in cash. Pat got the larger of the two farms, and two thousand pounds, while Fiona was left the smaller farm and a sum of three thousand pounds. Maeve received five thousand pounds, and the remainder of the money which was in excess of ten thousand pounds was left to Sr Dominica's Order. Hugh found it difficult to understand how Peggy could have been left out, for the second time; but Maeve and Sheila gave her a thousand pounds each, and Hugh was very happy for her. Peggy put a large sum of money aside for Neil's education, and she made great improvements to the cottage. Gráinne stayed at home with her for a month, helping with the decorating, and she had no intention or desire to return to O'Dowds at all. Peggy was glad to have her around the house, because it was plain to be seen by all, that she was her favourite, but as the time went by, she became worried lest the O'Dowds would be concerned at her long absence, because they were very straight-laced people. She confronted Gráinne one morning about the situation.

'Isn't it high time you were going back to your husband's house?' she said, Gráinne's face fell and she blushed.

'Please don't ask me to go back to that lonely house, Mum. I absolutely detest it.'

'But your place is in your husband's house, and not here

with your mother. You're a married woman now, you know.'

'Married indeed, is it?' snapped Gráinne, 'with my husband away at sea, God only knows where, and me stuck up there on top of Beach Hill with his parents. I tell you, Mum, I was nearly dead from loneliness, with not a christian to talk to all day long.'

'You knew how it would be before you married Eoin, and that should have been sorted out before he left.'

'I'll sort it out when he comes back,' replied Gráinne, 'but meanwhile, I want to stay here, and if you won't allow it, then I'll find some place else.' Peggy knew that there was no point in arguing the point any further with Grainne, because when Gráinne made up her mind about something, that was it.

'You had better go and tell the O'Dowds, so,' Peggy said 'and don't have them getting annoyed and maybe writing and complaining to Eoin. You have a good man now, and you had better mind him.'

'He had better mind me,' Gráinne said, 'there are plenty of others only waiting to get me.'

'Less of that foolish talk now,' said Peggy, angrily, 'you don't know how lucky you are and you should appreciate that fact.'

Pat married Clodagh Breen in June, and because of the circumstances surrounding his father's absence, a small, quiet wedding was decided on, with only the immediate families of the bride and groom invited. Clodagh looked beautiful, dressed all in white, and it suited her sallow skin and big brown eyes. Eoin was home for the wedding, and Peggy thought Gráinne and himself looked as radiantly happy as the bride and groom. Fiona brought her boyfriend, and Sheila was terrified at his appearance. He wore skin-tight jeans and a pink shirt, and his black hair was almost shoulder length, and very unkempt, as was his thick, black beard. Alana told Peggy that he was an artist, and that they both intended to emigrate to America in the fall of the year. Sheila hadn't yet been informed, and Peggy felt that this would be a big blow to her, just when she was beginning to recover from the shock of George's disappearance. She would be completely alone now after Pat's marriage; but Alana decided to stay at Clover Road with her every night, until she settled down a little. She had plenty of company during the day, what with a steady flow of customers, coming in and out of the pub, and of course, Maeve and Sr Dominica were frequent visitors. George's only sister, Imelda, and her husband, Ken Dunphy, were very kind and attentive to Sheila. Ken was George's best man, and they had been very close friends all through their lives, and Ken was a tower of strength to Sheila, as well as to Imelda, who had also been very disturbed by her only brother's departure under such a dark cloud.

Alana was at everybody's beck and call, like a ministering angel, concerned about everybody's happiness and welfare, with never a thought for herself. Outwardly she seemed very happy, and was always very cheerful; but deep down, her heart was troubled. She longed to be back behind the convent walls, where everything she did seemed to have a meaning and was to her, a labour of love. She hadn't the slightest interest in material things, and she felt that the world and all that it stood for was superficial and insincere. Sr Bernard was very sorry for her, but all she could say was I told you so! which annoyed Alana intensely. Still, she was grateful for the friendship and support of the sisters at St Annes, where she could freely visit at any time of day or night, and she regarded them as her true family. She applied to be re-admitted to the order, but it was decided by the powers that be, that since she had received a dispensation from her vows, they felt it necessary to reject her application. Although she was bitterly disappointed, she

212

accepted the decision as a sign from the Lord that He had some other plan for her.

Neil was four, and going to school, and Hugh and Peggy loved him dearly. He was their pride and joy, and Alana was absolutely delighted at the way he seemed to have brought them very close to each other again. She gave her mother a very generous allowance each week, and apart from what she spent on the bare necessities for herself, the remainder of her salary was used to purchase clothes, toys, and almost anything else that Neil wanted. He was the next best thing to her own son, and it was he only, who gave her life any purpose at all.

Alana bought him a Shetland pony, and rigged Neil out in full riding regalia. 'Trigger' was kept in a stable at Clover Road, and Dave was teaching Neil to ride. As soon as Neil had a good seat on the saddle, and was able to trot reasonably well, Dave brought him along the road one day, with the pony, held on a long lead rein. Neil was thrilled to bits, and was doing very well. Biddy Leary, who seemed to be always walking the roads, passed by and when she saw little Neil astride the pony, she came over to him.

'If you'll be half as good a rider as your grandmother was, you'll be doing very well,' she said.

'He'll be better,' replied Dave, walking on about his business. As they neared home, Neil asked Dave.

'Who is my grandmother that Mrs Leary spoke about?'

'Peggy, of course,' answered Dave.

'But she is my Mum, you silly goose!' Neil said.

'Ah! sure of course,' said Dave, realising he had goofed. 'What was I thinking about at all.' Neil said no more, but he decided to ask Alana about it. He was highly intelligent, and it wasn't easy to fool him, or fob him off with an evasive answer.

On the way home with Alana in the car soon afterwards, he asked.

'Where is my grandmother who rides ponies well?' Alana was startled by his question, and had to think quickly.

'Both your grandparents rode horses well' she explained, 'As a matter of fact, in those days, everyone was able to ride, because there were no cars to take them from place to place.' That explanation seemed to satisfy Neil, but his question set Alana thinking about the day when Neil would have to know the real truth about his parents. That was something she didn't look forward to at all.

Coming events cast their shadows before them, and some months later, Ken Dunphy received a letter from George. Deirdre had given birth to twin sons, who were now a year old, and he enclosed a photograph of them. They were identical, and the very image of George himself. Imelda burst into tears when she looked at them.

'My God,' she cried, 'They're moulded out of him, the poor little darlings,' and she continued to sob.

'Shall I read George's letter to you?' asked Ken.

'Yes please, if you would,' Imelda replied, pulling herself together slightly. Ken sat down beside her and began to read.

Dear Ken,

I am virtually in tears as I write this letter to you, in tears because of the sorrow and anxiety I have caused my family, especially my beloved Sheila, and in tears for the little family you see in the photograph enclosed.

I am at my wits end with Deirdre. Believe me Ken, that girl is big trouble, and I cannot take any more from her. She has plagued and persecuted me from the day we set foot in this country. I come home from the office in the evening, tired and hungry, to find her either very drunk and absolutely violent, or in my bed with other men. This was going on even before the twins were born, and though I tried all in my power to change things, it was impossible. I

214

had to have her committed to a nursing home, three months before the birth, for fear she would seriously injure herself, and the babies. She took an overdose of tablets on three occasions, and the third time almost proved fatal.

Since the day the twins were born, she hasn't even looked at them, and threatens to kill herself and them if she is forced to take care of them. I couldn't take the risk of leaving the boys with her, so I had to employ a woman to look after them. Meanwhile, she continues to live a notorious life, and spends money like water. I work the round of the clock, and I haven't a dollar in the bank. She's ruining me, Ken!

I realise that I don't deserve your friendship after what I have done, but I beg you not to turn your back on me now, because I really need your help and advice, or God knows where we'll all end up.

Enclosed is a letter for Sheila. I want you to hand it to her personally, for fear anybody else might get hold of it. Give my love to Imelda, and please write soon. Do not tell Sheila of my troubles with Deirdre for the moment.

Your loving friend,

George.

Imelda was horrified at what she had heard.

'What on earth are we going to do about him?' she asked Ken, her face as white as a sheet.

'Try not to worry, darling,' he replied. 'I'll think the whole thing over very seriously, and we'll find some solution. In the meantime we had better take this letter to Sheila.'

'I wonder what her reaction will be!' Imelda said.

'Get yourself ready now,' Ken said, 'and we'll soon find out.'

Sheila was serving behind the bar when they arrived, and Alana was in the kitchen preparing the evening meal. They were glad Alana was there, and they decided to have a chat with her before giving Sheila George's letter.

'Someone is cooking something delicious,' Ken said as he entered the kitchen. Alana turned around from the cooker, and wiping her hands on her apron, she greeted them warmly, but she had an almost uncanny, intuitive sense, and she immediately got the feeling there was something amiss.

'Whatever it is, just spit it out,' she said to Ken. He handed her George's letter.

'Read this,' he said, 'and if Sheila comes in, put it away.' Alana sat down, and began to read. When she was finished, she studied the photograph for a while and then she looked up at Imelda and Ken, and in a slow, deliberate tone, she said.

'Deirdre is mentally ill, and will have to be committed for psychiatric treatment without delay. I'll have to go and bring her home.'

'That's going to cost a lot of money,' Ken said.

'I'll borrow from the bank, but it must be done, or there will be a severe tragedy.'

'But what about George and the children?' asked Imelda, anxiously.

'When Sheila reads George's letter, I feel she will co-operate with my plan'

'What is your plan?' asked Ken.

'George will be accepted back by Sheila with his children, in the same way as she accepted Pat. I know she will do this,' said Alana, 'and I would even be prepared to place a large bet with you on it.'

'I hope you are right,' said Ken, as he went to the bar to call Sheila.

216

Everything happened just as Alana had predicted. Sheila's heart melted when she read her husband's long letter.

'He has never stopped loving me,' she said to them, 'and I really believe him, and I fully understand now, why he had to do what he did. It's all over now,' she added 'and arrangements will have to be made to bring him back home.' Alana and the Dunphys were overjoyed, but a little puzzled, because they did not know how much Sheila knew. Alana broke the silence.

'What about Deirdre?' she asked.

'George didn't mention her,' Sheila replied, 'but I must tell the three of you now that he will bring twin sons, one year old, back with him, and we will be a family again.'

'Deirdre is very ill,' said Alana, 'and I must go to Australia and bring her home to a hospital.' Then Sheila's face lit up.

'That's it,' she said.

'You can bring them all home, and I'll buy all the tickets.' Alana threw her arms around Sheila.

'You're one in a million!' she said, 'and thank God you have decided to do what you're doing. You will be very happy soon again.' Ken and Imelda stayed to dinner, and all the arrangements were finalised during the meal.

'This is the happiest night of my life,' Sheila said.

Sheila wasted no time getting the travel arrangements made. She seemed to have got a new lease of life, and Tommy and Maeve were very happy for her.

'It will be nice to have children around this place again,' he said in his gruff voice.

'I'm so glad you feel like that Tommy. You're the best brother-in-law in the world,' and to his great embarrassment, Sheila gave him an affectionate kiss. Maeve was in the kitchen at the time, and she nearly choked with laughter.

'It's a pity Dominica wouldn't accept George's return in that spirit,' Sheila said to Maeve.

'Why? What did she say when you told her?'

'Oh the usual. "I don't know what the O'Flaherty family is coming to, swallowing your pride, and running to the end of the earth after those who are not fit to wipe our shoes."'

'My God! She never lost it,' said Maeve, 'after all those years in the religious life, wouldn't you think she'd have learnt a bit of humility?'

'Never mind her!' Sheila said, 'Alana is off, tomorrow, and it won't be long until they're all back. Can you believe it, Maeve. Isn't it wonderful?'

'I'm really very happy for you, Sheila, and I must say, you deserve it.'

Meanwhile at Rosebud Cottages, Hugh and Neil were very excited, as they tried to map out Alana's itinerary on the atlas.

'Imagine. You're going to the bottom of the world, Alana,' said Neil, 'You'll be upside down.' Alana laughed, as she packed some last minute items into her case.

'I hope the aeroplane doesn't crash,' Neil said, nervously.

'Don't worry one little bit about that, son,' assured Hugh, 'Sure, we'll be saying a very special prayer for her after the rosary every night.' Peggy was in a sarcastic mood.

'If you ask me, the people who step out of line in this world, are far better loved and respected than those of us who work hard, and constantly toe the line.'

'That's not true, my love,' said Hugh. 'Don't think like that. It's just a question of the prodigal son and the lost sheep. But sure, aren't you my only consolation and my pillar of strength!'

Alana set off next day for Brisbane in Queensland. She went to Dublin and flew from Collinstown airport to Heathrow, where she got a plane to Brisbane. The journey was long and tiring, and Alana was anxious about arriving at the other side. Would George be there at the appointed place? If he wasn't, what was she going to do, all alone in that far away land. Pat had spoken to George on the telephone, and he had assured Alana that his father would be there.

After almost three days, the plane finally touched down at Brisbane airport. Alana's heart was thumping with a mixture of joy, anticipation and anxiety. After collecting her luggage and going through all the other tedious formalities, she was finally walking towards the information desk, which was the appointed meeting place. Please God let him be there, she repeated to herself, and then she saw him. He was standing there, looking in every direction for her. He had aged a lot, and his hair had gone a lot more grey. He looked run down and shabby too. He saw her coming and he ran towards her.

'Alana! What a joy to see you?' he said, throwing his arms around her, the tears streaming profusely down his cheeks.

'It's great to see you, George. How have you been at all?'

'I'm fine now, Alana, but God, did I go through it!'

'I know. I know,' Alana said, 'but it's all over now.'

'Thank God for that!' he said, taking her luggage, and leading her towards the car park, 'We have a long drive ahead of us,' he said.

George settled Alana comfortably in his black station wagon, and they began the two hour journey. Alana slept most of the way, and didn't waken until George tapped her on the shoulder.

'Here we are, Alana. This is Vanessa Vale, and here is our little bungalow.'

'Isn't it pretty,' Alana said, drowsily, 'and what a nice, quiet place. Why, it's almost like Ireland here.'

'If Deirdre is here, don't be shocked,' George warned Alana, as he opened the front door. She wasn't there; but

Pam, a very pleasant middle-aged lady greeted Alana warmly.

'Welcome to Australia, Miss O'Grady. We have heard quite a lot about you.'

'Thank you, Pam,' replied Alana, 'but where are the boys? I'm dying to see them.'

'They're out in the back garden. I'll get them right away.' She came in with two darling blonde boys, who were absolutely identical.

'Which is which?' queried Alana.

'This is Gavin and this is Graham,' said Pam, pointing out to Alana a slight difference in the shape of their ears. Alana hugged them both, and then opened her case and gave them both a farmyard set that Sheila bought for them.

'You must be tired now, Miss O' Grady.'

'Alana please Pam!'

'I'll run a hot bath for you, Alana, and then you will be just in time for dinner.'

Pam left for home as soon as the twins were in bed and George and Alana sat by a big, log fire in the lounge.

'Where is Deirdre now?' Alana asked.

'That's a good question. Your guess is as good as mine. I never know what time she'll roll in, or whether she'll come home at all.'

'That's really terrible,' said Alana, 'but you do realise she's ill and needs psychiatric treatment.'

'I tried that approach,' said George, 'but it didn't work. She didn't want it to work.'

'I'm putting her into a private nursing home, as soon as we get home. I have heard that a Doctor Breen, who works there, is an excellent man.'

'I wish you the best of luck, Alana, and I will be eternally grateful to you for all you are doing.'

The door opened and Deirdre was there. Alana hardly knew her. She was a peroxide blonde, and her face was

220

plastered with make-up, which made her look cheap and debauched. She took a long cigarette from her mouth and threw it indiscriminately on the floor. Alana got up, and went towards her.

'How are you, Deirdre?' she said. Deirdre laughed.

'Look at my poor little Alana, all the way from the old sod, sober as a judge, and pale with worry about her problem sister. How am I? I'm drunk as a skunk, drunk as a skunk. Isn't that right, George mate.' George remained silent.

'Come on to bed now, Deirdre,' said Alana. 'We're going back home and I'm going to have you taken care of.'

'I'm incurable, Alana,' she said,'but yes, I'll go back home with you. The sooner the better. The drink is better over there, and I'm dying for a good Irishman again!' Alana was horrified and utterly disgusted, and it showed clearly on her face. Deirdre was quick to notice Alana's expression. 'Oh, you're shocked, aren't you? Well, you have a lot to learn, big, little sister. You were always a prudish little spinster, weren't you?' Then she staggered to her bedroom, and when Alana went in some time later, she was sprawled on the bed, fast asleep, and with all her clothes on.

'We will have to go home almost immediately,' Alana said to George. 'I couldn't bear to stay around watching her behave in this manner.'

'But surely you'd like to spend a little holiday here, after travelling so far,' said George.

'No honestly. I couldn't stand it. I came to bring you all home, and that's what I want to do, as soon as ever possible.'

'That's OK by me,' replied George, 'I have no possessions here, and I can be ready in less than a week.'

'That's settled then,' said Alana.

They were all back in Glenbeg two weeks later.

Chapter 17

Alana took Deirdre to a private nursing home in Cork, and put her in the care of an excellent psychiatrist. Pat and Clodagh were at Clover Road with Sheila to welcome George and his little sons home, and George wept with joy as he was welcomed back again into the bosom of his family. The only black cloud on that happy day was the absence of Fiona his only daughter, but he hoped and prayed she would return some day.

Hugh and Alana visited Deirdre regularly, but Peggy was still adamant that she never again wished to see her.

'Surely you won't turn your back on your own daughter, and she a very sick girl,' said Hugh.

'Her sickness was brought on by her own bad living, and it is a punishment from God, for the damage she has done to so many people,' Peggy argued.

'But when she is well, mum, she will have to be allowed back to her own home, so she can be rehabilitated,' Alana said.

'Over my dead body will she ever put a foot inside this door again, for it wouldn't be long until she would disappear again, and maybe take my Neil with her. Oh No! You can forget about her coming back here.'

'Neil is Deirdre's son,' Alana reminded her mother, 'and if she ever feels she wants him, she has first claim.'

'She'll never get that child from me,' Peggy replied. 'I will fight her for him in any court of law, and she wouldn't

222

stand a chance with her bad reputation.' That was the end of the discussion for that day, and Alana and Hugh continued to worry about Deirdre, her mother's hostile attitude towards her, and most of all about Neil, who was growing up and would soon to be told about his mother.

Doctor Butler was pessimistic about Deirdre's chances of a full recovery. She was heavily sedated all the time. Sometimes she didn't know Alana or her father; other times she spoke a lot of nonsense, and then there were the rare occasions when she was perfectly lucid; but even then, here speech was slurred. The nursing home was very expensive, and Alana had to sell her car to help pay the bills. Deirdre had a very plush room all to herself, on the ground floor with a balcony overlooking a large paddock, where cattle and horses grazed peacefully. The door of the room had to be kept locked, because she was not allowed to leave it, her treatment was so severe. Night after night, Hugh and Alana went to see Deirdre, hoping in their hearts to find some improvement in her; but night after night their hopes were dashed as she lay there with a vacant stare in her eyes and her tongue passing frequently over her dry lips in an effort to moisten them. 'How is my little girl to-night?' was the first thing Hugh always asked her, and then he would rub his hands across her forehead and through her hair. She just looked at him, and either muttered a few incomprehensible words, or close her eyes and return to the other world in which she now lived. It saddened Alana intensely to see her father cry.

'What in God's name have they done to her at all?' he cried one night, 'She wasn't half as bad as she is now, when she came in here.' Alana had been thinking exactly the same thing, and was beginning to feel very guilty herself for committing Deirdre to the hospital.

'We'll call to Nurse Creedon's office,' Alana said, 'and find out what the situation is.' Nurse Creedon was the sister in charge of the ground floor, and she was a big, stong, capable woman, of middle age, but she spoke with a very soft voice.

'Deirdre suffered acute trauma when she was forced to marry and leave the country, and then she was deserted immediately afterwards?,' explained Nurse Creedon. 'It was this trauma that sparked off her very serious mental disorder, and this troubled state of mind caused her to drink and commit other foolish acts, which in turn, caused her further trauma, until the whole series of events became a vicious circle. She is now undergoing severe shock treatment, which is intended to blot out these traumatic memories from her subconscious mind, and this, combined with heavy sedation, is the reason you see her as she is.'

'But when will this treatment finish?' asked Alana.

'It may take some time yet,' Nurse Creedon answered, 'but even when it is over, she has a very long, arduous road to recovery, and she will need the full support of her family.'

'She will be perfectly cured, will she?' Hugh asked anxiously.

'We'll only have to wait and see,' replied Nurse Creedon, 'and hope and pray. She couldn't be in better hands than those of Doctor Butler.' This was a consolation to Alana, and somewhat allayed her feeling of guilt; but Hugh was very down in himself.

'Mental sickness is the last word,' he said, 'and to think that your mother was in some way responsible for it, breaks my heart.'

'Come on now Dad. Cheer up! We must keep the bright side out for Deirdre's sake.' She opened her purse, and took out a ten shilling note. 'Here you are,' she said, 'call into Mac's on the way home, and have a few pints. I think you need them.'

Chapter 18

After nine years, and three trips to sea with Eoin, Gráinne eventually gave birth to a little baby daughter. She was in labour for two full days, and in the end the six pound baby had to be taken by caesarian section. Eoin spent every minute of the time with her in the hospital and as soon as he was perfectly satisfied that his wife and daughter were doing well, he came out to deliver the good news to all concerned.

'I'm a daddy at last,' he shouted, excitedly, as he burst into the kitchen to Peggy, 'and my daughter is a little beauty!' Peggy was overjoyed.

'I'm worn out from praying,' she said, 'and to be quite honest, I was beginning to get a bit worried.'

'It was a very worrying time, indeed,' said Eoin, 'especially when the baby's heart beat weakened, and they decided on the caesarian.'

'Poor Gráinne,' exclaimed Peggy, 'she must have had a very difficult time.'

'She's very happy now, anyway, and so am I. I can't believe I have a baby all of my own.'

'The first one is always the most exciting and wonderful,' Peggy remarked.

'That's the first and last,' answered Eoin, 'I could never see Gráinne going through all that again.'

'It's amazing how quickly the pain is forgotten,' said Peggy, wistfully.

Neil came home from school. He was ten years old, and

very mature and intelligent. Eoin couldn't get over how tall and grown up he had become.

'How's school?' he asked.

'Fine,' replied Neil, 'but aren't you going to tell me whether it's a niece or a nephew I have?' Peggy and Eoin looked at each other, and then Peggy answered.

'You have a pretty, new niece.'

'Congratulations, Eoin,' he said. 'Little girls are much cuter than boys.'

'We are going to have the christening after last mass on Sunday,' Eoin said, 'and we would like Alana to be the godmother.'

'She'll be delighted,' replied Peggy.

'There will be a little bit of a party afterwards at the house, and you are all invited. I'll call to Mossy and Mary on my way out.'

'Oh! Great!' Neil said, 'I'll be able to show off the new suit that Alana bought me.'

Alana and Hugh were delighted to hear of Gráinne's safe delivery, and Alana felt very happy and privileged to have beeen asked to stand for the baby.

'You ought to get your hair done, and buy something nice to wear,' Peggy said to her. 'After all, we don't want the O'Dowds to think we are the poor relations.' Alana looked at her father, and as she threw her eyes up to heaven, she thought to herself: There she goes again, the old O'Flaherty grandeur.

'I'll wear my royal blue suit, with the pale blue hat that I bought for Pat's wedding.'

'Sure, they have all seen that outfit on you already,' answered Peggy.

'And what's wrong with that?' said Alana, indignantly.

'Well! They'll think it is the only decent thing you have to wear,' Peggy said.

226

'And aren't they right?' replied Alana. Peggy was furious.

'If you weren't keeping your debauched sister in luxury at St Helen's Nursing Home in Cork, you could have a fine wardrobe.'

'That's a most unkind and evil thing to say about your own daughter,' Hugh said, almost in tears.

'Oh! the truth is always bitter,' she said 'and there is no use in sweeping it under the carpet.' Alana changed the subject.

'Where's Neil?' she enquired of her mother.

'He went to Mary's house a little while ago, to Elaine's birthday party, and he wasn't at all happy about spending the evening with a crowd of girls.'

'In another few years it will be a different story,' remarked Hugh. 'We won't be able to keep him away from them.'

'He won't have anything at all to do with them,' replied Peggy, 'because if I have my way, I'll make a priest of him.' A cold shiver passed through Alana's body when she heard her mother talk in that vein, and the snobbery that had been bred and engendered into her mother struck Alana very forcibly yet again. She was beginning to see that maybe the Lord did want her in the world after all, because who knows to what lengths her mother would go, to make of Neil what she wanted him to be. Alana was definitely not going to tolerate any interference of this nature, and she could visualise many big clashes between herself and her mother in the future.

Peggy was up at the crack of dawn on Sunday morning, making quite sure the little cottage was gleaming, and trying to put on a show of grandeur for the O'Dowd family, who were calling at ten o'clock to bring Alana to the nursing home in Cork, where the baby was to be collected for the christening. Sheila had given her a silver tray and six

Waterford crystal wine glasses, and they were placed on the highly polished side-board with a bottle of Sandeman port.

'You pour the drinks when they come in,' she ordered Hugh, 'and be careful not to fill the glasses too much. It's not the done thing.' She gave Neil a long lecture on how a young gentleman should behave, and she persecuted Alana so much about her pale face, that Alana was finally forced to use make-up for the first time in her life. Hugh was so unnerved by her fussing that he felt like pouring himself a large glass of port. When finally the O'Dowds arrived and he was serving drinks, his hands were shaking with tension. Conor and Eoin O'Dowd enjoyed their brief visit to the O'Gradys, and Hugh thought they were great company; but Maura seemed anxious to be on her way to the hospital and she badgered the men so much, that they were reluctantly forced to refuse the last drink. 'You know I have to dress the baby in the christening outfit, and that will take sometime.' Then she asked Eoin to go to the car and bring in the large box containing the clothes. 'This calls for another drink,' said Hugh, and Conor and himself drank a toast to their granddaughter, while Maura showed off the magnificent lace christening robe, the little bonnet and the elaborate crochet shawl.

'It only seems like yesterday since I dressed Eoin in these very clothes,' she remarked, nostalgically, 'and now I am to dress his daughter in them. My God! doesn't time fly?'

'Aren't they absolutely beautiful!' said Peggy, as she held up the christening outfit to Alana.

'It's amazing how well you kept them,' Alana said to Maura, 'they are as new as the day they were first bought.'

'I hope Gráinne will mind them as I have done,' she replied, 'and that they will be there for her children's children.'

'I was getting anxious,' said Gráinne, looking at her

228

watch, as Alana and the O'Dowds walked into the luxurious private room at the nursing home.

'You look beautiful this morning, my love,' said Eoin as he kissed her tenderly.

'Congratulations, Gráinne,' Alana said, 'I'm very happy for you.'

'Wait until you see the baby,' she exclaimed, excitedly, 'she's an absolute darling.'

There were flowers and cards everywhere, and Gráinne looked the picture of health and happiness, her pale, pink lingerie perfectly matching her lipstick, and her hair combed up in a pony tail, and tied with a pink ribbon.

'You had better ring for the baby,' said Maura O'Dowd, 'It's time to get her dressed up.' Gráinne rang the bell at the back of the bed, and almost immediately, a pretty blonde nurse wheeled in the cot.

'Would you like me to dress her?' the nurse asked.

'Oh No!' replied Maura O'Dowd, 'I'll do that myself, thank you.' Then she lifted the baby out of the cot.

'Isn't she beautiful!' she said, showing her to Alana.

'She's a little dote,' Alana replied, lost in admiration at her tiny niece.

'Who is she like?' asked Gráinne.

'It's difficult to say yet,' said Alana, 'But that mop of black hair is definitely an O'Grady feature.'

Gráinne never took her eyes off Maura O'Dowd, as she dressed her daughter, and Alana knew that she was nervous lest she might hurt her. Conor O'Dowd must have also seen the worried expression on Gráinne's face, because he turned to her and said.

'She's a fine, strong, little lass, and not half as fragile as she looks.'

'Do be careful of her, and bring her back safely to me,' said Gráinne, as they left for the church.

'You just relax there now,' replied Eoin, 'and we'll have her back to you in no time.'

The mass was just over when they arrived at the church. Peggy, Hugh and Neil were already seated in the back seat with Mossy, Mary and Elaine. Ian Morgan, Eoin's best man was also there, and he was to be the godfather. Eoin introduced him to Alana, and also introduced Peter Doolan another friend of his. The three of them were at sea together, Ian and Peter being engineers on board the ship. Father Seamus came down the centre aisle, and gathered the family together around the christening font.

'What is she to be named?' he asked.

'Margaret Anne,' replied Alana. Then he began the ceremony, and Alana felt quite nervous as she held the tiny infant over the font while Fr Seamus poured the cold water over her head. She gave a loud cry, and Father Seamus winked at Alana and smiled. 'That's the aul' devil going out of her now,' he whispered, in his typically humorous manner. Alana gave Margaret Anne to her mother, while she and Ian Morgan went into the sacristy with Fr Seamus to sign their names on the register, recording the fact that they were the godparents of the baby. Ian gave Fr Seamus a crisp twenty pound note and Alana thought that was a very generous offering; she could see by the broad beam on the priest's kindly face, that he thought so too.

'You are a decent young man, Ian,' he said, 'and may God reward you.'

'Thank you, Father,' replied Ian with a slight stammer in his speech.

'How are things with you, Alana?' Father Seamus asked.

'Oh! Never better thanks, Father.'

'And how is poor Deirdre? Is there any improvement at all in her?'

'None that I can see, Father, unfortunately. Pray for her, will you please, Father?'

230

'Don't you know I am already doing that, and be sure the good Lord will cure her.'

'Thanks Father! I had better go out and join the crowd again.'

'God love and bless you, Alana!' the priest said, 'and I hope that some day soon, I will be doing this job for a child of your own.'

'That's hardly likely, Father,' she said, leaving the sacristy.

Everyone went to the hospital to see Gráinne, and the hospital room assumed a very festive atmosphere, with Gráinne and Margaret Anne the centre of attraction. Maura O'Dowd put the baby into Gráinne's arms, 'Kiss her now,' she said, 'because her soul is shining and full of grace, and she's a little angel.' Eoin opened bottles of champagne, and everyone drank several toasts to Gráinne and Margaret Anne. Neil was allowed to wheel the baby out to the nursery, as Gráinne thought the noise and the smoky atmosphere would do her no good. He was as proud as punch in the navy blue suit Alana had bought for him.

'He's a lovely looking boy, and so mannerly,' Maura O'Dowd remarked to Peggy.

'An ounce of breeding is better than a ton of feeding,' replied Peggy, in her most polished tone. Alana was mortified, and although her father was smiling, she knew by his eyes that he felt the same.

'Your mother really fancies herself,' remarked Ian Morgan, who was sitting beside Alana.

'That's a trait she inherited from her own family,' Alana replied, the colour rising to her face. Ian was small and chubby with a nice round, soft face, and big blue eyes; but his attire was very shabby and untidy, and he wore a grey overcoat which was far too long for him. Alana caught her mother eyeing him several times, and she knew by the disgruntled look on her face each time, that she didn't think much of him. His friend, Peter Doolan, was the exact opposite; tall, blonde, and impeccably groomed, and Alana thought he was very handsome.

Ian asked Alana to travel in his car to O'Dowd's house, where the party was to be continued, and for the remainder of the night, he paid great attention to her. He sat beside her all evening, and made sure she was well supplied with refreshments at all times. He was a bit shy at first, but after several drinks, he became quite talkative.

'I hear you were in the nuns for a while,' he said to Alana. 'What a waste of a lovely girl!' Alana was highly indignant at this remark.

'Any time spent doing God's work is not a waste,' she argued, 'and I can assure you, were it not for extenuating circumstances, I would be still in the nuns, where I belong, and hope to return some day.' Ian blushed and looked puzzled.

'I'm sorry if I offended you. I didn't mean to. I hope you will come out with me sometime. I would very much like to get to know you better.'

'Forget it,' answered Alana, 'I haven't the slightest interest in men.'

'Ah! maybe you would change your mind,' he said. 'You are the type of girl I like and admire, very intelligent and plenty of character.'

'I'm very flattered,' Alana said, 'but I'm sure if you looked around, you could find plenty of girls answering to that description.'

'I'll phone you at your office. Eoin gave me the number. I don't give up too easily you know.' He was getting very drunk at this stage, stammering more than ever, and Alana couldn't stand him.

'It's time for me to be going now,' she said, 'my little nephew is getting tired.' She got up, and went across the room to where Neil sat with Hugh and Peggy.

'Let's get out of here,' she said, 'that Ian Morgan is annoying me intensely.'

'He's a funny looking fellow,' remarked Peggy 'and very fond of drink.' Conor and Maura O'Dowd saw them all out to Mossy's car.

'Thank you for a most enjoyable day,' Peggy said.

'You went to a great deal of trouble, and we appreciate it very much,' added Alana. Mossy and Mary also conveyed their gratitude, and Hugh, well and truly merry, declared as he warmly shook Conor O'Dowd by the hand, 'I hope we'll all be here again next year.'

Ian Morgan rang Alana at the office every day during the following week, but Alana refused to accept his calls, and warned Marie on the switchboard to say she was out. It came to Mrs Buckley's attention that Alana was avoiding someone, and she challenged her about it.

'Is there a man ringing for you?' she asked.

'That's right,' replied Alana, 'but I haven't a notion of talking to him.'

'Who is he?'

'His name is Ian Morgan, and I met him at Gráinne's christening party. He wants me to go out with him, but you know I haven't the slightest interest in men or the slightest intention of ever getting married. I can't wait to get back to the convent again.'

'That's a very silly way of looking at things,' remarked Mrs Buckley, 'You don't have to marry a man because you go out with him, and who knows, it might be God's will for you to marry. The next time that man rings, I am going to make sure you talk to him, and accept his invitation. It cannot do any harm.'

'He may not ring any more,' said Alana, 'But if he does, I'll do as you advise, but only because you asked me to.'

He rang again, and Alana made a date with him for seven o'clock on the following night, outside the church on the

Ashe Road. From the time she awoke that morning, she dreaded the thought of meeting him; but because she promised Mrs Buckley, she had to turn up. She was at the appointed place on the stroke of seven o'clock, having been well trained to be punctual. There was no sign of Ian, so she went into the Church to say a little prayer, and to light a few candles for all her intentions, especially for Deirdre, who was very much on her mind. When she came out, she was amazed to see that there was yet no sign of him. She looked at her watch. It was seven-fifteen. I'll give him another ten minutes, she said to herself, and if he's not here by then, I'll go with dad to the hospital to see Deirdre. Alana waited and waited in spite of herself thinking that maybe something urgent and unforeseen had delayed him, and when she looked again at her watch, it was eight o'clock. There was a phone box about twenty yards down the road, and she decided to ring her mother from there, to find out if perhaps Ian had tried to get in touch with her at home. Peggy answered.

'It's me, Mum,' Alana said, 'Did anyone ring looking for me?'

'No,' replied her mother, 'were you expecting to hear from someone?'

'Not really,' Alana answered, and she was about to hang up when Peggy asked.

'Where are you anyway?'

'I'm in the phone box by the church,' Alana replied.

'What are you doing there?' Peggy enquired.

'I'm waiting for Ian Morgan.'

'And at what time were you supposed to meet him?'

'Seven o'clock,' answered Alana. Then there was an irritable sigh from the other end of the line.

'Come home at once, and don't be making such a fool of yourself. I don't know what kind of an idiot I reared,' and she banged down the receiver.

Alana came out of the telephone box, and was walking back in the direction of the church, when a car pulled up beside her. It was Ian's blue Anglia, and Ian was sitting in the driver's seat, grinning from ear to ear, a big, fat, old gentleman seated beside him in the passenger seat. He got out of the car and came towards Alana.

'I'm very sorry to be so late,' he stammered, 'but we came up from the country, and the traffic was bumper to bumper all the way.' Alana had the feeling he wasn't telling the truth, because she got a strong whiff of drink from him.

'You have drink taken,' she said, curtly.

'It's like this,' he drooled on, 'Billy Hennessy and myself transacted a nice little bit of business over a few pints.' Alana was disgusted, and she turned to walk away, but Ian took hold of her hand, and led her over to the car. She didn't want to give a display of rudeness in the presence of the older man, so when Ian opened the back door of the car for her, she went in. To her absolute horror, there were two greyhounds inside before her, and she was scared to death, and very angry.

'This is my old buddy, Billy Hennessy. This is Alana O'Grady.'

'Pleased to meet ye miss,' said Billy.

'How do you do,' Alana replied in a voice like caustic. She was edging out of the way of the greyhounds who were jumping excitedly around the back seat.

'Take no notice of Flip and Flop,' said Ian, 'They won't do you any harm at all.'

He was driving the car in a most dangerous manner and Alana thought he would never arrive in Cork. She couldn't be civil to either of them, and she was almost overcome by the smell of drink and the stench of the dogs. He pulled up outside a public house on the western side of Cork. Alana was relieved to be out of the car; but she was damned if she was going into the pub with two men and two greyhounds.

'I don't make it a habit to frequent public houses,' she said, sharply.

'Yera, come on in and don't be such an oddity,' Ian said, 'We'll only have a few quick ones, and then we'll leave.'

'I don't drink,' Alana emphasised.

'You can have a few glasses of lemonade, can't you?' Billy Hennessy answered, very impatiently. Alana walked in behind them, feeling more than a little degraded and humiliated. They found seats at the end of the bar, and Ian pointed to Alana's stool.

'Sit down there,' he said 'and hold on to Flip and Flop while I go up to the counter.' He handed the leads to her.

'Lemonade for you, is it?'

'Yes thank you,' she said, a terrible anger mounting inside her. What a cheek that fellow had to treat her in this appalling manner. If her mother could see her now, she would definitely disown her. He brought back a glass of lemonade to her, and then went back to the counter to Bill, leaving her there, alone with the dogs. They must have consumed about five drinks, and there wasn't a sign of them leaving. Alana was furious. How dare they leave her here like this. Everyone was looking at her, she felt. She couldn't stand it for another second. She tied the dogs on to the leg of the table, left her seat, and walked out the door. She would hitch a lift home, or walk. Anything was better than being with these two ignorant men. She hadn't gone far, when she heard the horn of a car hooting. She looked back, and there they were.

'Get in,' Ian said, 'and I'll drive you home.'

'But you're drunk!' she said, 'and you're not capable of driving.'

'He's a very capable driver,' Billy Hennessy interjected. 'Get in now, and don't be making a scene.' Alana did as she was told, and Ian drove off out of town and headed north towards Glenbeg. He was mounting kerbs, and taking both sides of the road, and Alana was terrified.

'Watch the ditch!' she screamed. 'My God! you are a wicked driver!'

'Nobody ever said that to me before,' he said angrily. 'You're a prim, starchy old bitch!' Alana said no more, and suffered in silence until the car pulled up at Mac's bar.

'Let me out here,' she demanded. Then Ian turned back to her, fire in his eyes.

'Get out, ye bloody ghoul!' he shouted.

Alana ran all the way home, her heart pounding and tears in her eyes. She didn't stop until she flopped on to the settee in the kitchen.

'What's the matter with you?' asked Peggy, 'You look as though you've seen a ghost.' Alana burst into tears, and then told her mother about the horrific experience with Ian Morgan.

'You have nobody but yourself to blame,' her mother said. 'I told you at eight o'clock to come home, but you never listen to me. That Ian Morgan is not your type. He is nothing but a drunkard and a very ignorant one at that. I hope you have learnt your lesson now.' Peggy put on the kettle and made her a cup of hot tea.

'Drink this,' she said, 'And don't ever mention that fellow's name to me again.'

As Alana sat there sipping the hot tea, her mind wandered back to the sweet, joyful contentment of the convent life which she had regretfully cast aside, and the full realization that she was a complete misfit in the world, caused her, for the millionth time, severe pain and heart-ache.

She pulled herself together quickly when she heard the key turn in the front-door. It was her father returning from the hospital, and she didn't want him to see her upset. He was worried enough about Deirdre's condition, and he totally depended on Alana's support with this great problem.

'Well! How is the patient?' Alana enquired, as he walked into the kitchen, although she could tell from the glint in his eyes that the news was good.

'She's as well as I've ever seen her. I would go so far as to say that she is better than she has been for years. She has a completely positive outlook on everything, and she discussed her past mistakes with me to-night, in a most open, frank fashion.' Alana was delighted. Deirdre had been making steady progress, but Alana never expected such a drastic change so quickly, and it happened on the only night she herself was missing.

'That's absolutely wonderful Dad. Isn't it fantastic, Mum?' she said. Peggy was ironing and hadn't displayed any interest in the conversation up until then.

'I hope she's well enough to take care of herself,' she replied, 'for I hope you both know that I meant it when I said she was not returning to this house.' Hugh decided to ignore Peggy's statement, and continued addressing Alana.

'She asked if you would call to see her to-morrow morning. She has an urgent matter she wishes to discuss with you, and she said that Doctor Butler would like to have a chat with you as well.' Peggy put down the iron.

'Ah! She's scheming something again,' she warned. 'Mark my words, she's up to something. Her kind are cute and coniving, but no doubt you will both fall for her deceit, and end up in trouble again. Nobody can save you from yourselves, but don't say I didn't warn you.' Alana was getting very annoyed with her mother's attitude, in the face of what she considered to be a very hopeful turn in Deirdre's state of mind.

'I think you are being most unkind and unfair, Mum,' she said 'and if you are not prepared to treat Deirdre as a mother would, a sick daughter, then I am prepared to treat her with sisterly love and ordinary charity.'

'Good for you,' snapped Peggy, continuing to iron with vengeance. Alana turned to Hugh.

'I will take the day off from the office to-morrow, and I will take the bus to the hospital to see Deirdre.'

'You're a star,' Hugh replied, and kissing Peggy on the brow, he returned to his bedroom.

As Alana walked through the hallway of St Helen's Nursing Home at exactly ten-thirty next morning, she saw Deirdre coming down the wide staircase. She was wearing her blue dressing gown, and although she was pale, she looked perfectly normal, very well groomed, and in great form.

'I knew you would come up on the nine o'clock bus,' she said, 'so I was just coming down to meet you.'

'That was good timing,' said Alana 'shows you are really back to normal. Dad was thrilled with you. He hasn't stopped talking yet about how well you are.'

'Thank God! I feel really well again. It's a marvellous feeling, Alana. It's just like I've come out of this endless black tunnel to the light of day. You could never understand it, until you've been there yourself, and I sincerely hope you never do.'

'I'm very happy for you,' replied Alana, tears of joy appearing in her eyes.

'You were very good to me, and I owe you a lot. I hope I'll be able to repay your kindness, some day.'

'Your recovery is the best reward I could get,' answered Alana.

'Come on upstairs to my room. I want to have a serious talk with you,' said Deirdre, leading the way, as Alana followed.

They sat down together on two red leather arm-chairs by the window, and Deirdre lit a cigarette.

'I had a very long talk with Doctor Butler, and he told me that I have made an almost miraculous recovery.' She produced a small bottle of tablets from the pocket of her dressing gown. 'This is the only medication I am taking now, just one of these tablets, three times daily, and I will be required to take them for some time yet. Dr Butler says he will be discharging me in a week's time, but he wants me to live at a geographical distance from mum.' Alana was relieved to hear this last bit, because she wouldn't have to hurt Deirdre by telling her she couldn't go home anyway. 'You know Alana,' Deirdre continued, 'Dr Butler reckons that mum was responsible for this whole mess I got myself into, and he doesn't want me to come under her influence any more.'

'But where will you go? and what will you do?' asked Alana.

'I have applied to be reinstated in my job in the civil service in Dublin, and I will stay with Aunt Kate. Doctor Butler has some influential friends, and he is going to speak to them on my behalf.'

'That sounds just perfect,' said Alana.

'That's not all,' Deirdre went on. 'I am now mentally strong enough to face up to the mistakes I have made in the past, and before I leave this hospital, Dr Butler wishes me to do two things.' Alana was listening attentively and taking in every word.

'What have you to do before you leave?' she asked.

'First of all I have to make my peace with George and Sheila. I realise that I have caused both of them great unhappiness, and how George kept his sanity with the way I behaved in Australia, I'll never know. All I do know is, that in spite of all, he was good and kind to me. You know Alana, he suffered a lot for one mistake, for which I was one hundred per cent responsible. I bore him twin sons, and I am very glad and happy that they are being raised by

Sheila, and that they are a family once again. I must meet them both, face to face, and acknowledge to them my wicked behaviour, apologise to them for the trouble I have caused them, and legally sign over the twins to them. Dr Butler says it is important that I do this, because that will close that bad experience, and block it out of my mind forever.'

'I think I can arrange to have George and Sheila up to see you to-night,' replied Alana, 'and I am in full agreement with Dr Butler that this is a very good thing, both for you and them. But tell me, what is the second thing you must do?'

'The next thing may not be so easy,' said Deirdre, as she lit another cigarette. 'You see, Alana,' she went on slowly and deliberately, 'Neil is my real son, my legal son, born into my unfortunate marriage, and he is my responsibility. I must face up to that too.' Alana felt her body go numb, as she waited for what was coming next. 'Neil must be told that I am his mother, and also about his father's disappearance. I am quite willing and able to tell him myself, but I fear that because of my illness, and the things he must have heard about me, that he may not believe me. I am asking you to tell him, as soon as possible.'

'Are you going to take him away with you?' asked Alana, anxiously.

'Not yet, Alana. I realise he will need a lot of time to adjust to the shock he is about to receive, and it would be too traumatic for him, to take him from the only home and parents he has ever known; but I do want to see him after you have broken the news to him. When I get back to work, I will write to him every week, and send him some money to save for himself. Then, as time goes on, and I establish a relationship with him, and win back his love and trust, who knows what might happen?'

Alana was relieved.

'That seems very just and fair to me,' she replied, 'and I was always aware that sooner or later he would have to know the truth, and I know I must tell him now.'

'I will write to Mum,' said Deirdre, 'and put her in the picture, at the same time making her aware that my decision is final.'

'When you have those two points fully tackled, there will be no turning back for you Deirdre,' said Alana.

'The only remaining problem is Minnie Burke, but I can do nothing about that, because she is in America, being well taken care of by her brothers, and anyway she didn't love Johnnie.' Deirdre began to cry, and Alana didn't stop her. Then after a few minutes, she dried her eyes, and continued. 'Johnnie is dead now, so that chapter in my life is closed, but believe me, Alana, I truly loved him, and I made him very happy at the end of his life.'

Alana stayed with Deirdre for lunch, and Doctor Butler joined them. He confirmed to Alana all that Deirdre had said.

'You need have no further worries about her now, Alana,' he said, as he left the table. 'She is ready for anything.' He patted Deirdre on the head, shook hands with Alana, and left the room. Sheila and George called that very night, and Deirdre made her peace with them. She never forgot what Sheila said: 'Out of evil cometh good, they say, Deirdre. The twins you gave us have more than compensated for any heartbreak you caused. They are the most precious gems in our lives.'

Peggy was sceptical about Deirdre's very drastic reformation.

'I don't trust her, Alana. That girl can change like the wind, and you can never tell what she'll do next.' Alana had related the whole story in detail to her mother, bubbling over with joy and enthusiasm as she did so, and this response was a severe disappointment to her.

'But, Mum,' she pleaded, 'She is doing her best now, and obeying all the doctor's orders, and think what joy she'll bring to George and Sheila, waiving her claim on Graham and Gavin. You yourself should be relieved that she is not taking Neil away with her.'

'Have sense, Alana,' retorted Peggy, 'Sure you know as well as I do, that the girl hasn't an ounce of maternal instinct. Deirdre loves Deirdre, and anyway, how could she fly her kite in Dublin, with three children tied to her.'

'I have faith and confidence in her, anyway,' replied Alana, 'and I must do as she wishes, and tell Neil.'

'I suppose that has to be done,' Peggy agreed, 'but rather you than I, and I sincerely hope you will break this news very gently to him. Remember, Neil is a highly intelligent and super sensitive boy.'

'Don't worry about that, Mum,' Alana said. 'I plan to take him away with me for the evening, and give him a nice treat, to take the trauma out of the unfortunate situation.'

'How would you like a trip to Cork, a meal out, and the pictures afterwards?' asked Alana, when Neil returned from school.

'Wow! Goody!' he exclaimed, jumping for joy, 'I'd adore it, but what have I done to deserve such a fabulous treat?'

'You work hard at school, and you do what mum tells you, and those are reasons enough for an occasional surprise,' answered Alana. He threw his school-bag on the floor.

'I'll go and change into my new suit,' he said, still very excited, 'I won't be a minute.'

They went by bus to Cork, and then to a very trendy, new restaurant 'Mr Munch'. Alana waited until Neil had polished off a big meal, followed by a tall ice-cream sundae, with several minerals in between, and then she caught his hand across the table.

'I have something to tell you, Neil,' she said, very quietly,

'OK then, go ahead,' was his reply.

'You are a big boy now, Neil,' Alana said, 'and soon you'll be a fine man, and I am pretty sure you can handle what I am about to tell you,' Alana said.

'Oh! sure I can,' he answered, looking rather puzzled, and blushing a little.

'Well,' Alana explained, 'Mum and dad are not exactly your real parents.' He began to fidget with his tie, as was his habit when he was nervous, but otherwise showed no sign of distress. Alana continued. 'You see, Neil, before you were born, your real dad disappeared, and left your unfortunate real mum, who was only twenty, all alone in London. She was very frightened and upset, and the shock made her very ill, and she came back to Ireland and asked me to help her. I was a nun in the convent at the time, and I came out to take care of her, and my nephew whom she was carrying, and who was so precious to me. Deirdre gave birth to you, but she hadn't recovered from her terrible ordeal, and she had to hand you over to the care of your other mum, who is, of course, your grandmother, and she and grandad have loved and cared for you ever since, while your mum was trying to recover.' Neil was stunned, but he remained calm, and Alana could see he was repressing his tears in order to act like a man.

'But Deirdre has done bad things, and I could never love her, and if my friends knew, they would jeer at me for having such a wicked mum.'

'You mustn't think like that, Neil. Deirdre is my sister and I love her, and your grandad loves her also. We are not ashamed of her, because we know she didn't mean to be bad. She was just very ill and frightened; but now she has recovered, and is trying to be good, and to make up for the things she has done wrong. Please give her a chance, Neil.

Just be friends with her, and get to know her. That is all she wants, and it would mean a lot to her, and to grandad and myself.' He thought for a while.

'I will try Alana, but please do not tell my friends, until she is fully better and really good like mum.'

'That's a deal,' said Alana, 'and now, let's go to the pictures.'

The following night Hugh and Alana brought Neil to St Helen's to see his mother. Deirdre didn't try to force herself on him that night. She just chatted to him about school and other little topics of interest to a boy of his age. He behaved in a very friendly manner, and even gave her a kiss on the cheek when he was leaving. He went every night for the remainder of the week, and on the night before Deirdre left the hospital, she asked to be left alone with him for a while. She spoke intimately to him, like a mother to a son, apologising to him for deserting him, and explaining to him as simply as she could, how her life had gone wrong.

'I love you very dearly, Neil,' she said, 'and I hope that in time you will grow to love me too. I will be waiting and praying for that day to come, and in the meantime, everything I do will be for you, because you, and you alone, are my reason for living now.' She took him in her arms, and held him there for a long time, and she became very emotional. Neil took a handkerchief from his pocket and wiped the tears from her eyes.

'Don't cry, Mum,' he said, and her heart leapt for joy. She had done much better with him in a few days than she, in her wildest dreams, had ever imagined.

'I feel better already,' she said, 'and I will try hard to get to know and love you more and more. This is the happiest moment of my life,' she said, as she kissed him good-bye for the moment. Hugh and Alana were sitting downstairs at reception, when Deirdre and Neil came downstairs hand in hand.

'You're the best boy in Cork,' Hugh said to him on the way home, 'and I am very proud of you.'

Chapter 19

As Alana made her way to the office next morning, she was feeling happier and more contented than she had done for a long time. She felt a great sense of fulfilment, and a sense of freedom too. She had done her duty, to Deirdre and Neil, and now she was free to resume again her life for God in some convent. She would apply to a few whose work appealed to her, and surely she would be accepted by one. As soon as she walked into the office, Mrs Buckley greeted her.

'The long week-end has certainly done you a power of good. Why! I haven't seen you look so well in ages. You must definitely be in love.'

'In love!' exclaimed Alana, 'Now, with whom would I be in love?'

'Hadn't you a date with Ian Morgan on Sunday night?' Alana had almost forgotten about that incident.

'Oh. That!' she answered. 'I can tell you that that was an absolute fiasco.'

'What do you mean?' queried Mrs Buckley. Alana then began to relate the story to her, and the tears of laughter rolled down Mrs Buckley's cheeks as she did so.

'I'm glad you find it so amusing,' Alana commented 'because, believe me, I was anything but amused at the time.'

'You have a lot to learn, Alana,' Mrs Buckley said, 'he seems to me like an innocent and very original type of lad.'

'You can have him if you want him, but I wouldn't be seen dead with him ever again.'

'He rang a few times yesterday, looking for you,' Mrs Buckley said, 'and he said he would ring again to-day.'

'I'm not taking any calls from him,' replied Alana.

'Ah! Listen to what he has to say, anyway. That cannot do any harm.'

The dreaded phone-call duly came in the afternoon, and Mrs Buckley insisted that Alana should take the call. Ian was profusely apologetic for his behaviour, and asked Alana out again.

'I accept your apology, Ian,' she said, 'but I have no interest in going out any more with you, or with anyone else for that matter.'

'Would you just come out once more,' he begged her, 'just so I can apologise in person, and make up to you for Sunday night.'

He finally succeeded in persuading her, and she met him again. This time he was waiting for her at the appointed place, and although he still wore the funny long, grey, tweed overcoat, he took her to a posh restaurant, and afterwards, to a show. He behaved like a thorough gentleman, and couldn't have done more to make the evening a very pleasant one. He drove her home to the door.

'Will you meet me again?' he asked, his big blue eyes pleading with her. She didn't want to, but she felt sorry for him, and she hadn't the heart to refuse him. Another date was made, and another, and the affair drifted along for some weeks, in spite of the fact that Alana hadn't the slightest interest in him, and would have preferred to be at home with Neil. Besides, she had got the smell of drink from his breath on a few occasions, and Alana had an abnormal horror of drink She made up her mind to end the relationship at the next meeting.

Alana was helping Neil with a rather difficult Irish essay, and had lost all track of time. There was a knock on the front door, and she knew it must be Ian, because she had told him to call to the house for her. Peggy answered the door, and Ian, expecting to see Alana, became so nervous that he stood there, red in the face, stammering frantically. Peggy's cold haughty attitude towards him, served only to increase his anxiety and tension, until after a few seconds he failed miserably to utter a syllable.

'I presume you are looking for Alana,' she said impatiently, to which he just nodded his head. She left him at the door, feeling acutely embarrassed and humiliated, and walked back into the kitchen.

'The quare fella is at the door,' she said, 'and 'tis only the mercy of God that he didn't break a blood vessel trying to ask for you. I eventually had to tell him what he wanted to say.'

'You probably frightened him to death, Mum. My God! You can be so cruel at times.'

'I don't know what you're doing with him, Alana, but I think you can be so stupid at times,' retorted Peggy. Alana ignored the last remark, and went out to Ian.

He was sitting in the car outside, and when he saw her coming he got out and opened the passenger door to let her in.

'I have made an awful fool of myself in front of your mother,' he said.

'Never mind that,' replied Alana.

'I don't think she likes me,' he went on, 'she probably thinks I'm not good enough to you.'

'Don't worry too much about her,' Alana said, feeling very sorry for him, 'She has an odd manner, but deep down she's not that bad.' He relaxed a little then, and began to drive off.

'Where are we going to-night?' enquired Alana.

'Gone with the Wind is showing in the Star Cinema in Cork, and I thought you would like to see it. It's an excellent film, I believe.'

'That would be just lovely,' said Alana, very excited, as she had heard a lot about it.

On the way to Cork, Alana noticed Ian's driving a bit erratic, and she also noticed his stammer more severe than usual. She attributed these factors to his encounter with her mother, because Ian was a very nervous and excitable type of fellow. He also had a huge inferiority complex, because of the fact that he was not very well educated, and his job as a fitter in the Ford plant in Cork was, as far as he was concerned, very much beneath Alana's excellent position as clerical officer in the civil service. It was very obvious to Alana that he was highly intelligent and super sensitive, and she never missed an opportunity to boost his morale; but her mother had undone a lot of her good work to-night, she felt.

During the film, Iam moved close to Alana, and putting his arm around her, he kissed her affectionately. To her horror and disgust, she got quite a strong smell of drink from his breath, and Alana was allergic to drink. She was disappointed also, because although she had intended to end the relationship to-night, she was beginning to change her mind, and in a rather strange and sudden way she was becoming quite fond of Ian. Now, her original decision would have to stand, and she would definitely not see him any more after to-night. He must have sensed her change of attitude towards him, because he moved back to his own seat, and was very fidgety and ill at ease for the remainder of the film.

'Will you come for a cup of coffee?' he asked, as soon as they came out.

'No, thank you,' replied Alana, 'I would prefer to go home please.' They walked in silence to where the car was parked, and as soon as they were on the homeward journey, Ian broke the silence.

'There's something wrong, isn't there, Alana?' he said.

'There's a little boreen about fifty yards or so down the road,' said Alana, 'and if you pull the car in there, I would like to have a talk with you.' Ian did exactly as Alana asked.

'Don't pull any punches with me now, Alana,' he said, 'just give it to me straight. I am not your type. Isn't that it?'

'Nothing could be further from the truth, Ian,' she replied. 'As a matter of fact I have very strong feelings against categorising people into types.'

'What is it then?' he asked.

'Well, Ian,' she explained, 'We have been going out together for five weeks now, and through no fault of yours or mine, this relationship will never go anywhere; so rather than lead you on, I have decided that it's best that we do not meet any more.' Ian's face fell, and she could detect tears in his big blue eyes.

'But why are you so sure after five weeks that things could never work out between us?' he asked.

'First of all, I intend to re-join the nuns, and even if I did intend ever to marry, I would not choose a man who drinks. I have an absolute horror of it.' His eyes lit up.

'So that's it. But if I thought you would continue with this relationship, I would give up drink altogether. I would even become a pioneer, and take the pin,' he said.

'I wouldn't expect you to do that, Ian, just because of my aversion to it. It wouldn't be fair to you,' she said.

'But I want you, Alana, more than anything else, so please give me an opportunity to prove that to you. Just give me another chance, please,' he pleaded. Alana couldn't resist the sincerity and childlike earnestness in his attitude.

'If you feel you want to give up drink, Ian, then I am prepared to continue the relationship; but remember, I am not forcing you into this decision.' He threw his arms around her.

'You won't regret this, Alana, I promise you.'

When next they met, he was wearing a pioneer pin on the lapel of his coat, and though Alana was slightly amused at this drastic change, she was nevertheless very touched by it. He took from inside his tweed overcoat, a large parcel.

'This is for you,' he said 'in gratitude for giving me this chance.'

She opened the parcel, and inside was an exquisitely ornate brush, comb and mirror set for her dressing table.

'This is beautiful, Ian,' she exclaimed, 'and it is the first time anyone has ever given me a real present. I will treasure it forever.'

'It was my sister, Rose, who chose it. She thought it would be suitable,' he said proudly.

'She made an excellent choice,' said Alana.

'You must come and meet my family soon. They are all dying to meet you, especially my mother.'

'I would be very happy to do that,' replied Alana.

'That's settled then,' Ian said.

Ian lived in a quaint but charming house in Rockmore, a small fishing village on the outskirts of Cork. As Alana sat in the large, tastefully furnished drawing room, with the big bay window overlooking the water, she felt very much at home in the bosom of Ian's lovely family. His sisters, Margaret and Rose, were identical twins, two years younger than Ian, and were absolute beauties. Alana had never seen such beautiful heads of jet black, naturally curly hair. Theo, Ian's father, was very like Ian, though a good deal taller. He was shy and retiring, but very gentle and kind. In his capacity as a guard in the local station, he had a record for never issuing a summons on anybody. Alana could well believe that, because he seemed as quiet and docile as a lamb. Monica, Ian's mother was a real lady, small and thin, with a wonderfully affectionate nature. It was perfectly obvious to Alana that Ian adored her, and she him, and Alana herself took to her from the very first moment she saw her. How totally different she was from her own mother, Alana kept thinking.

'Ian is a new man since he met you, Alana,' she said, 'and we are all delighted with the great influence you are having on him.'

'Any change in Ian comes from himself, Mrs Morgan, and I too am very proud of him.' Ian was beaming all over.

'Don't be giving me a swelled head now,' he said, 'or I might go into reverse gear.' Margaret and Rose served up the most delicious supper of bacon, egg, sausage, tomato and mushrooms, followed by mouth watering home-baked confectionery.

'You'll have to teach me some of your culinary arts,' said Alana, 'because Ian would never survive on my cooking.'

'There's nothing to it,' said Monica 'it's just practice, and sure we all had to learn.' Margaret and Rose didn't have very much to say during the evening; but when Alana went to the cloakroom for her coat just before she left, Margaret followed her in. She closed the door behind them.

'I don't know whether or not you intend to marry Ian, Alana; but if you do, I feel it my duty to warn you that you must never, under any circumstances allow him to drink. He is the best and most lovable person in the world when he is sober; but drink changes his personality completely, and he becomes like a monster. Believe me, we have experienced it here, and I would hate to see you have to go through these dreadful experiences, so do be careful.' Alana was shocked for a moment.

'I am very grateful to you, Margaret, for putting me in the picture, but I have made it perfectly clear to Ian that drink and I would never get on.'

Peggy and Hugh were sitting by the fire when Alana came home.

'Had you a nice time at Ian's house?' asked Hugh.

'Oh yes,' replied Alana, 'He has a magnificient home, a wonderful family, and I was treated like a queen.'

'They know what they're doing,' said Peggy, 'trying to palm him off on you.'

'I could do worse, Mum,' answered Alana.

'You could do a hell of a lot better too, than a tradesman, who has neither appearance nor personality, not to mention the fact that he can hardly talk.'

'He is a very nice person, Mum, and highly intelligent too, and I must tell you that I am extremely fond of him.'

'Nobody can save you from yourself, Alana,' Peggy replied, 'And if you make your bed, you'll have to lie in it.'

'Hush now, Peggy,' said Hugh, 'I have made enquiries about Ian Morgan, and he is very well respected and thought of, and by all and every account, he is the best fitter in Cork.'

'What a wonderful attribute!' retorted Peggy, sarcastically, as she went down to her bedroom, leaving Alana and her father to figure that one out for themselves. Hugh got up to follow his wife, and as he was passing by Alana, he put his hand affectionately on her head, and whispered, 'Don't pay her too much heed. She can't help it. That aul' class distinction is deeply engendered in her.' Alana smiled to herself at the irony of it all. Fifty years ago, Peggy was at war with her father to break this loathsome mould; and now, here she was, almost as bad as he was then. Breeding goes a long way, Alana thought to herself.

Alana and Ian travelled to Dublin to see Deirdre, and

they brought Neil with them to see his mother. It made Alana very happy to see how really close they had become. He had been to visit her twice already, with Mossy and Mary, and every Wednesday morning, her letter arrived to him by first post. He treasured those letters, keeping them all together neatly, in a box beside his bed. He also kept his own special album with photographs of Deirdre at the various stages of her life. He got along famously with Ian, who had a very winning manner with children, especially with boys.

'I hope you get married to Ian soon,' Neil said to Alana one night, on their way home from confession.

'Why do you hope for that, Neil,' she asked.

'Well! Because he is loving and kind, just like grandad, and besides, he always talks to me as though I were a real grown-up.'

Deirdre and Kate were very impressed with Ian.

'He's one of these sincere, genuine fellows that are so hard to find,' Deirdre said, while Kate thought he was soft and cuddly. Sr Bernard thoroughly approved of him.

'He's a fine, decent boy, Alana, and if you think he will make you happy, then in the name of God, marry him.'

'But I still believe I have a vocation to the religious life, Sister.'

'You have given that life a trial, Alana, and for one reason or the other, you left it. I think it's time you stopped regretting this decision now, and start getting on with your life. Remember, marriage is also a very high vocation, and who knows, maybe some day a child of yours might continue the good work you began in the service of the Lord.'

Alana and Ian became engaged in the spring, and to mark the occasion, they invited both their parents to a meal in a hotel in Cork. At first, Peggy declined the invitation.

255

'This would be an endurance test for me, Alana,' she protested, 'You know quite well I have nothing in common with these people.'

'You cannot possibly know that until you meet them,' Alana argued, 'and apart from that, your failing to attend would be a most disrespectful and discourteous act.' Gráinne, who invariably echoed her mother's sentiments in almost everything, and who, like Peggy, thought that Alana wasn't making a proper match, finally influenced her to go; if only for appearance's sake. Peggy was agreeably surprised when she met Monica and Theo Morgan, who were a bit in awe of her. She definitely had that cold, arrogant and uppish manner, which was, to say the least, very off-putting. She only spoke when she was addressed, and then her answers were monosyllabic. Hugh more than compensated for his wife's attitude, making everybody feel relaxed with his cheerful and stimulating conversation. Theo Morgan was sitting beside Peggy at the table, and Alana felt very sorry for him. He was naturally very shy and retiring, and Peggy made no effort whatsoever to converse with him. Monica and Hugh, on the contrary, were enjoying themselves immensely.

'I have been praying for years that Ian would get a good girl,' said Monica, 'and now Thank God, my prayers have been answered.'

'You had better continue your prayers,' answered Hugh, jovially, 'because this good girl here can't boil an egg, and if Ian can't live on love, then he is likely to die of starvation.'

'I'll settle for living on love anytime,' said Ian, putting his arm around Alana.

'And when the pangs of hunger bite,' added Alana, 'sure there's always the chipper.' As the evening came to an end, Hugh was well and truly tipsy, and he began to make a speech.

'On behalf of pompous Peggy, my wife over there, and

256

myself, humble Hugh, I wish to say how happy we are that our eldest daughter has become engaged to a fine trades-man. She may not be able to cook, but she has a heart of pure gold, which is her most valuable asset.' Peggy's lips were pursed as they usually were when she was angry.

'Sit down, Hugh,' she ordered. 'You've had too much to drink, and you are making a fool of yourself.'

'Your wish is my command,' he replied, and then kissing the hand of Monica Morgan, he added, 'You are a sweet lady, and I have thoroughly enjoyed your company.'

'I hope we'll all meet soon again,' she replied, as they left for home.

Hugh was in the dog-house for a long time after his speech that night, and when she finally did condescend to speak to him, it was to inform him that they had been invited to a party at O'Dowds, to celebrate Margaret Anne's birthday, and that he was to be on his best behaviour.

Ian bought a plot of land at Blossom Grove Heights, in the suburbs of Cork, and his next door neighbour, who was an architect, designed a charming bungalow for him. He commissioned a builder to erect it, and the date for the wedding was fixed for August 12th. From the evening Alana made this announcement to her mother, Peggy was on a collision course with her straight away.

'So, you have definitely decided to marry Ian Morgan,' she said.

'That's just what I've told you, mum.'

'I sincerely hope you won't regret it. Remember, you made one mistake already, and you were able to get out of it. But there's no getting out of marriage. 'Til death do us part. Isn't that how it goes? It's a sobering thought, my girl.'

'I love Ian, mum, and he too loves me very dearly, and he has proved his love for me by becoming an absolute model

257

of sense. He is still a pioneer, and attends the meetings regularly. Actions speak louder than words. Isn't that how it goes?'

'I hope it will last. A leopard doesn't change its spots you know.'

'I am prepared to take a chance anyway, and I have full faith and confidence in him.'

'Where will you be married?' Peggy asked, after a brief pause.

'The ceremony will be held at St Anne's convent chapel, and the sisters will give us a little wedding breakfast in the parlour afterwards. It's just going to be a small family affair, nothing elaborate at all.'

Peggy was taken back at this.

'You will be married in white I presume?'

'No,' answered Alana, 'I will wear a simple blue dress which Sr Oliver is making for me, and Deirdre, who is to be my bridesmaid, will wear a lemon one.'

'You cannot possibly be serious, Alana,' Peggy exclaimed, horror in her face and voice.

'I'm deadly serious, mum. That's it. Remember, I am almost thirty years of age, and Ian is thirty-two, and we have a great deal of expense with the house. Besides, you know how much I detest pomp and glamour.'

'I hope you know, and realise what the neighbours will think.'

'No! I do not,' answered Alana, 'and anyway, I don't care what anyone thinks.'

'Are you all right, Alana?' Peggy asked very seriously.

'What do you mean?' Alana replied.

'I mean are you pregnant?' Alana threw her head back and laughed.

'I am not pregnant, Mam.'

Well, if you're not,' Peggy continued angrily, 'You are making a silly joke and a big skit of this whole thing, and I, for one, have no intention whatsoever of attending such a wedding. Why, the tinkers of the road do better than that.'

'I am sorry to hear you will not be there, Mum, but I suppose it will have to go on without you. As long as Dad gives me away, that's all that matters.'

'Don't speak to me any more, Alana,' Peggy warned. 'I'm ashamed of you, and I think you behave in this manner to annoy and torment me.'

Very few words passed between Alana and Peggy for the next few months, and the atmosphere at home was so tense, that Alana could hardly wait for her wedding day to dawn, so she could be finally apart from her mother. Hugh tried to reason with Peggy; but she remained adamant to boycott what she called an excuse for a wedding.

'She'll come round in the end,' Hugh said to Alana.

'If she does, I'll be delighted,' Alana replied, 'but I wouldn't be as optimistic about it as you are. She's a tough nut to crack.'

'Oh! She's tough all right,' replied Hugh. 'She was tough fifty-two years ago when she defied her father, and I'll always be grateful to her for that.' Alana was very touched by her father's remark.

'You still love her dearly in spite of everything. Don't you Dad?'

'My darling Alana! I couldn't live without her, and I always pray that the Lord will deign in his mercy to take me out of this world before her, because I would be nothing without her.'

'I hope Ian will say the same of me in thirty years' time,' Alana said wistfully.

Chapter 20

On the morning of August 12th, nineteen sixty-four, Alana, accompanied by Hugh, Deirdre and Neil, left the cottage for the waiting car to take them to St Anne's. Peggy, true to her word, remained in her bedroom. Alana had gone in to say good-bye to her.

'Aren't you even going to wish me luck, Mum?' She said.

'What I wish you, Alana, will remain in my heart; but what will also remain forever in my heart, is the fact that you, because of some stupid hang-up have always had about even the most basic of social standards, have made it impossible for me to be with you today.'

'I'm sorry if you see it in that light, Mum but, I am what I am, and this is the right way for me.'

'Your sister, Gráinne, is coming to spend the day with me,' Peggy added. 'She also sees things from my point of view, and neither will she be attending your wedding.' Her mother's last words to her had hurt Alana deeply, and she felt like bursting into tears; but she quickly took hold of herself and put on a brave face. After all, this was her wedding-day, and she must be happy.

As the car pulled up at the convent door, all the sisters were waiting there to welcome Alana. She was showered with kisses and embraces, and Sr Oliver had a hard task to whisk her into the parlour, to put the finishing touches to her hair, and the little blue lace head-piece she had made for her. Sr Bernard was already in the organ gallery playing a piece from Handel's Messiah, and as soon as Alana and her father appeared at the end of the chapel, she struck up the Bridal March. Alana walked slowly down the centre aisle on her father's arm, followed by Deirdre and Neil, and as they came to the top, Ian and Peter Doolan, the best-man, took Alana to the altar. Fr Dominick, the convent chaplain, performed the ceremony, while the nuns' choir sang the most exquisite anthems. Sr Anne, a young pro-fessed sister, who had a glorious voice, sang Panis Angelicus during holy communion, and it was really heavenly, caus-ing many tears in the little congregation.

When Alana arrived at the parlour for the wedding breakfast, she could hardly believe her eyes at the spectacle that confronted her there. How did the sisters manage to do such a magnificent job, and did she really deserve their goodness and kindness to her! The tables, three in all, were covered with spotlessly white, linen, table cloths, had little posies of white and red roses placed here and there, and were laden with the most exotic foods. One of the tables was placed horizontally at the top of the room, and the two others vertically, one on either side of it. The three-tier, beautifully decorated cake was placed in the centre of the top table, and was greatly admired by all. Sheila had certainly made it to perfection, and Monica Morgan and the two girls called it a work of art. Taking pride of place in the middle of the table to the right, was a large stuffed salmon on a silver dish, lying on a bed of lettuce, and tastefully decorated with slices of tomato, cucumber, egg, onion, and red and green peppers. For those who didn't like fish, there was a golden brown turkey, and a large baked ham, surrounded by silver platters of fresh, buttered veget-ables, succulent salads and creamed potatoes, all on the third table. The sisters were all dressed in gleaming white habits, and served up course after course of the delectable food in the most efficient manner, making the guests feel very much at home, with their very pleasant and cheerful manner. Sr Bernard had even thought of printing special, very ornate souvenir cards for the occasion, and each guest received one with his or her own name printed on it.

'Your mother missed a veritable treat,' Sheila said to Alana.

'She's as stubborn as a mule!' Maeve added, 'and when she gets an idea into her head, it's absolutely impossible to influence her.'

'Dad is putting up a great show,' Alana said, 'in spite of mum's absence, and the absence of any intoxicating liquor to help him on. Mrs Morgan seems fascinated with him.'

Ian was a bit ill at ease in the midst of all the nuns, and he seemed to be clinging for dear life to his bestman, Peter Doolan. Peter, on the other hand, was brim-full of poise and self-confidence, and he was a most eloquent master of ceremonies. Deirdre wasn't too keen on him at all.

'He's full of himself,' she remarked to Alana, 'I'd give anything to bring him down a peg or two.' He read a telegram from Sr Dominica wishing Ian and Alana God's grace and blessing on their marriage, and apologising for her absence. She was very seldom absent from any function, and Alana believed that she too was in sympathy with Peggy and Gráinne. They were definitely three of a kind. Mrs Buckley also sent a telegram, as did Aunt Kate, who, due to illness, was unable to travel. Hugh made a lovely speech, during which Alana observed Mary in tears, as she tried to hide behind Mossie's back. 'This is the second time I have given my eldest daughter away,' he said. 'She came bouncing back to me the first time, but I feel very happy to-day, to be putting her into the loving care of Ian, who I know will keep her for ever, and cherish her as I have done for the past thirty years.'

Alana was very lonely when evening came, and she had

to leave for her honeymoon. The good-byes were heart-breaking, and everybody was in tears, even the nuns.

'Take good care of Alana now,' Ian's mother said to him.

'There's no need to tell me that, Mother. You know I will.'

'Of course he will,' said Hugh, giving him a hearty handshake. Deirdre called Alana aside as she was about to get into the car.

'I know, Alana, that you have never in your life been with a man, and that you have lived a very sheltered life. You are still very innocent in the ways of the world and very vulnerable. When you go to bed with Ian to-night, don't be frightened. Just relax and be patient. Ian is very gentle, and if you have any problems, he will help you I'm sure. Don't worry! Everything will be all right.'

'Thank you, Deirdre,' Alana replied, but she really hadn't the foggiest idea what these words of advice and warning were all about. Deirdre meant well. She knew that; but she also knew that she loved Ian and Ian loved her, and as far as she was concerned; all else would follow from there.

'We'll head for Kerry,' Ian said, as they drove down the convent avenue, out of sight of their relations, who were gathered at the door to see them off. 'Then we'll travel up the west coast, across the North and down the east coast.'

'That will be lovely,' Alana replied, feeling excited at the prospect of her first holiday. She felt Ian was a bit strained and uptight.

'You're very quiet in yourself,' Alana commented after a while, 'Is there something troubling you?'

'Not a bit in the world,' Ian replied. 'It's just perhaps delayed action after the excitement of the ceremony, and the breakfast, and most of all those nuns hovering around me.'

263

'Strange, isn't it?' Alana went on, 'but I am more at ease in their company than I am in anyone else's in this world. They have been like family to me since I was four years old.'

It was dark when they arrived at Tralee, and they checked into one of the large hotels there. As they entered the beautiful bridal suite, Alana suddenly began to feel very nervous, and she wasn't helped in the slightest by Ian, who seemed to be lost in another world altogether. He went straight to the window, and stood there motionless, looking through it for a long time, without ever uttering a syllable. Alana began to unpack her clothes, arranging them neatly on hangers in the wardrobe.

'Shall I unpack your bag?' she asked Ian.

'What's that?' he said, after some time. Then, stammering badly he answered, 'Oh! yes, if you would please, Alana.' She proceeded to arrange Ian's clothes, all the while wondering what was on his mind, and feeling herself very much alone and ill at ease. Her mind wandered back to her father and Neil, and she could feel the tears beginning to blind her. She was very tired, and longed, more than anything else to fall into bed, and sleep for hours; but how could she possibly do that, with Ian still standing there with his back to her, and in this silent pensive mood. Perhaps Ian was nervous too, and possibly this was what Deirdre spoke to her about this morning. Deirdre had told her to be patient; so that was what she would do, and given time, Ian would surely come back to himself again.

As she was thinking these thoughts, he turned around.

'I must go downstairs to make a few telephone calls,' Ian told her, 'and I may be some time away, so shall I have a tray sent up to you?' He handed her the room service menu. 'Pick anything you fancy from this,' he said, 'you must be feeling a bit peckish now.' She studied the menu for a few seconds.

'I'll just have a pot of tea,' she said, 'and if you don't mind, I'll go to bed. I feel rather tired after the long day.'

'That's what you'll do,' he agreed. 'Have a good rest for yourself, and before you know it, I'll be back to you.' He kissed her gently and left the room. Soon afterwards a waiter brought her the tea, and after she had taken a few cups of it, she felt a good deal better. She was still a bit bewildered by Ian's strange behaviour; but she dismissed it from her mind, and took a nice hot bath. Then she donned the fancy pink nightdress and dressing-gown that Deirdre had given her, and after watching television for a little while, she went into bed.

Ian had been gone a long time now, and she was getting worried. There was a telephone beside the bed, and she decided to ring home and have a chat with her father and maybe Neil and Deirdre. She felt she needed to be close to them, if only by telephone, at this moment. It was Neil who answered when she rang.

'This is me, Neil,' she said.

'Oh! Hello Alana,' he replied, excitement sounding through his voice.

'How are things at home?' Alana asked.

'Just fine,' he replied, 'Grandad is inside telling Grandma about the brilliant day we had, and I think she's sorry she stayed at home.' Alana was chuckling to herself. 'Oh! and Alana! Mum is taking me to Dublin with her to-morrow for a holiday.'

'That will be lovely for you. Have a nice time now, pet. I'll see you when I get back. Would you put Grandad on to me for a minute.' She heard him call her father. 'It's Alana for you,' he shouted, and almost immediately she heard Hugh's voice.

'How's my girl?'

'Fine, Dad,' she answered, a lump in her throat.

'Where are you now?' he enquired.

'We're in the Grand Hotel in Tralee.'

'That's a very swanky place,' he said. 'Ian does it in style.'

Little does he know, Alana thought to herself, how lonely and heart-broken she felt. She wished she could open her heart to her father, and tell him how things were right now, how she was sitting alone in a hotel room, her heart pounding with fear and anxiety, and no sign of Ian. Deirdre came on the line and cheered her a little.

'Let your hair down now,' she advised, 'and live it up, and don't forget to call to see us in Dublin, on your way home.'

'I won't forget,' Alana promised, saying good-bye and putting down the receiver. She was back again in the lonely room, the voices of those so very dear to her, silent now, and still no sign of Ian.

She lay back and tried to sleep, but as tired as she was, sleep would not come. Then she heard footsteps coming along the corridor, a key turning in the door, and then the door opened and there was Ian at last. She breathed a sigh of relief, but as he approached her, she thought he looked different, in a strange sort of way that Alana couldn't figure out. His face seemed very flushed, and she imagined his eyes were watery, as though he had been crying.

'Thank God you're back, Ian,' she said. 'I was beginning to think you had deserted me already.' He looked at her there sitting up in the bed, and stammering fiercely, he replied.

'I had some business to attend to which took longer than I expected.'

Alana did not reply, but wondered to herself what business he could possibly have that could keep him such a long time from his bride on the first night of his honeymoon. He went into the bathroom and had a shower, and after some time he emerged, wearing wine colour pyjamas. This is it now, Alana thought to herself, fear of the unknown gripping her.

He came into bed beside her, and turned off the lamp on the locker next to him. Then he turned in towards her and took her in his arms. She yielded to him and he began to kiss her; but as he did, to her horror and disgust she got the strong, vile smell of alcohol from his breath. She immediately stiffened, and pulled away from him.

'You've been drinking, Ian,' she said, almost in tears. 'You have deceived me, and it is impossible for me to allow you to make love to me in that state. You have turned me off completely, and I am bitterly disappointed and very upset. I made my feelings in this regard perfectly clear to you before we even became engaged.'

'Oh, shut up! You stupid, frigid bitch of a nun!' he yelled, 'Have it your own way.' Then he turned his back on her, and in a short while he was snoring loudly. Alana sobbed herself to sleep, and wished at that particular moment that she had never been born. She thought once again of Mother Teresa's stern warning to her when she was leaving the convent: You'll rue the day. How right she was.

The following morning Ian was very apologetic for his dastardly behaviour.

'I was never with a woman, Alana, and I was very nervous. I thought a few drinks would give me courage.'

'If you were nervous, you should have told me. I would have understood. I was nervous too, and we could have worked things out together. You took the cowardly way out, and ruined everything.'

'Please forgive me, Alana,' he begged, 'I made a mistake, but I promise you it will never happen again.'

He was very persuasive, and Alana took him at his word, and they both dressed and went down to breakfast. They spent a very pleasant and enjoyable day together, and travelled to Salthill, where they spent the night in one of the best hotels there. Ian never made any approach to Alana in bed that night, or indeed, any other night for the duration of the two weeks' honeymoon. She didn't question his reason for this, and he never made any reference whatsoever to it. Although they had a very enjoyable holiday, Alana was puzzled by his odd behaviour, but she hoped that maybe when they got home to their new bungalow, things might change. They spent a night in Dublin with Deirdre and Kate, and Deirdre was very eager to find out how Alana was getting on with Ian. She followed Alana into the kitchen during the night.

'Well,' she asked. 'How did things go for you on the honeymoon?'

'Nothing at all happened,' Alana replied. Deirdre was flabbergasted.

'You mean you are still a virgin?' she asked.

'That's right,' replied Alana.

'My God!' exclaimed Deirdre. 'He certainly is a very slow starter. But not to worry, you have the rest of your lives, and sure maybe he'll be a good finisher.'

'Let's hope so,' said Alana. 'It might even be to-night.' She winked at Deirdre as Ian and herself went upstairs to bed.

It was a warm, sunny Saturday afternoon when Ian and Alana drove in through the gate of their new bungalow at Blossom Grove Heights. Ian was in the best of form, really back to his own good-humoured self again, and for that Alana was very glad. They got out of the little green mini car, and looked in admiration at the splendid view from their garden at the top of the hill.

'It's great to be home,' Ian said.

'I agree wholeheartedly,' replied Alana, 'especially to a heavenly spot like this. We're really very lucky, aren't we?'

'We definitely are,' he replied, and then he took the key

from his pocket and opened the front door. 'Come on now,' he said to Alana. 'I must lift my bride over the threshold.' She was tickled pink when he took her in his strong arms, and landed her down in the hall. He kissed her tenderly. 'Welcome home, my love.' he said.

'Thank you, Ian,' Alana replied, feeling very happy and encouraged, and becoming secure again in his love for her.

Inside the bungalow they roamed from room to room, admiring the soft wool carpets and the plush new furnishings. They tested the big double bed, and they both agreed it was soft and comfortable. On the dining room table, they found a large bunch of pink and white carnations, artistically arranged in a pretty glass vase, and a card which read: Welcome Home—The Morgan Family.

'That's definitely your mother's idea,' commented Alana. 'I think she's a real pet.' The kitchen table was set for two, and the note said: The meal is in the fridge. Alana opened the fridge and, wild with excitement at what she saw, she called to Ian, who was bringing the cases in from the car.

'Come and see what we've got here,' she said. 'We won't have to cook for a week.' There were two plates, wrapped in grease proof paper, each containing a chicken and ham salad, and these were obviously intended for this evening's meal. Then there was a shepherd's pie, a steak and kidney pie and a beef casserole, all ready cooked, only to be heated, as well as plenty of cheese, pickles, tomatoes, eggs and butter.

'This is great,' Ian said. 'Sisters are useful commodities after all.'

''Tis the best surprise I've had for a long time,' replied Alana, 'and I will always be grateful to your family for such a kind, thoughtful gesture.'

'I'll tell you what,' Ian said eagerly. 'Why don't I light the fire, and we can pull up the sofa and eat in comfort.'

'What a lovely idea?' exclaimed Alana. 'It will be so warm and cosy.'

In a very short while, the room was aglow with the bright, red flames of the fire, and they sat down together on the soft, beige sofa and relished the delicious chicken and ham salad. Ian was perfectly relaxed, and Alana was acutely conscious of his closeness to her. She was ready to make love to him now, if he so desired. She thought he felt the same way as she did, and her heart was beating fast in joyful anticipation of their very first union. Then the loud knock sounded on the front door.

'Don't answer it,' pleaded Alana. 'We need to be alone to-night.' Ian hesitated for a moment.

'It may be urgent,' he argued. 'I had better see who it is.' He went to the door. 'Hello Peter,' she heard him say. 'Come on in. You're very welcome to our new home.' Alana's heart sank, and she could have screamed with sheer frustration and disappointment. Peter Doolan came into the room, smiling in what Alana thought was a rather cynical sarcastic manner, and he sat himself down on the sofa with Ian and Alana. Alana couldn't get herself to be civil to him. There was something about him, something devious and wicked, Alana believed.

'Are you coming out for a while?' he asked Ian, and Alana could immediately feel her temper mounting.

'Is it alright if I go out with Peter?' Ian asked her.

'I would prefer if you didn't go out to-night,' Alana answered, 'it's our first night home, and the house feels a little strange to me yet.'

'You can't tie a man down like that,' argued Peter. 'After all, he has just spent two full weeks with you.' Alana ignored his remark, and then Ian said to her.

'I won't be very long, love.'

'If you are going out,' Alana replied, 'then I will join you.' She noticed Peter Doolan's face redden.

'This is his night out with the boys. No women allowed to-night.' Alana could contain herself no longer.

'I beg your pardon, Peter,' she said disdainfully. 'I addressed myself to my husband, and I am perfectly sure he can speak for himself.' She looked directly at Ian for his answer.

'I am going out with Peter to-night, Alana, and I cannot bring you along. Perhaps another night.' She could see the vindictive glint of satisfaction in Peter Doolan's eyes, and she pleaded with Ian.

'Please Ian, I am asking you to stay. Do not leave me here alone, to-night. Please stay. I really do not want you to go out.' She began to cry, but Ian ignored her tears and pleadings, and walked out of the room with Peter Doolan. She called after him. 'Please come back, Ian. Please, please come back.' But to no avail. She heard the car door bang, and she ran into the bedroom to look out through the window, to see if he was really going. She got the biggest shock of her life when she looked into the car. Was she dreaming or hallucinating, or maybe she was cracking up. But no, she wasn't. She could see the two of them quite clearly before her eyes. They were sitting in the car, and they were kissing and caressing each other. 'Sweet Jesus!' she exclaimed, feeling physically sick. 'What am I going to do now?'

They drove off, leaving her standing there in the bedroom, all alone, in a dazed, numbed state. Everything was beginning to make sense to her now; the honeymoon, the drinking, the complete absence of any physical contact and the stark reality that she was still a virgin, and her husband was a homosexual. What a terrible mess she was in now. This was a severe problem, and one which she couldn't possibly share with anyone. She began to shiver all over. Then, feeling quite weak, she went into bed. As she lay there, her mind tortured and in turmoil, she thought that this must surely be a punishment to her from the Lord for turning her back on him when she left the convent. After all,

271

she couldn't expect to get away scot-free; so she must suffer it now, and live out this most difficult life with Ian, and above all, she must keep it a secret until the day she died.

She tossed and turned, waking and sleeping, for several hours, and at three in the morning she heard him turn the key in the door. She knew by his footsteps that he was drunk, and she pretended to be sound asleep. He kicked open the bedroom door and stormed in. She was so terrified that she thought her heart would stop beating. Then he undressed and fell into bed beside her.

'Wake up, you lazy bitch,' he shouted, shaking her violently, and eventually pulling her roughly towards him. She opened her eyes and looked at him. His face was transfigured, and his eyes were glazed and popping out of his head. 'Come on now,' he yelled. 'Let's see if I'm not man enough for you, Miss O'Grady.' She jumped out of bed, but he jumped out after her, caught her, tore her nightdress from her body, and threw her like a rag doll back on the bed. Then he threw himself down on top of her. She struggled fiercely, kicking and pushing, in an effort to fight him off.

He became violent, like a wild animal. He beat her fiercely, punched her, all the time hurling vicious obscene abuse at her. She escaped again; but he caught her and banged her head hard against the wall several times. Then he punched her on the nose until the blood came gushing from it, and spattered on to the newly decorated walls. He kicked her and kneed her in the abdomen. She was groaning in agony, and she thought she was going to die. She begged for mercy, and when she did, he only beat her more fiercely until she collapsed to the ground unconscious.

When she awoke, she was lying on the floor, stark naked, her body completely black and blue, and aching all over. Her two eyes were almost closed and very swollen, and her nose and mouth were covered with congealed blood. She looked in the bed, but he wasn't there. She struggled to her feet, and with great difficulty got into her dressing-gown. Then she searched the house to see if he was anywhere there. He was gone. She knew she was very badly bruised, because she could hardly walk. She needed a doctor, but she was miles away from nowhere and too weak to travel unaided. She prayed to God to send help, and wondered what on earth she should do. Then she heard the postman coming to the door. She called to him through the letterbox.

'Please phone for a taxi for me as soon as you can. I am very ill, and I need to get to hospital.'

'I'll phone from the coin-box down the road.' he answered. 'Don't worry now. Your taxi should be here in about half an hour.'

'I'm very grateful to you,' Alana said faintly.

The taxi duly arrived, and Alana got into it, still in her dressing gown and slippers.

'St Anne's Convent, Glenbeg,' she said to the driver.

'Yes miss,' he replied, and drove off. He could clearly see that Alana was in a bad way; but he was discreet, and she was grateful that he didn't ask any questions, or even try to hold a conversation with her. She sat in the back seat, still very distressed, and in deep shock, and even during the half an hour's journey to the convent, she felt herself lapsing in and out of consciousness. Her head was fuzzy and numb, and she was trembling from head to toe.

'Here we are now,' she vaguely heard the driver say, as the car came to a halt outside the convent door. 'That'll be thirty shillings, miss,' he said, and Alana put her hand into the pocket of her dressing-gown, and gave him all she had in it. She didn't know, or didn't care how much was there, but she knew it must have been enough, because he thanked her, and opened the door to let her out.

She rang the bell, and almost immediately, Sr Oliver appeared at the door. Alana just fell into her arms, and broke down into a fit of convulsive crying.

'Dear God!' Sr Oliver exclaimed. 'You are badly injured. Was there an accident? Is Ian with you? Oh! You poor child! What has happened to you at all?' Alana just continued to cry, and she was unable to answer. Sr Oliver brought her into the kitchen, and sat her down beside the Aga cooker. She wrapped a shawl around her, and gave her a cup of hot, sweet tea. 'Here now, pet. Drink this, and you'll feel a wee bit better. I'll go and gong for Sr Bernard.' Alana sipped the tea, and just sat there staring vacantly into space. She heard the quick sound of Sr Bernard's footsteps coming along the corridor, and then she saw her coming through the kitchen door and over towards her. Sr Bernard pulled up a chair, and sat down beside Alana.

'Alana,' she said. 'Can you try and tell me what has happened to you.' Alana could never tell Sr Bernard the gory details; so she just remained silent, and continued to cry. Sr Bernard held her hand. 'Come on now, Alana. You have never kept any secrets from me, and whatever it is that has happened, you know you can tell me. I'll understand, and I'll help you.'

'I need a priest, Sister,' was all Alana could say. 'Get me a priest, please.'

'You need a doctor, first,' said Sr Bernard. 'Why, my Divine God! Look at the state you're in. Come along with me to the nuns' infirmary, and I will get you to bed and call the doctor. Maybe when you get some medication and a good night's rest, we can talk.' Alana followed like one in a daze, and allowed Sr Bernard to put her to bed.

Later the doctor arrived and examined Alana thoroughly.

'You have a few broken ribs, and you are still slightly concussed and suffering from severe shock; but apart from that, your bumps and bruises, though sore and painful, are superficial'. She had managed to tell Doctor Horgan of Ian's vicious onslaught on her, and of the circumstances surrounding it. 'That man has a really serious problem,' he said, 'And you can count yourself extremely lucky that he didn't murder you, or that he didn't actually rape you, or you could be carrying his child. Are you going to press charges against him?'

'Oh no. I'm not,' Alana replied.

'But you'll have to take things very easy for a while. Your whole system is shaken and upset, and your body will take time to heal. Take these tablets now, and you should sleep soundly until morning. I'll be around then to see how you're doing.' 'Thank you, doctor,' Alana said, and Dr Horgan picked up his bag and left the room. She could hear him in deep conversation with Sr Bernard and some of the other nuns in the office outside. She couldn't quite hear what he was saying, but no doubt he was telling them of her horrific ordeal, and saving her the embarrassment of having to do so herself. She began to feel drowsy after the tablets. She closed her eyes, and a beautiful, relaxed and happy feeling swept over her.

Chapter 21

'What the hell have I done?' Ian Morgan said, as he struggled out of bed in Peter Doolan's flat. His head was pounding with severe pain, and he was shaking all over with a terrible hangover.

'Take it easy now, man,' Peter Doolan said, 'and don't panic.'

'I'm in dire trouble. You do realise that? She may even be dead by now. I've got to get out of here before I'm arrested.'

'Don't jump the gun,' Peter advised. 'Things are not as bad as that. Anyway, you were definitely provoked. If a man can't have his woman after a few drinks with his friend, 'tis a bad job. I told you women were trouble, and anyway, you were never cut out for marriage, not to mind being a pioneer husband.' He poured out a large stiff whiskey. 'Here! Drink this. It will help you to think more clearly.' Ian grabbed the glass in his shaky hand and swallowed it back.

'Give me another, please.' He had another, and another, until he felt quite capable of handling all problems. 'We'll go to the house and see how the land lies,' he said.

'That's a good idea,' said Peter. 'Come on. I'll do the driving.'

The bedroom was just like a battlefield, and when Peter saw the blood on the walls, he began to get worried himself.

'By God,' he said, 'You certainly gave her a fair hammering.' Ian looked all over the bungalow.

'I wonder where she is now?' he asked.

'To hell with that now,' replied Peter. 'It's high time we got our asses out of here. Grab your bits and pieces fast. There's a boat sailing for England tonight, and we'll be aboard.'

'But what about my mother?'

'Just drop her a line, and tell her the marriage is over. Make some plausible excuse about mutual agreement or something like that. She'll swallow anything you say. Sure, aren't you her white-haired boy?' Ian was hesitant. 'Come on, man,' Peter said impatiently, 'Snap out of it, and put yourself in my hands. I'll take care of everything. Never fear—Peter is here,' he said jokingly. Ian locked up the house and left with Peter. They drove to Dublin, and from there Ian wrote to his mother before he sailed to Holyhead.

Neil usually answered the phone at home.

'It's Sr Bernard for you, Grandad,' he said. Hugh took the telephone from Neil.

'What can I do for you, Sister?' he said, in his usual cheerful tone of voice. Then he was reduced to silence when he got the terrible bombshell from the other end of the line. Peggy could see the look of severe shock and terror on his now ashen countenance, and she heard him say, 'Oh my God! Sister. This is awful. What are we to do?' She knew instinctively that Alana was in trouble, and she could hardly wait for him to put down the receiver, to find out what had happened. She knew it must be serious, and she was now very worried herself. 'I'll come up right away,' she heard him say, as he finished his conversation.

'It's Alana, isn't it?' she said. He sat down, put his face in his hands and cried silently. Peggy panicked when she saw his terrible reaction. 'She's not dead, is she? Please Hugh, tell me. What's wrong?' He lifted his head and looked blankly at her.

'She has been very badly beaten by Ian Morgan, and she is now in the convent infirmary.'

'Jesus! Mary! and Joseph!' exclaimed Peggy. 'What a brute! But I knew it. I never liked a bit of him. There was something peculiar about him, and I sensed it. I was right again. I'm always right, but I'm never heeded.'

'Never mind that now,' said Hugh, irritably. 'I cannot comprehend how any human being could be so cruel to a defenceless woman. Think of what our poor daughter has gone through. It's breaking my heart.'

'She's lucky to be rid of him, if you ask me. Better sooner than later. She'll get over that. She's a fighter.'

'Her body will heal,' Hugh replied. 'But what about the effect it could have on her mind. Sure that's bound to leave a scar.'

'We'll cross that bridge when we come to it,' Peggy replied. 'Pull yourself together now, and don't let Alana see you in that condition. She needs your strength now if ever she needed it.'

Fr Dominick was sitting with Alana when Hugh came into the room. Hugh could hardly recognise her, her face was so distorted. He felt ill, and inadvertently, he ignored the priest and went straight to Alana. He kissed her on the forehead.

'My poor child,' he said, 'How are you feeling?'

'I've done it again, Dad,' she replied, trying to be cheerful for his sake, because she knew the terrible effect any form of violence against womankind had on him, and for his own daughter to be so violently assaulted, must have been a devastating blow to him.

'You've done what again?' he asked.

'I've come bouncing back to you again.' He tried to laugh, but it was very strained. 'This is Father Dominick,' Alana said. 'This is my father.' The two men shook hands warmly.

'I'm very happy to meet you, Mr O'Grady, though I would prefer the circumstances to be more pleasant.'

'Father Dominick is applying for an annulment of my marriage, Dad.' Hugh looked very seriously from Alana to the priest.

'What exactly does that mean, Father?'

'Well! Mr O'Grady, it means that, in the eyes of the Catholic Church, your daughter Alana will no longer be married; but unfortunately, in the eyes of the state, her marriage will still stand.' Hugh was puzzled.

'That seems rather odd, Father. But will she be free again, free to do what she wishes with her life, even to re-marry?'

'It's a bit complicated, Mr O'Grady. But yes, basically she will be completely free.'

'How long will that take to go through, Father?' he enquired.

'Well! Some of these cases take years; but in Alana's case, since the marriage was not consummated, there are no complications, and it shouldn't, I hope, take too long.'

'It's a great pity the Church and the State are not on the one word, Father. Isn't it?' Hugh added.

'It's a pity all right, but at least the Catholic Church has taken the initiative in this very important matter, and Alana is lucky now that it did.' Alana could detect anguish in her father's face.

'Don't worry about it, Dad,' she said. 'The wheels are now in motion, and we just have to wait and see what happens.'

'I'll leave you two alone now,' Father Dominic said, as he got up to go. 'I'll keep in touch with you, Alana. May God bless you for now.'

When they were alone, Alana told her father the whole gruesome story.

'I'll kill the blackguard,' Hugh said. 'I'll kill him with my bare hands.'

'Leave him to God,' Alana replied. 'Wherever he is now,

he must be very miserable. He is a mentally sick man, Dad, and he is more to be pitied than blamed. I thank God I'm still alive.'

'What will you do now?' her father enquired.

'I'll remain here until the doctor gives me the all clear, and the Reverend Mother has told me I can live in the convent lodge. I am fortunate that it has just become vacant.'

'So you won't come home, will you?'

'No, Dad. I would prefer to be alone here, for the moment anyway. I have been given a teaching post here at St Anne's, and I will have all my meals here.'

'God bless the Sisters,' said Hugh. 'They are certainly our best friends, and sure aren't you yourself one of them anyway?'

'I count myself very lucky to have them, Dad, and don't think I do not appreciate that fact.'

'Mum will call to see you to-morrow,' Hugh said. 'She is very concerned about you, Alana.'

'Mum was right all along the line,' Alana admitted. 'I have to hand it to her. Tell her I look forward to her visit.'

Monica Morgan got Ian's letter. She read it over and over again, not really believing at first what the words were saying. There must have been some very serious obstacle in the marriage, she thought to herself; otherwise they would not have decided to separate after just two weeks. She wondered what on earth could have happened. Ian didn't give her the full details; all he said was that by mutual agreement, they decided to separate. There was something more to this than met the eye. She called Theo, who had just come in from night-duty.

'Read this,' she said. He took the short letter and began to read it.

'Well, at least he had the sense to leave the country,' Theo said. 'That boy was always a poblem. He never knew what he wanted, and to tell you the truth Monica, I was very wary about that marriage from day one.'

'But what about Alana, and she such a nice decent girl?'

'It's obvious from Ian's letter, that for whatever reason, she realises it's all for the best. It was agreed mutually. That's what he says in the letter.'

'We should really call and see her, and find out what exactly happened.'

'Let it rest for the moment. It's a private matter between the two of them, and we shouldn't interfere. We can't do anything about it anyway; so there's no use in fretting or upsetting yourself.'

'It must have been the shortest marriage in history,' Monica remarked.

'Better a short marriage than a long, miserable one,' Theo replied.

'I suppose you're right,' replied Monica, 'But it puzzles me, and I cannot understand it for the life of me.'

'Leave it rest now woman. Leave it rest.'

Alana was soon up and about again, and as buoyant as she ever was. She busied herself decorating the little lodge, and threw herself wholeheartedly into her teaching. Sr Bernard watched over her like a guardian angel, and her kindness and generosity to Alana was something she could never forget. As they walked in the garden together one evening after supper, she said to Alana.

'The Lord must really want you for himself, and he must have something very big for you to do for him. You know I can see his hand all through this whole affair. He is adamant not to let you stray from him.'

'When will I know what he wants of me?' Alana asked.

'In God's own time, Alana. Not a moment before.'

'Then here I am Lord! Send me where you will,' was Alana's prayer on that day.

Epilogue

Alana walked down the long tree-lined avenue of the convent, to her quaint little lodge home just inside the big blue gates. She was beginning to come to terms with her life, and she felt very much at peace with herself.

As she turned the key in the door, a taxi drove in the gate, and she saw the white veils of two novices in the back seat. She had heard they were coming to St Anne's on their outing and she felt the pangs of pain and regret again momentarily. She quickly dispelled the thoughts and went inside.

The evening was chilly, so she decided to put a match to the fire in the sitting room. She then went into the kitchen and put on the kettle to make herself a cup of tea. She had some test papers to correct and she would do them in comfort by the fire. Afterwards if time permitted, she would write to Deirdre. She owed her a reply to her last letter, and Deirdre who was progressing so well now in every way, was one of Alana's main sources of consolation.

There was a ring on the door bell. That could be Neil, Alana thought to herself. He often called when he had some problem or other with his home-work. As she threw the door open, she was very pleasantly surprised.

'Hello, Dad, and Father Seamus! How really wonderful to see you! Come on in. You are more than welcome to my new home.' The old priest embraced her lovingly.

'Thank you so much Alana, my dear child. I am so very glad to see you looking so well again after all you've been through.'

'She made a wonderful recovery, Father,' Hugh commented, looking proudly at his daughter, 'but then our Alana was always very ebullient.'

'Thank the good Lord for that, Hugh, me boy, for 'tis a great blessing, a great blessing indeed.'

Alana went to the kitchen and brought in a tray to the fire where the three of them enjoyed hot buttered scones, appletart and cups of strong tea. Father Seamus enquired about all the family, and Alana gave him a long glowing account of Deirdre and Neil. 'I hope Deirdre will never forget what you have sacrificed for her,' Father Seamus said, and Hugh couldn't help feeling a lump in his throat.

Father Seamus then took a white envelope from his pocket.

'This is a letter from the bishop's secretary, Alana, concerning the annulment of your marriage.'

The words hit Alana like a bombshell, and she felt suddenly sick again. She remained silent for a minute, and then taking hold of herself, she asked.

'What does it say, Father?'

'Here you are, Alana,' replied the priest, 'Read it for yourself.'

He handed Alana the letter and she read it carefully, noting every word. Then, turning to her father, she said.

'The committee have succeeded in locating Ian and he has agreed to come to a meeting with them, with a view to signing the annulment papers. As soon as that is done, I will sign, and soon afterwards the marriage will be annulled.'

'That's great, news Alana.' Hugh said. 'I am very happy for you.'

'Are you happy yourself?' asked Father Seamus, noticing the wistful look in her pale face.

'Well,' replied Alana, 'It's the only thing to do I think. Isn't it?'

'That's a question for yourself, Alana, my child. May God and his Holy Spirit direct you. But what will you do with your life now?' asked Father Seamus.

'That's a question for heaven, Father,' answered Alana, 'and we will have to wait patiently until the answer comes'.